Dedalus Africa

The Fire Within

Touhfat Mouhtare

The Fire Within

translated by Rachael McGill

Dedalus

This book has been selected to receive financial assistance from English PEN's "PEN translates" programme, supported by Arts Council England. English PEN exists to promote literature and our understanding of it, to uphold writers' freedoms around the world, to campaign against the persecution and imprisonment of writers for stating their views, and to promote the friendly co-operation of writers and the exchange of ideas.

Supported using public funding by ARTS COUNCIL ENGLAND

Published in the UK by Dedalus Limited,
24-26, St Judith's Lane, Sawtry, Cambs, PE28 5XE
info@dedalusbooks.com
www.dedalusbooks.com

ISBN printed book 978 1 915568 86 1
ISBN ebook 978 1 915568 88 5

Dedalus is distributed in the USA & Canada by SCB Distributors
15608 South New Century Drive, Gardena, CA 90248
info@scbdistributors.com www.scbdistributors.com

Dedalus is distributed in Australia by Peribo Pty Ltd
58, Beaumont Road, Mount Kuring-gai, N.S.W. 2080
info@peribo.com.au www.peribo.com.au

First published by Dedalus in 2025

Printed and bound in the UK by Clays Elcograf S.p.A.
Typeset by Marie Lane

The Author

Touhfat Mouhtare grew up between her island and several other Sub-Saharan African nations. Today she lives in France where she studied foreign languages at the Sorbonne.

Her first novel, *Vert cru,* was published in 2018, and she is the author of the short story collection *Âmes supendues* (2011) as well as poetry.

Le Feu du Midi (*The Fire Within*) is her second novel.

The Translator

Rachael McGill is a playwright for stage and radio, prose writer and translator of novels and plays from French, German, Spanish and Portuguese. Her short stories have been published in several anthologies and online.

She has translated four books for Dedalus: *The Desert and the Drum* and *Saara* both by Mbarek Ould Beyrouk, *Co-wives, Co-widows* by Adrienne Yabouza and *The Fire Within* by Toufhat Mouhtare. Her translation of *The Desert and the Drum* was shortlisted for The Oxford-Weidenfeld Translation Prize and her translation of Kerstin Specht's play *Marieluise* won the Gate Theatre/Allied Domecq translation prize.

Her first novel *Fair Trade Heroin* was published by Dedalus in 2022 *for H., I. and M.*

[...] He rebuked the wind and the sea. 'Silence!' He commanded, 'Be still!' And the wind died down, and it was perfectly calm.

Mark 4: 39

Words in italics are defined in the glossary at the end of the book.

SA'FAS

سعفص

It was harvest time, in the month of Muharram. I'd always had trouble correctly identifying the two winds that blew over my island; could never remember which was the *kashkazi*, which the *kusi*. This knowledge still escaped me at the time of my eleventh birthday. All I knew was that the year had two seasons—the rainy season and the season of blossoms kissed by a crisp wind—and that during the second season, Tamu always caught a cold. The leaves of the mango trees rasped against each other in the breeze, like the wings of crickets. The palm fronds bowed to the left, then the right, and I laughed to see the *lesos* of my friends flapping around their ankles.

On New Year's Eve, we'd gone to look for branches in the forest that bordered the town of Itsandra. We called it Ahmad's Wood. It hadn't rained for a month, so the branches were just dry enough to burn. The soles of our calloused feet sank into the sandy, rocky soil. We walked with the purposeful stride of children who've been trusted with an important mission. There were five of us: Mlima, Ramla, M'maka, Olympe and me.

When the scent of mango and eucalyptus reached our nostrils, we knew we'd arrived at our destination. We had two hours to collect as many of the driest branches as we could carry. Olympe marked out the plot we were to work on, and divided it into five sections, one for each of us. Once we had our wood, we were to meet at the entrance of the forest to bind the branches into bundles and help each other to load them on our heads.

I set off in the direction of the henna grove. I was delighted with the patch I'd been allocated: male mango and lychee trees shaded the bushes there, and the ground was littered with their sun-baked branches. I'd be able to collect some leaves too, for Tamu, the woman I thought of as my mother.

When I got to my area though, my joy receded. Someone had been there before me: all they'd left were small piles of branches that were too thin to burn for long. I'd have to venture further afield. Foliage obstructed my path; I had to hack my way through wild lemongrass and nettles.

By the time I found a place where some large branches had fallen, I was out of breath and angry. All my life, it seemed to me, people had amused themselves by putting obstacles in my path, trying to thwart me in whatever I wanted to do. My mother was the first culprit: too young to raise a child, she'd decided to get rid of me. Tamu had caught her, eyes blazing, hand pressed over my mouth and nose. They struggled, Tamu pulled me free, and my murderous mother fled, to somewhere no one would find her.

Then there was my father. People said he was a trader from the Indies, the sort who came only occasionally to our shores, looking for vanilla, ylang-ylang and clove plants to sell for perfume, or the medicinal herbs that grew on our beaches. According to Tamu, it was my mother who had seduced him.

However it happened, my father had bequeathed me the straight hair typical of the bastard children of foreign traders. Because of that, and because the name seemed to suit me, I began to be referred to by the surname of a trader everyone knew, a man who passed through often: Hardie.

The only unobstructed path I'd ever known was the one that took me to Tamu. And occasionally, the one to my schoolmaster.

My friends and I worked as maids in different people's houses. We were put to service from the age of about five: it was customary to keep child slaves to do simple housework and food-preparation until they were able to take on more demanding chores. We were the third generation of slaves, our parents born on the island. Our grandparents had been taken from their own country, but nobody knew which country that was, and it was so distant that we never thought about it. Slaves arrived here from different places and in different ways: Tamu's grandparents had been given as a wedding present to a princess. They'd been paraded through the city during the festivities, carrying dishes and chests filled with gold and jewels on their heads. Tamu had no more idea of where her ancestors came from than I did. When I annoyed her, she sometimes called me 'cat-face'; apparently, I looked like the descendants of a slave convoy who were said to have come from the land of the cats. They were compared to felines because their eyes were slanted, their bodies small and lithe, and they moved around so stealthily they were barely noticed. No one knew where the land of the cats was, or what it was really called. What our elders had to say on the subject was this: one day, a very long time ago, smooth stones the size of mountains had fallen from the sky. The people had taken them for gods. Allah, the god worshipped by our masters, had punished them for this belief by enslaving them. The slaves had adopted the religion and the prophets of their masters, but on some nights, they still gathered secretly in caves to honour the gods of their ancestors, trembling in fear of Allah's wrath.

The lives of my friends and me rarely presented us with opportunities to feel indispensable. Collecting the wood needed to cook the big Muharram meal was a chance to demonstrate our usefulness to our community.

I found a mango tree that had been freshly cut and abandoned. I greeted it by placing my hand on its trunk, as Tamu had taught me. I closed my eyes and asked the tree's permission to take some of its wood. A dull rumbling, like the creaking of a door, rose up from the heart of the trunk, where the last of the tree's life-force still thrummed. My request had been accepted.

After removing the thickest branches from the majestic trunk, I set off again, planning to continue deeper into the forest. I found my path blocked by a pile of branches. They bore deep gashes where they'd been hacked at inexpertly. I bent down to gather them up and was surprised to see even more butchered branches strewn far in front of me. It was as if they'd been torn off the trees haphazardly, thrown around, then finally abandoned, crushed into the ground where someone had run over them, snapping them as they went.

The someone who'd been here before me.

I didn't think too much of it at first. Collecting wood was a task for maids: whoever it was who'd disturbed the path I was on could only be a girl or a woman. A beginner, judging from the clumsy incisions and the branches scattered messily on the ground. A few more months and she'd be a proficient woodcutter like the rest of us.

On second thoughts though, my master's school was the only Qur'anic school that accepted maids. This whole estate belonged to my master, so only his pupils could gather wood in this forest. Who could have passed through here before us? A mango thief? It wasn't mango season. A hedgehog hunter?

Shouts from the clearing interrupted my reverie. I'd collected enough branches for a decent bundle. I tore a vine from a banana tree to lash my branches together.

The journey home was by my favourite road. I tried to press the entire surface of each of my toes against the warm earth as I walked. It was both painful and pleasant: the sun warmed my feet while the rocks grazed and massaged my skin. The others called me 'barefoot Hardie'. I pitied them for missing out on such joy.

All the way home, I wondered about the state of disarray I'd found in my section of Ahmad's Wood. Based on how tiny the pieces of discarded branch had been, I decided the person who'd been there before me must have very small hands.

The master's house was at the crossroads of Thin Beard Junction.

The story was that on this spot a man had challenged the sultan Fe Fum, the *mafe* of our region. During one of his morning rounds of the Itsandra farms, the *mafe* had passed by a ylang-ylang plantation, a place where only women worked. One of these women was called Urango. Her skin was smooth but her hands were rough from labour. She dragged her portly body around like a burden. Urango's curves and her hard-working hands caught the eye of the *mafe*. But Urango was already taken: her husband was the spiritual guide of the neighbouring town of Milembeni. When he heard this, Fe Fum retorted, 'I don't care; I will have that woman.' He summoned the local *qadi* and ordered him to dissolve the union between Urango and her husband. The *qadi* replied that he could not desecrate the sacred bond of marriage for no other reason than a man's desire. The *mafe*, convinced the *qadi* was siding with the husband because he was a scholar like himself, had the *qadi* imprisoned. The *qadi* did not protest. Instead, he raised his eyes to heaven with devotion while muttering a curse: that the sultan and all his male descendants should be struck with madness, that the sultan's posterity should be ensured only by children born out of wedlock, and that his offspring should be recognisable by their perennially patchy beards.

The very next day, the prophecy came true. The *mafe's* eldest son, who was in line to succeed him, woke up with the word 'vanilla' on his lips. All day long, he could say nothing else, answering every question he was asked with this word. The next day he did the same. No matter how hard he tried to pronounce other words, his mouth could shape only 'vanilla'. This situation drove him mad. He ended up having a child out of wedlock with a woman he was forbidden from marrying. This son grew up normally, albeit in the shadow of an overprotective father who could speak to him using only one word. When the boy was ten years old, one of his friends told him what his grandfather had done to the *qadi.* At that moment, the boy split into two people: by day he was called *Nyoha*, 'snake' in Comorian, and by night *Hannâs*, 'snake' in Arabic. When he went on to have children, they were all boys, all with patchy beards. The place they lived in came to be known as Thin Beard Junction.

*

We laid our bundles in front of the kitchen hearth, at the feet of the master's wife. She was an elderly woman with dark skin and hair as soft, smooth and white as raw silk. She always squinted, as if she was searching for something tiny. When we arrived, she was peeling green bananas. When the oil began to boil, she threw the peeled fruit into the pan. I watched as the bubbles multiplied. She ordered us to wait until the bananas were cooked.

'Eat before you go and learn,' she said. She handed two

crispy bananas to each of us. When she got to me, she fixed me with her gaze.

'How's your mother?' she asked. I looked into her eyes, trying to gauge whether they expressed anger or concern.

'Tamu's fine,' I murmured.

'I know she's fine. Tell her I know that.' I nodded without understanding, wondering why the woman was staring at me so intently. Then it was time to go to the *shioni*.

When we got there, the master was teaching the older pupils. Sitting cross-legged, the pupils formed four concentric semicircles around a bench on which the master sat. The arrangement meant the master could address any one of them individually, as well as the group as a whole, and could lead the chants of praise that ended the class. In the centre of the circle was a wooden pole. Firmly planted in the earth, it seemed to stare at us with absent eyes. We were terrified of this pole. Recalcitrant or unruly pupils were tied to it, shirtless, and brushed with bunches of nettles. The punishment was called *ndjeni*. Anyone condemned to *ndjeni* knew they had at least two sleepless nights ahead of them: none of their mother's oils would relieve the itching.

We took our places on the raffia mat beside the other younger children, who were busy revising their *surahs*. Whatever we were doing, we always kept our ears open to what the master was telling the older pupils. Today he was outlining the rules that governed how a person should behave in daily life; alone, in a group, with his spouse, parents, children and brothers and sisters.

This wasn't of much interest to my friends and me. What we were waiting for were juicy details about certain aspects of married life. We were fascinated by this world that wasn't yet ours, by the idea of lifting the veil on what our elders experienced. But as soon as the master noticed we'd gone quiet to listen, he returned to his usual boring sermons. 'We are all brothers and sisters,' he intoned. 'Allah means unity; the unity of God, because he is One.'

I found these lectures tedious. I preferred it when the master guided us through the meaning of the Qur'an, sentence by sentence. The Qur'an was exciting, filled with the adventures of men and women who'd lived long before us. We listened to the letters that formed their names, felt the imprint of the words on our lips and our tongues, sometimes even felt as if we'd grasped their essence. The slither of '*sss*', the brisk melody of '*bâ*', the hiss of '*ha*'... I always asked the master lots of questions, some of them fanciful. Had King Solomon really passed through here on his chariot pulled by *jinns*, accompanied by Queen Bilkis? Had she really lost her ring in the crater of the Karthala volcano, and would she come back for it one day, as the legend said? Had the king locked up *jinns* in the caves by the sea and the marshes?

We listened to the master while day-dreaming about the conversations we'd have with our friends later. That was the pattern of our lives back then.

But that day, while my friends were dreaming up tricks to scare each other that evening, I was mulling over what I'd seen in the woods. I realised that whoever had been there before me must have been running. Running away from something.

Tamu was at the beach. She stood knee-deep in the water, washing clothes by rubbing them against a dark stone. Her silhouette stood out against the blue expanse and the surrounding rocks, looking like the cross section of a flower head. In her hands, I recognised my pink hemp dress and my blue *leso* with the yellow flowers. It was Tamu who'd dyed them: dyer to every master in town, she spruced up the other servants' clothes with beautiful tones in her spare time. We called her Tamu-of-the-magic-fingers: plants and flowers willingly offered up their most intense colours to her touch. She'd crush henna leaves against a stone to extract their sunset-coloured juice; the hibiscus flower provided her with a whole spectrum of pinks, reds and yellows. Sometimes, when harvesting vanilla, she'd grab a few pods that were still purple and use them to draw patterns on the yellow cloth. That was what she'd done on the dress I was wearing that day. It was the envy of all the girls at the *shioni*.

I ran over to Tamu and showed her my bag of henna leaves. She gave me a broad smile. Her teeth were as white as the foam on the waves. Her voice had the dry, lilting sound of the wind in the trees.

'Who gave you that henna, you little thief?'

I smiled back. 'It came from Abé.'

'Liar! Queen Abé, our Creator, has more pressing matters to attend to. Give me that. And recite me today's *surah.*'

She gently took the pouch of leaves from me and slung it over her shoulder. I helped her to rub the clothes as I recited my *surah.*

And the first ones, yes the first ones.
They are the closest to the Truth.
Many are the truthful among the first.
And so few, so few, among the last.

That evening we dined on stingray tail, sea snails and manioc. After dinner, we heard the sound of footsteps crunching on the pebbles outside. I knew then that it was time for me to go to one of my friends' houses. Fundi Ahmad had arrived.

*

I met up with Olympe, Ramla, Mlima and M'maka on the neighbour's verandah. The stray wisps of hair that had escaped from their plaits shone in the moonlight. I sat down among them and unwrapped the slices of cardamom cake I'd brought. We shared our spoils: Olympe had *mkatra sinia*, a rice cake made with coconut pulp; Ramla had *gudu gudu*, a caramel and coconut milk cake. Mlima began by making excuses: 'We haven't cooked dinner at my place yet tonight.' We tutted at her, 'You say that every night. You should all have died of hunger by now!'

We didn't hold it against her, though, because sometimes

it was true, and it could happen to any of us. Also because Mlima was the most talented storyteller in Itsandra. We called her 'Mlima-of-the-sweet-saliva'. Not only had she committed the entire repertoire of tales from our grandmothers to memory, she also knew how to add just the right amount of spice to rumours and to reality, and to adapt them to suit her tastes. Thanks to her, we'd invariably leave our gatherings either trembling with fear, shuddering with sadness or choking with laughter.

Our favourite stories were about the *jinn*. We were always greedy to hear about their latest exploits, and Mlima knew how to satisfy us. As soon as she opened her mouth to speak, the starry sky turned black, the stones shifted in the earth, the crickets stopped singing and every one of us stopped breathing.

'You'll never guess what happened to Bahati, the maid from Fundi Mkaya's house,' Mlima began, widening her eyes and flashing us a mischievous smile.

'The one who the *jinns* forbade from opening her mouth in the month of Ramadan, to stop her bitching about people?'

'That's the one.'

'Tell us, tell us!'

'Well, a few days ago, she was visited by an… unusual *jinn*.'

'What do you mean 'unusual'?'

'Not like the others. You know how it usually goes with *jinns*: you're all sitting there, eating, chatting, when all of a sudden someone starts sighing, throws her head back, rolls her eyes, as if she's about to faint but she's enjoying it?'

We all nodded vigorously: each of us had witnessed a scene of possession at least once. It could happen to anyone, anywhere, at any time: just as fire could penetrate the earth, *jinns*, beings of fire, had the power to penetrate us. Our island was home to three types of *jinn*, all of them travellers who'd been stranded off our coast centuries ago. The *rumbu*, from the neighbouring island of Pemba or Dargubei,[1] spoke Swahili; the *trumba* spoke Madagascan; the *rawhân* spoke Arabic. The language they used told us which Qur'anic master or sorcerer to call on to exorcise the victim. The most troublesome *jinn* was called Ahmad Bin Sultân: when he possessed a man or a woman, he compelled them to wear the *kandu*, the men's prayer robe, and wander the streets of the city reciting the Qur'an until they collapsed from exhaustion.

'Well, Bahati's *jinn* was of a completely different kind,' continued our friend. 'She let out her first sigh, then threw her head back. But instead of fainting and waking up babbling something in Swahili, Arabic or Malagasy, she started speaking in Hindi!'

Olympe and I widened our eyes, then burst into laughter.

'Hindi? What are you talking about? Those people don't even believe in the same god or the same things as us!'

'Well, that's how it happened with her. She sat with her ankles crossed, her hands resting in her lap. And you won't believe it, but suddenly she looked as if she was wearing make-up. Her skin took on a blue-ish tinge, her lips were very red, and there was kohl around her eyes. I swear to you, *wallahi, billahi wa rasul*!'

'If you say so,' I conceded. 'But something about your story doesn't ring true to me.'

1 City on the African coast, probably Durban (South Africa).

'I swear it's true, and it's not over yet! There was a woman in the group who knew a bit of Hindi, because she worked as a maid for some Indian traders. According to her, Indian *jinn* are called *bhûta*. They're people who've been dead a long time and who find it difficult to leave our world. They only take possession of the living when something prevents them from reaching their paradise. The *bhuta* who'd possessed Bahati had a message to deliver before he died, but he'd refused to do it. So that message had kept him in our world. Since the person he was supposed to deliver it to now lives on our island, he'd come to deliver it, because he was tired of being imprisoned.'

We couldn't suppress our shudders. A ghost! An undead! Was there really such a thing? Discussions like this pushed at the limits of what our master allowed. We lived for these transgressions. Like all children, we were drawn to the forbidden. We experienced these stories as secret passageways leading out of the fortress of the beliefs that were imposed on us, hidden windows through which we might escape. We knew nothing of our ancestors, we believed ourselves to be faithful servants of Allah, and yet our backs sometimes buckled under an unnamed burden, our lungs became choked by an invisible weight, our mouths sealed by something brought on the sea breeze itself.

'And what was this message?' asked Olympe.

Mlima fixed me with a serious gaze. 'It was: *watch out for the scientist's daughter*.'

She kept her eyes on me. Then her body jerked, she sighed and flung her head back. When she brought her head upright again, she stared up at the sky and said with gravity, '*Namaste-ji*'. Then she mumbled something in an unknown language.

We didn't speak Hindi, but it was clear that, apart from '*Namaste-ji*', the language she was speaking didn't exist.

It took us a moment to realise she was pretending. I felt a mixture of amusement and indignation. I pushed her against the wall. She burst out laughing. Olympe elbowed me aside, laughing too. Finally, defeated, I laughed along with them.

But I didn't feel as light-hearted as I had at the beginning of the evening.

How did Mlima know the names of Hindu ghosts? And, most of all, why had she stared at me like that while delivering her supposed message?

Fundi Ahmad was fond of me; I had no idea why. Said to be a descendant of the prophet, the *fundi* was proud of his Arab and Persian roots; less so of the African ancestry that had flattened his nose. He made full use of the right his complexion conferred to look down on those of more humble origins.

Yet he had an inexplicable affection for Tamu and me. Whenever he was irritated with one of his high-born wives, he'd come and stand outside our tin hut, announcing his arrival with a loud '*Hooodi!*' When Tamu opened the door, he'd follow her into her bedroom, which was separated from mine by a curtain we'd made out of old rice sacks. One evening we heard him approach, his steps curiously hesitant as he neared our door, as they were on occasion. At times like this, Tamu would let out an exasperated sigh. 'Here he is wanting to take a piss again…' she'd mutter, dropping her spoon into her steel dish and sucking her teeth in annoyance.

I didn't understand what she was upset about. Fundi went nowhere near the toilets; he just followed Tamu straight into the bedroom. Then they'd have one of their loud conversations, complete with 'Ah!' 'Yeee!' and 'Hee!' sounds—so animated, they'd both come out breathless and sweaty. Then, still without going to the toilets, Fundi would come and sit next to me at the table, his lower body draped in one of my mother's *lesos*.

He'd dab at his forehead, take a cardamom cake from the bag hanging at his waist and hand it to me with a smile. He'd get his tobacco pouch out of his pocket, pour a little of the black powder onto his palm, and bring it swiftly to his nose. Then he'd start his usual questioning.

'Have you memorised this week's *surah*?'

'Yes,' I'd answer proudly.

'Recite it for me.'

Each week, we were required to memorise a chapter of the Qur'an and recite it to Fundi. When I recited correctly, I earned a compliment. Fundi's compliments were a rare and sought-after commodity. If I mispronounced a word, Fundi would wait till I'd finished, then declare, 'Correct, but not complete!' That meant that at the next reading class, I'd have to re-recite the chapter I hadn't mastered as well as the one I'd been given to study that week.

On the evening in question, I inhaled deeply, to ward off the devils' breath, and recited:

I recite in the name of the one, of the lover, of the near,
And of the first; yes, the first!
For it is they who are closest to the truth.
There are many who know truth among the first,
And few, so few, among the last.

'Good, good, *djayyid*,' he said, before I'd finished. 'You're making progress with your pronunciation, but you need to lengthen the final vowels; they're still too short.'

'Yes, Fundi.'

'And what do you think about this 'first'?' he said, leaning closer, an expectant look on his face. 'Have you thought about what that might mean?'

'Y-yes,' I stammered. 'I think about it every time I read the *surah*, but—'

Tamu interrupted us at this point in the conversation, probably because it was getting boring.

'Fundi, dear, finish your tea before it gets cold. Then go back to your wife before she suspects you of something you're not guilty of.'

Fundi cleared his throat and sat up straight, almost reluctantly. He contemplated the designs on his fine china cup with interest. A flowing river, two women on each bank, four women in all, each pouring water from a jug. He was the one who'd given this cup, and the rest of the tea set it was part of, to Tamu. It was rare for a master to give a gift to a servant, but Fundi bore a love for us that no one understood.

'You're right, my dear Tamu,' he replied. Turning to me, he said, 'Think carefully about my question, Hardie. It's important for your learning.'

'Yes, Fundi.'

Finally, he put his clothes back on and left us. Once he was out of earshot, Tamu sucked her teeth again and muttered, 'You come to do your business, then don't wipe up afterwards!'

I had no idea what she was talking about, took it to be some sort of coded grown-up language. All that mattered to me was that, despite her grumbling, there was a radiance to Tamu after Fundi's visits, one that none of the old man's wives could match.

After dinner, we always went out into the cobbled communal courtyard to wash our soot-stained pots. The neighbours would be there too, gossiping about this or that nobleman's daughter, delighting in the tribulations of their betters. I think it reassured them to know that wealth didn't bring happiness to privileged women. It made them feel they shared something with those who were fair of skin, born into faith and bathed in the sacred language. Tamu joined in enthusiastically with the gossip, until Fundi's visits became more frequent.

After that, as I rubbed at the cooking pots with coconut fibre, she'd gaze up at the stars, eyes shining. She taught me the names of all the constellations we used to count the passing of the years. The neighbours would stop talking and Tamu would tell stories that had been passed down by our ancestors from across the sea.

'The shape of the stars is a story,' she began. 'The elders have entrusted me to celebrate this story. Let me tell you the epic of the five princes whose names have been erased.'

In those moments, I forgot I had neither father nor mother. I forgot the strange feeling I had about the relationship between Tamu and Fundi, the things my friends said about the sighing and the loud conversations. My friends called me naive, but it might be more accurate to say that I preferred dreams to the truth. My own dream was one day to sail between the brightest star in the constellation of Asorotan, the biggest star in Asumbula and the whitest star in Alakarab.

Tamu told me of her childhood in the land of Msumbidji; a place inhabited by spirits, sorcerers and fish-women.

Afterwards, I fell asleep curled up in her arms. Before drifting from consciousness, I'd hear her prayer, the meaning of which I would not understand until many years later: 'May you never cry down below.'

It was Ramla who pointed it out. Two weeks after our previous outing, we were back collecting branches in Ahmad's Wood. We stopped at the edge of the forest first to dig up some cassava and pink taro roots to roast in the hot ash the next day. Everything was as it always was; on the path I took, there was no sign of anyone else having been there. On the way home, though, when we asked Ramla why her bundle was so small, she said someone had already collected wood in her section, leaving only branches that were too thin to be of any use.

People were saying that Bilkis, the wife of King Solomon, had been roaming our forests of late; that her ghost was haunting our island in search of a ring she'd lost during a romantic escapade with her husband. An evil *jinn* had fallen in love with her and was threatening to break up her marriage to Solomon. Only this ring could save her.

There were other stories from closer to home. The chief of Itsandra, Charif Mohamed, had lost his daughter. She'd run away after discovering she was about to be forced into marriage with a man from the capital. Search parties had been sent out and mystics had entered into the spiritual sleep of *manamein* to try to find her. After several weeks of fruitless searching, she'd been declared dead.

Some people had invented a second life for this girl in the woods: transformed into a *jinn*, she wandered in search of little children, who she swallowed whole.

The next day, I got up before everyone else, long before the dawn prayer. The ground was still cold and the crickets still chirping in the tall grass. The whole town was asleep. I waited for Tamu to leave for work, then headed towards Ahmad's Wood.

Jamu, the night *jinn*, had just finished painting every blade of grass with dew. Vegetation tickled my soles as I crushed the green carpet under my feet. I slid between the trees, stealthy as a mango thief, chose an enormous male lychee with a three-pronged trunk and hid myself behind it.

All I heard at first were the tiny, fleeting noises of hedgehogs reclaiming their nests, mongooses shifting as they began to wake. Their delicate rustling sounds overlaid the sound of my calm, even breathing.

Then my breath quickened and caught. I'd heard a new sound: dry leaves crackling rhythmically under the weight of footsteps: heavy, halting. Human.

I strained to make out where they were coming from. It seemed to be just a few metres away and to my left. I moved my head so I was completely concealed by the trunk of the lychee and peered in that direction.

The voice came from behind me; soft, cool, crystal-clear.

'I knew you'd come.'

Her skin had the burnished tint of the setting moon. She was a study in harmony: eyebrows that formed perfect arches over huge eyes; long, curling lashes, as black as night; a broad nose that narrowed at the centre; full, sharply outlined lips; small hands with long, slender fingers. Exquisite in face and body. It was as if every girl who'd lived before her was just a step in the process, a practice run on the route to her perfection.

She was a master's daughter. What was she doing out here?

I don't know how long I would've stayed glued to the spot, staring at her, while she eyed me back warily. She considered for a moment, then said, 'If you tell anyone you saw me here, I'll say that you kidnapped me.'

I swallowed, already feeling guilty of a crime I hadn't committed. She'd managed to ask me not to expose her without relinquishing any of her power. She really was a master's daughter.

'You must be Hardie.'

I nodded. I opened my mouth to ask her how she knew my name. Nothing came out. I gathered my courage, forced myself to try again. She was in my world, I told myself, not in her own realm of carpets and incense.

'And who are you?' I asked, as casually as I could.

She laughed, a shrill, sing-song laugh, like the call of a bird. She raised her chin and gave the tiniest smile.

'I'm Halima. Come with me.'

She disappeared into the trees.

I was so surprised, it was a moment before I could persuade my feet to move. Then I hurried after her.

We moved quickly through the forest, past the mango and the eucalyptus. I pushed aside the dense ferns and spiky aloes that blocked my path. Halima ploughed through them without even registering the scratches to her face. We rushed down a slope I knew well: it led to Hatov beach.

Children were forbidden from going to Hatov beach: the legends said King Solomon had imprisoned the strongest of his disobedient *jinns* there. My friends and I occasionally broke the rule and sneaked off there to swim. As soon as we reached the beach, Halima turned to me. She wriggled out of her long white dress, revealing pale skin, and let it drop to the sand.

'Teach me to swim,' she said.

I gaped at her. Me, a servant, risking being seen swimming with a master's daughter?

'I don't know how to swim.'

She smirked again, wrinkling her left nostril slightly. The shadows of the palm leaves caressed her flawless face. They seemed reluctant to let it go, despite the breeze that blew them.

'You're Hardie,' she said. 'That is your name, isn't it? You're the one who catches the bluefin tuna.'

Her directness surprised me. I planted my feet firmly in the sand and shook my head.

'I keep my feet on the ground. I don't go where it's deep.'

She stared at me, still smiling. 'Bluefin don't live on the surface. You have to go a long way out to find them. Of course you can swim.'

I had no response to that. Finally I ventured, 'How do you know that if you can't swim yourself?'

'A fisherman told me.'

'How? Girls like you don't talk to people like us.'

It was her turn to be surprised. We were even. But she soon regained her composure.

'He told me because I ordered him to. Abé has given me the gift of being able to make anyone talk.'

Abé was the name we gave to God, but only in secret. We could never speak the word aloud in front of the masters: to them, Abé was the goddess of ignorance, imported from the land they'd taken us from. They believed in Allah, and that was the only name by which we were allowed to refer to divinity. What was this girl doing talking about Abé?

As if she'd read my mind, Halima said, 'Mercy, clemency, greatness: it's all the same thing. You call him Abé, my father calls him Allah. They're the same being.'

'Ours is a woman. Queen Abé.'

'Male or female, it makes no difference.'

'Which name do you use?'

'Whichever I feel like, depending on my mood and the person in front of me.'

'And you have the power to make others answer you?'

'According to my father. Unfortunately, that's where my power ends.'

She walked towards the shoreline. Her feet caressed the sand beneath the foam. She held her back straight; at the base of her spine was a smooth arch. She lifted her chin, as if trying to keep her head above water. Her voice was clear and carried further than her delicate frame suggested. It was strong and a little nasal, like the sound of an Indian sitar.

Halima's body was more mature and sculpted than mine; still childlike, but with extra contours. She must have been a little older than me, thirteen or fourteen. Already she'd been taught to command, intimidate, provoke fear.

'If only my power could take me far away from here, far

away from my fate!' she shouted at an imposing wave that was advancing towards us. 'But it can't,' she continued, turning back to me. 'So you're going to have to show me how to swim. Then, when I'm ready, I can leave this place and never come back.'

My heart caught in my throat. Helping a young girl run away from her marriage? That was what this would be. They said a group of young women had once fled to Mount Djabal to escape the Malagasy king who'd invaded our island. They threw themselves in the sea, one after the other, all apart from one. She lived to tell the story, but after that she was never seen again.

Halima was born too late to be that young woman, though.

There were three rules about interactions between servants and the daughters of masters: don't help them escape; don't plait their hair; don't become attached to them. If I did what Halima asked, I risked being locked up with her at the top of Mount Djabal, where lepers and people with tuberculosis were confined, at the mercy of evil *jinns*.

So I have no idea why I stripped off my clothes beside Halima, before plunging into the warm, briny water.

*

After that we met often. Long before dawn, I'd make my way towards Ahmad's Wood, then veer off and head to the sea. Halima would be waiting at the bottom of the slope, naked and ready to swim. She seemed to have no fear of being caught.

'A light-skinned girl naked on the beach is either a

dangerous *jinn* or a master's daughter. And no master's daughter is brave enough to venture out here!' she said, with her crystalline laugh. Her long hair clung to her back as she dived into the water. Then it fanned out, black as coal, and floated in front of her eyes, impeding her progress.

'I'd love to have your hair,' she said, 'It's so easy to plait! Hey, would you do my hair like yours?'

Braiding the hair of a master's daughter: another breach of the rules. They said a person who braided another's hair was passing on a part of her soul through her fingers. No master wanted a servant's soul mixing with his daughter's. No servant wanted to be the first to commit such a transgression.

The strands of Halima's hair slid through my fingers like delicate snakes. I twined them together with care. Her head rested on my thigh. Her hand, perfectly co-ordinated with mine, held back the hair so I could braid each section. I gazed down at the fine line of her jaw, the curl of her eyelashes, her long, velvety-soft neck. Did I mention that her skin was fair? I hadn't looked at it properly before, but now I saw it was the colour of an almost-ripe mango. A fresh, sweet yellow, full of tender promise. The tight braids I was creating exposed channels of amber skin, which I stroked with my fingertips to massage out the tension of the hairstyle.

The second rule was well and truly broken.

Sometimes Halima wanted a swimming lesson, at other times she just wanted to talk. She talked about her mother, whom she'd never known, and her father, who'd taught her everything usually taught to boys, though she was never going to become a *cadi* or a *mufti*, as a son of his would've done.

'Of course he'd have preferred a boy,' she said with bitterness.

I got the impression she yearned for a friend. She might have been a master's daughter, but she was powerless against loneliness. For my part, I was unable to resist the urge to try to soothe her pain. In spite of my fear of breaking the rules about exchanges between master's daughters and lesser humans, I was already under the spell of her upside-down cashew nut eyes. I kept on going to meet her.

One morning, when I returned from the beach at Hatov, Tamu was standing at the front door, a stern look on her face. She asked me where I'd been.

'In the forest, collecting wood for Fundi Ahmad,' I lied.

The truth was, I'd surrendered to Halima's repeated demands and had skipped one of Fundi's lessons. What I didn't know was that Fundi had sent Ramla and Olympe to tell Tamu about my absence and pass on the warning that I'd be excluded from class if it happened again.

I couldn't tell if Tamu was furious about my absence or because I'd lied. I didn't have time to think about it, though; she grabbed me by the ear and twisted my earlobe with a ferocity I hadn't known she possessed.

'Absent from the *shioni* on the eve of Ramadan!' she roared.

I cried out in pain. Tamu gripped me harder and dragged me inside. Just then, a downpour started. I wished I could run back outside and dance in the rain.

Behind the curtain of my room, Tamu stood facing me. Her black eyes flashed. Her neatly-oiled hair and the smooth, dark skin of her rounded face shone in the flame that flickered behind the smoky glass of the lantern. Outside, huge raindrops splattered on the ground. Despite the reprimand, my mind drifted towards where I could've placed calabashes around the house to collect the water.

In a sudden movement, Tamu grabbed the collar of my dress. I was so stunned I took a step backwards.

'This,' she hissed, 'Is all you have in this world. If I take it off, you'll be naked. Do you hear me? Naked, *bo daba*!'

She lunged at me, gasping with fury, and ripped a strip off my dress. She tore the strip in two. I shivered in the rain-cooled air, hugging myself instinctively.

'You think you're alive? You're an empty carcass, rotting flesh! You think you're worth something to these people? You're worth nothing. Nothing! You're just a body, like a head of cattle. At best, you're another plate of food, another belly to fill. You're a miserable, worthless wretch!'

Her voice quivered with rage and also, I understood then, with despair. Tamu wasn't screaming, she was crying. She moved away from me, behind her curtain, and I thought she was going to leave me there, in the middle of the room, naked and shivering. But she came back, armed with a copy of the Qur'an. She brandished it at me.

'This is all you've got, idiot girl. It's all that's real. It will save your life. Things are going to change in the future, and if you don't take this book seriously, you'll still be a slave while other girls your age are free women, teaching their masters' children. Do you hear me, bird-brain? This book is all you have! I have nothing to give you. Absolutely nothing. I don't even have the right to defend you if someone decides to hurt you one day!'

Her voice cracked as she spoke the last words, and I watched as her face dissolved in tears. As if by contagion, I started crying too. I didn't understand much, but I understood Tamu's despair. I'd known about powerlessness since I was a child.

What I hadn't understood, but could read in the gleam that still shone in Tamu's eyes, was her hope. It was a spark as fragile as the one dying in the lantern, yet it was there, in spite of my idiotic behaviour. I promised myself then that I wouldn't be the one to put it out. I'd obey Tamu, even if it wasn't clear to me how the Qur'an could rescue me from my condition. Never again would I miss a day of *shioni*. I'd find another way to see Halima.

'Hurry, the sun will be up soon!'

I'd met Halima before dawn, deep in Ahmad's Wood. My plan was to spend some time with her before joining my friends to gather branches. We talked as we walked. I taught Halima how to catch the insects that tasted good, even raw. She pointed out the stars that could still be made out as dawn broke and told me their names. Then we dozed off.

Now I was late for the firewood collection. I was going to get whipped!

'I have to go,' I spluttered, 'I can't come with you now!'

'But it's so close! Come on, I have to show you this!'

I looked behind me: we'd walked a long way from Ahmad's Wood. The damage was already done: my friends would have left without me. Fundi had probably asked them to gather *ndjeni* leaves at the same time, to make my whip. I pictured him preparing the coconut fibre ropes that would be used to tie me to the central post of the *shioni.* Then everyone would be invited to administer a stinging lash to my chest. I shuddered at the thought of those terrible spiked leaves attacking my skin, of the searing itches that awaited me. But I followed Halima.

We arrived at the beach. The sea was calm, smooth as a sheet of steel. The sun was sending tentative rays down from the hill behind us. They hit the water, making its tiny ripples sparkle like diamonds. I automatically picked up three stones, murmured *bismillah* and blew on them, before throwing them as far as I could; one to the east, one to the west and one to the north, to chase away the three *djinns* that lived at each of those points of the compass. Halima sat down on the sand a few metres away from me. Her silhouette stood out against the glowing sky. Her head was lowered and her fingers brushed the sand in front of her. I sat down beside her.

'Look,' she said.

I obeyed, chastising myself inwardly for being so obedient to a virtual stranger, so disobedient to my Qur'anic teacher.

Halima made a dot in the sand, lengthened it into a line, then drew another alongside it.

'Tell me, do you know when you were born?'

'No,' I replied. 'Servants don't have dates of birth.'

'Yes, you do,' she continued. 'And judging by your anger, you were born in the twelfth constellation, which is this one.'

She drew a series of figures that I couldn't make head nor tail of. I just stared at her two fingers, dancing on the sand, hypnotised by them.

'How old are you?'

'Eleven, I think.'

'Right. So you were born two cycles before this one.'

I should have felt impatient. Yes, she was beautiful, but she was wasting my time, putting me at risk of punishment, just for her own amusement.

'I know you don't see what I'm getting at,' she murmured.

'But bear with me.'

'It's just that… I'm supposed to be at Ahmad's Wood…'

'Are you eager to go and claim your punishment?'

I made no reply. She was right, it was too late. Although I was terrified of the punishment Fundi Ahmad had in store for me, I wanted to know where this was leading. I stared quizzically at Halima. She kept her eyes fixed on the sand and on her fingers, which were drawing perpendicular lines.

'*Two, four, house of peace. Six, eight, house of punishment. Ten, twelve… peace returns.*'

I couldn't understand a word she was saying. She turned to me, unconcerned.

'You won't be punished. As long as you comply with my request.'

She gave me a penetrating look. I was stunned. I wouldn't be punished? What request could possibly have such a profound impact on my fate? I wanted to tell her she was talking nonsense, but in spite of myself, a part of me wanted to believe her. My fear of the stinging nettles was very much alive; I thought I could already feel the poisonous caress of their tiny white spikes on my skin.

'What request?'

'First you have to promise me you'll accept.'

'But…'

'Promise!'

'I promise,' I said mechanically.

I simmered with anger at myself for giving in so quickly. The imperious tone she'd used was that of a master addressing a recalcitrant servant. She spoke again, still keeping her gaze fixed on the sand.

'I need your help.'

She said it quickly, whispered it, as if it were both urgent and dangerous. Her voice betrayed fear, but her face remained as serene as if we were playing a game of noughts and crosses in the sand.

I kept quiet and listened. Halima articulated each word carefully, as if to give me time to absorb it.

'I am the daughter of Charif Mohamed.'

The name rang in my ears, as shrill as the flute of Firimbi, the musician who announced the deaths in our town. 'OK,' I thought. I was in serious trouble. Halima was the daughter of the chief of Itsandra. What punishment would that man devise for a person who'd helped his daughter to escape? Surely something a thousand times more painful than the *ndjeni*. For a moment, I wondered whether I'd be better off slipping away now and reporting Halima immediately. It might mean a few lashes of the nettle whip, but that would be sweet compared with what awaited me if I kept quiet.

I made a move to get up, but my legs buckled beneath me. As I was to discover throughout my relationship with Halima, some unknown force was at work, pinning me to her side and preventing me from rescuing myself. She sat with her head bowed, waiting patiently for my response. She seemed relieved when, looking up, she found me still there. I looked away, let my gaze get lost in the ripples on the ocean.

Halima continued in a hesitant voice, 'My father wants to marry me off. I don't want it, but I have no choice. I'm surviving on lychees and manioc tubers. But I can't carry on like this for much longer. I know my absence is making my mother suffer in her grave. And if I swim away, either someone will recognise me and I'll be dragged back by force, or I'll become someone else's slave, on some other island where no one knows my father. All I can do is accept this marriage proposal and become the wife of a bookkeeper from Moroni. But there's something else…'

Her voice hadn't wavered as she told me about her tragic situation. She even seemed to have made peace with the idea of submission. I knew that kind of serenity. It was the same calm with which our mothers agreed to be concubines for our masters, or to deliver their daughters to them.

Halima reached into her pocket and pulled out something wrapped in cloth. She passed it to me. Her hand was trembling. She took my hand in hers. I felt her warm, smooth skin, the roughness of the cloth, and beneath it something hard. Dry wood.

'I want you to keep this for me. For the rest of your life, you're to look after this object and show it to no-one. No-one can see it, and no-one can remove the wrapping. Not even you.'

The object was cube-shaped. I could feel its edges pressing into my skin. It was barely bigger than my thumb.

I wondered what it was. I longed to unwrap the cloth. As if she'd read my mind, Halima grabbed my hand.

'The most important thing is never to reveal this object!'

'Why?' I asked boldly, 'What difference does it make, if it doesn't belong to me?'

'You'd be in great danger!' she said, suddenly distraught.

'All right, I won't open it,' I reassured her.

I hardly knew this girl, and already I was clinging to the

trust she'd placed in me, like a stray dog thrown a bone.

'Never unwrap that package, Hardie!'

'Why me?' I asked her.

She didn't answer. A light breeze blew across my cheek. I turned to look at her; she was gone.

Months passed. One night, Tamu came home early from work. She found me curled up on the mat we sometimes shared when Fundi wasn't there.

I was sobbing, groaning, crying hot, heavy tears. My arms were crossed over my chest. I was fighting the urge to scratch at my nipples, as if the prospect of that pain could be worse than what I was already feeling.

My mother immediately understood what had happened. She dropped her bag on the floor, rushed over and knelt beside the mat. Her hands scrabbled feverishly to get past the fortress of my arms. She dug under my dress and reached my chest. I screamed, though she'd touched me as gently as she could. Then she felt it. The absence. Instead of the gentle slopes of my fledgling womanhood, the flatness of a plain.

A shriek of horror rose from her throat, piercing the silence of the night. She forgot to be gentle as she pulled her hands away from my torso, still raw and sticky, and I screamed again. Like a just-circumcised boy, I was hypersensitive, shuddering at the touch of even the softest cloth: where my breasts had been there was now an open wound.

It had all started when my period came. The changes in my body had already begun; at least that was what the other women kept telling Tamu. I was growing up too quickly, ahead of all my friends. Soon I'd be attracting attention from the noblemen of Itsandra, and it would only be a matter of time before one of them decided to push me up against a mango tree.

On Fundi's orders, I'd stopped gathering wood for a few days to focus on my Qur'anic studies. There were two chapters in particular he wanted me to read: one about the dawn and one about the merciful. The repetition of certain verses interested him, and he wanted to hear my thoughts. I'd been at the *shioni* for several hours, reading and re-reading the verses, looking for something that might illuminate them, when suddenly I felt a dripping sensation between my legs. I clenched my private parts, terrified I'd somehow slipped back into childishness. But the warm flow continued, as if someone inside me were slowly pouring a stream of water as they did their ablutions. I froze and stopped reading. Fundi let a moment pass before speaking.

'Why aren't you reading? What is it?'

I was unable to respond; my breath was ragged, my brow beaded with sweat. Fundi waited, then pressed a hand to my forehead.

'Are you all right, my child? What's wrong with you? Look at me!'

Only then did I raise my eyes, and he saw my tears. He stared for some time at my dry lips, my trembling hands. Then he took the Qur'an from me and asked if I could stand.

As I did so, he glanced at the place on the ground where I'd been sitting. He gave a small nod: he'd understood what was happening before I had. He pulled the embroidered scarf from his neck and wrapped it quickly around my waist. Then he looked me in the eyes.

'Listen to me,' he said. 'You're a woman now. But whatever happens, don't you dare think you'll stop being my student. Whatever anyone else says, you mustn't let your knowledge slip out of you, the way your childhood is doing right now. Do you understand? Now, run back to your mother's house and don't come back here today!'

I followed my master's orders and ran. I had no idea what was happening to me. Tamu wasn't home yet, but the door of our house stood open. As I rushed in, I bumped straight into Ramla's mother. She stared at me as I ran towards the toilets, and I heard her let out a small shriek. In the toilet, I pulled off Fundi's scarf, then my dress. Down the back of it, like the petals of a hibiscus opening to the sun, was a red stain.

Tamu raced back to the house, likely alerted by Ma Ramla. Everyone understood what was happening apart from me. My body was sending signals to the rest of the world without bothering to tell me a thing.

'Oh my darling, are you a woman now? That snake Ma Ramla's been telling every person she meets. I'm so sorry.'

Tamu took me in her arms, and I sobbed my heart out.

'I'm crying down there, Tamu!' I spluttered.

'No, no, my darling, that's not what crying down there is. That will never happen to you, may Abé protect you. It's just that you're a woman now. Nothing else is going to change. I'll make sure of that.'

The next day, Tamu came home with a *hami*, a pearl necklace and a pair of silver earrings she must have paid the Indian merchant a fortune for. I stared at her in bewilderment. She said, 'I told the mistress my daughter had become a woman. She said every woman should start her life with a piece of gold or silver. I hope these earrings bring you luck, my daughter.'

*

It happened a few weeks later, one afternoon just before the *asr* meditation. The subject of my new womanhood had already been broached several times by Tamu's neighbours and cousins. Menstruating at eleven, they said, was far too early; I was at too tender an age to be contending with monthly flows of blood, and whatever else. I needed guidance, they said, at this new stage of my life; steps would need to be taken to fend off those whose gaze might start to linger on my developing body. I'd be bleeding again soon, and before that happened I had to shield myself from predatory eyes. They carried on and on in that vein. Tamu paid them little heed, and I let their whispers get washed away by the monsoon.

That season had begun with the return of the pilgrims, the *mihadji*, who'd travelled to kiss the ground at Mecca. That year, one of Fundi Ahmad's cousins was among them. Tamu had received no visits from Fundi for the last few days; he and the other masters were spending most of their time grilling the *mihadji* about their experiences in Mecca. My dedication to studying my *surahs* had waned; instead of reading feverishly, I now sometimes wandered into the kitchens to deliver the fish I'd caught for the masters, lingering for a chat or to scrounge a banana fritter.

One day I was in the kitchen where Ramla's mother

worked. She was peeling green bananas for a coconut milk ragout to be served that evening. The master of that house came from the capital, where people used spices imported from India; he liked his ragouts enlivened with tomatoes, cumin, garlic, cloves and the most fashionable spice, *dzindzan.* As vibrantly yellow as the setting sun, it was said to tantalise the tongue just as much as chilli, but without the irritation.

The scent of jasmine wafted towards me as I entered the kitchen, lingering only briefly, like the perfume of a visitor who'd just left the room.

I noticed Ramla's mother eyeing me closely as she tossed some banana skins into the still-warm ashes under a pot where a sauce had been cooking. Ramla noticed too. She immediately concocted an excuse to slip out, as if Death were hot on her heels.

The call to prayer sounded. I'd just stirred the crushed garlic into the already-bubbling sauce when Ma Ramla suddenly snatched the banana skins from the ashes. A split second later, she was standing in front of me, arms outstretched, feet planted, blocking my exit. Before I had time to make any movement, she yanked up my dress. I opened my mouth to ask her what was going on, but she was already pressing the piping-hot skins against my budding breasts. The force she used and the searing sensation made my breath catch in my throat. My body drained of blood and became limp, my arms dangling uselessly at my sides. Ma Ramla's face shimmered in the haze that swirled around my head. The *muezzin's* call reverberated in my ears. I was burning, being consumed. I could no longer feel any part of myself, or perhaps I felt so intensely that feeling disappeared, plunging me into a terrible void. All I was aware of was the stretching of my lips as my mouth opened wide and air escaping from my throat. I didn't know if the shrill whistling sound was my own scream or the noise of a coconut stake ripping through my throat after piercing my heart.

There were a few more seconds of haziness, the feeling that my head had detached from my body, then dizziness engulfed me and spat me out again at the feet of my aggressor. It was the gravel digging into my knees that told me I'd fainted from shock. When I tried to lift my head it felt as heavy as a stone. Ma Ramla was still in front of me, her eyes still boring into me, but not as deeply as the brand new pain I now felt: that of my skin being torn away. While I was floating in limbo, Ma Ramla had kept up the pressure on my chest. Now she was peeling the banana skins away. What I felt must have been like what manioc roots feel when they're ripped from the ground to be eaten. Ma Ramla had ripped out my breasts. From deep inside my body, I could feel them separating from me, whole root systems of burning hot veins. I saw them, glowing red in the dusk, blood dripping from their filaments.

While I struggled to get my breath back, I heard Ma Ramla mutter triumphantly, 'Now you're safe from wayward looks. Nobody should have breasts so young. They'll grow back when you're old enough to marry.'

But my breasts would never grow back. She'd ripped out every last part of them.

My mother rushed to press a cloth soaked in olive oil to my chest.

'Good Lord,' she whispered, in a trembling voice, as she

daubed gently at my scalded skin. ‘My poor girl, you’re as boiled as the cow skin that goes in the servants’ soup!’

Confronted by this kindness, this all-too-rare demonstration of Tamu’s affection, and certain now that she didn’t want this life for me, I finally sobbed. The tears rose up from a well I’d kept scrupulously sealed. The river was in spate now, and I let it empty itself into my mother’s free hand as I met her eyes through the blur.

In the days that followed, Tamu treated me with a poultice of henna and crushed turmeric root wrapped in banana leaves. It was meant to help speed up my scarring, and its coolness eased the pain. Tamu never spoke to Ma Ramla again after that. I heard she also made her opinion known with a fist to the face.

Once my scars had formed and it was clear my breasts were not going to grow back, no-one ever called me anything other than Hardie again. Instead of nipples, around which soft, womanly mounds should have ripened, two huge, lumpy red blotches stared back at me in the mirror.

QARSHAT

The sun was at its zenith and it was hot enough to splash among the crayfish. In fact, I thought, if I could manage to fertilise my quota of vanilla flowers quickly enough, I could risk the stings of the sea urchins and jump into the salty water at Hatov with the more daring of my friends. We could go straight across the vanilla field, then cut through the forest, steering clear of the nettles. We could gather bunches of thyme as we went, pick some henna leaves for our mistresses, eat a few cashew apples.

If we did get stung by a sea urchin, it wasn't hard to find some little scamp willing to help out by pissing on us. We just had to make sure we got to the beach early enough to allow time, if it came to it, to find a friendly urinator, let the sacred balm do its work, wash and be rid of the smell by the time we got home. Fundi Ahmad would beat me to a pulp if he ever found out I'd let a boy piss on me, not to mention that I'd seen the equipment he used to do it.

These thoughts were in vain, though. By the time I'd fertilised my last flower, the sun had dipped low and the sky was turning red. I had to go home.

*

Ten years had passed since I'd last seen Halima. Our paths had never crossed again. I didn't think about her often, only when I found myself in Ahmad's Wood. At those times, I sometimes thought I heard a rustle of fabric between the branches, or a light, hesitant breath behind a tree trunk. But no one used those paths now apart from Fundi Ahmad's pupils.

My master continued to visit my mother. Their discussions went on long after their lovemaking was over. When he arrived, I'd retire to the new verandah we'd built and find myself something to do: sorting the grains of rice from the hollowed husks and the weevils, or weaving prayer mats from fresh palm fronds. Sometimes I went to see my friends. Olympe was now the servant of a rich family. Ramla had a baby boy, probably by her master. I'd bring her gifts I'd made for the baby: a hat, or a square ball woven from palm leaves.

We were no longer children. At harvest festivals, we danced the *wadaha* in the town square. One by one, draped in our young women's *hamis,* we stepped out into the night, to the centre of the circle of dancers, and swayed. I'd pick up one of the pestles placed at an angle on the edge of the mortar and dip it in the dry rice before throwing it to my neighbour, who'd do the same, passing it on to the next dancer. When our performance was over, we'd go back to shimmying our hips in the circle while the next performers entered one by one. The men beat frantically on their drums, their eyes closed, no doubt imagining one of us on their laps instead of the instruments. Some turned their dreams into reality at the end of the evening, with or without the consent of the woman involved. Ramla, Olympe and I always slipped away before the dancing finished.

One evening, Firimbi, the musician who announced the

dead by playing his flute, intercepted us as we were passing Thin Beard Junction. Two of his friends were with him. The men were visibly drunk, and their breath reeked of ginger liquor, despite the cloves they were chewing to mask the smell. They staggered towards us, eyes glazed. I heard Ramla and Olympe's breath, quick and damp, as they drew closer to me. Firimbi approach, panting with impatience, and shouted to me, 'Come on, then!'

I walked towards him, head bowed, feigning submission.

'You want me to come?'

Firimbi hadn't thought to wonder why his two friends were hanging back. He should have.

When he put his paws on my chest, he had just enough time to be surprised by the absence of breasts. I gave him an impish smile. With one hand, I grabbed his wrist, as if to encourage him to explore further; with the other, I grabbed his private parts and twisted, so fast and hard that he gasped. Then I pushed him roughly against one of his friends. They fell on top of each other on the ground. I bared my teeth at the third, who staggered backwards, stammering an inaudible threat. They ran off and left Firimbi lying there, breathless with pain.

As I watched them fleeing, my eyes lingered for a moment on the second man. His name was Soulé. He was terrified of me. For my part, though, I felt a tingling sensation on my skin whenever I saw him. It was a pity he couldn't choose his company better.

We went on our way.

'You're so brave, Hardie!' murmured Olympe. 'I just froze.'

'Me too,' I replied. 'My hands froze on his stinking balls.'

We all burst out laughing. I saw my friends to their houses before heading home myself.

When I got there, Tamu was waiting for me on the verandah, staring up at the stars. She seemed pensive and melancholy. I sat down beside her. Those ten years had wrinkled her smooth skin a little, but had done nothing else to diminish her beauty. In the evenings, she always told me legends from her ancestors: The zebra star that used its ingenuity to escape the lion star, and the trail of their chase across the sky; the milk that spurted from the teats of Dxui, the half-man half-woman fruit god, and flowed across the vaults of heaven. And my favourite story, that of the five princes with the forgotten names.

But when I sat down that night, Tamu told me a completely different story.

'Fundi Ahmad's going to take a wife,' she murmured. 'For the third time.'

She paused.

'It's not me.'

She turned towards me. Her eyes were clouded with rage and despair.

'I told you,' she added bitterly. 'If you haven't mastered their Qur'an, you can never be a part of their world. Without that bloody book, we're nothing, *bo daba.*'

*

So Fundi had chosen a third wife. According to Tamu, the reason the man was so insatiable was because he had an extra ball. Also because, according to the other women in the neighbourhood, the bride-to-be was breathtakingly beautiful. Fundi's other two wives were so jealous that one of them broke out in hives and the other had diarrhoea for a week. As for Tamu, she started laughing every five minutes for no apparent reason, as if a *jinn* was standing next to her and amusing itself by tickling her without warning. None of this changed the fact that Fundi Ahmad had found himself a pearl of a woman.

As a dyer, Tamu had to go and prepare the new bride for her wedding night.

'Her hair falls all the way down her back,' she told me in a monotone. 'It's as black as a guinea fowl's feathers, with the same blue highlights. It's as soft as the silk skeins of *Mzee* Mbaba, the weaver. It's as voluminous as the waterfalls on the island of Mwali.'

I wanted to see this woman.

Ramla's job was to bring the hot water the women would place under the bench that had been specially made for the bride-to-be. It consisted of two planks with a space in the middle. When she sat on it, the woman's private parts would be exposed to the steam escaping from the pot beneath her. The wedding rituals dictated that this part of her body be purified. The steam would melt away any foul-smelling secretions that might repel her husband. They'd fall, drop by drop, into the scalding water.

The house was always cleaned before the master entered.

Ramla burned her fingers carrying the pot, because the water had to be boiling. She'd poured a whole jar of incense resin into it; another woman had thrown in some jasmine petals, the Rahatul-Layl variety, 'Delight of the Night'; another had added a sprinkling of musk powder. The beautiful woman had placed her bare buttocks on the bench, then her white shawl had been unwound, revealing the yellow blush of the skin on her back and that magnificent hair. At least that was how Tamu described it.

'Her back glowed like the moon,' she told me, her eyes still shining with wonder. 'The water was so hot, I think I would've died if I were her. As that hell-fire reached her flesh, she flinched, then shivered, as if she'd never been so cold in her life. She cried too, but so quietly I'd never have known if I hadn't seen the tears trickling down her cheeks. She was staring into space, and her eyes… like two huge inverted cashew nuts with a black pearl at the centre! Poor thing, she was suffering in silence. Those women really are superior to us; they're so delicate!'

The wedding was a grand affair. The men danced day and night for a week. Thursday was the women's dance. I stood holding Tamu's big steel plate next to a band made up of drums, tambourines and young female singers, only one of whom had a good enough voice to soften the din made by the others. Coins rained into my dish, contributions towards the bride's trousseau, of which I was the temporary guardian. As each married woman danced past my dish, she stroked my face with her coins before dropping them in. By the end of the evening, I smelt like a mixture of aged steel and sweat.

I was in a good mood that day; cause for celebration, as joy had been in short supply in our tin hut of late. Tamu had gone from playful and witty to cynical and surly. Since his new marriage, Fundi's visits had become less frequent. He only came during the time he'd allocated to his other wives, which had also been curtailed, since to the four days a month he was supposed to spend with each of them had been added the five days he'd allotted to the new one. He never allowed the new wife or her servants to go to the market, preferring to shop for her himself. He alone had the right to know which clothes and perfume she wore. He decided on her weekly menu and oversaw the preparation of her tea and any other beverages she liked, for fear that someone would try to poison her. He'd become suspicious of the servants: he often sent them to take money or food to his old wives, and he worried they might play on the common grievances of servants and somehow bribe them to plot against the new wife.

People said Fundi was in the habit of putting drops from the Meccan spring of Zamzam[2] into his wife's water glass, while

2 The Meccan spring is said to have first sprung up when the son of Abraham's wife Hajer trampled the ground in anger because he was thirsty, and to have reappeared thanks to Abu Talib, the grandfather of Muhammad (Mohammed). It is said to have many physical and spiritual benefits, and is held in the same esteem as the fountain at Lourdes.

uttering invocations intended to inspire love.

A year had passed since the marriage, and no child had appeared.

The absence of a child was not the only source of Fundi's worries. He'd shared these with Tamu during one of his rare visits. First he'd apologised, saying he did respect people's feelings and servants were, after all, women, even if, in his opinion, they were closer than non-servants to the vile, animal side of human nature. I pretended to snore, so I could listen to their conversation.

'I'm having trouble arousing this girl,' he'd murmured.

'Woman!' Tamu retorted. 'Don't forget she was already no longer a girl when you married her.'

'Yes, well, you see what I'm saying, though. She's a girl to me now; my girl. And I'd like it so much if she could want me, if she could join in my ardour, help me out a little when I take her. She just lies there, stiff as a board! What's more, you've seen her, there wasn't much flesh on her to start with, and she's lost half her weight since we got married! Whatever I do, I can't get her to show the slightest sign of pleasure. She's never wrapped her legs around my waist. I feel as if I'm pushing a stick into a lock, it's a disgrace! Not to mention the terrible pain it causes me, which makes me less ardent with my other wives. People are going to think I'm impotent!'

'I see, so that's why you're not good for much these days,' said Tamu, with a rather silly laugh.

'Hey, have some respect,' replied the master half-heartedly.

This had little effect on Tamu: she laughed so hard she became breathless.

'Can't you help me instead of making fun of me?' Fundi protested, 'It's not right, it's not good behaviour towards your benefactor and your daughter's teacher. You should always respect the turban of the *fundi*, the work of the judge and the office of the imam!'

Tamu responded by nearly choking with mirth.

'The imam…' she breathed between hiccups, 'The imam under your loincloth can't seem to get up from his prostrations!'

She gave in to another wave of giggles, her breath becoming wheezy.

Finally, she pulled herself together and offered some advice. This included that spitting invocations into teas and sauces wasn't going to win him his wife's heart—she had another good laugh at this—and that he needed to give the girl time to get used to him. He should wait, she said, until his wife was in a better frame of mind before trying to be intimate with her. That way, he would demonstrate both kindness and resolve, a combination that refined women needed.

'Show her your heart before you show her your private parts,' Tamu said in a mocking voice, before bursting out laughing again. Her laugh was so contagious, I had to get up discreetly and go out on to the verandah so they couldn't hear me chuckling.

Once there, I whistled for my friends to come over. That was the signal we used. They all emerged from the surrounding huts to join me under the palm roof. I told them the story in a whisper. They tried to moderate their laughter too, but it was always hard for us not to giggle like teenagers when we heard about the romantic woes of the adults we looked up to.

This story, and the light it shone on the tribulations of

those who called themselves the masters of the world, put me in a very good mood.

I don't remember when I started to doze off.

'Hardie, you're falling asleep!' Ramla whispered.

'No, she's falling into a daydream,' retorted Mlima.

I laughed again. Mlima was right.

'Actually,' I replied, trying to make my voice less sleepy, 'I was wondering if men sometimes experience the same thing we do. Do you remember Firimbi? After the harvest dance?'

They all nodded. Olympe gave me a knowing smile.

'Let me guess, you're thinking about Soulé?'

I laughed.

'Did you see the way he looked at me? The fear in his eyes. I wonder how he'd react if the situation were reversed. Is it possible to embrace a man against his will? I think I'd have enough strength to kiss him and press him against me if he tried to squirm away…'

The guinea fowl clucked.

'Yes, but we don't know if he even goes to the vanilla field.'

'Wouldn't it be wonderful!' we sighed in unison, before letting our eyes wander up towards the stars.

Finally I was going to catch a glimpse of the famous wife.

The monsoon was stripping the leaves and the last-remaining fruits from the trees, spreading a sweet smell of rotting pulp.

Sometimes I'd go and help Tamu cook for one of her masters. This time it was for the one who lived in the house next to Fundi Ahmad's at Thin Beard Junction.

At that time of the late afternoon, Fundi Ahmad's new wife was in the habit of taking a bath in coconut milk and dried flowers in the courtyard, which was separated by a wall from the house where Tamu was working. Tamu had told me the smell of coconut milk perfumed the whole neighbourhood. My friend Olympe had recently become the new wife's maidservant. She poked her head over the wall that separated us to ask me to lower the fire over which my fish and banana was cooking, so the smell wouldn't bother her mistress.

I was about to get irritated at this intrusion by the precious wife into my affairs. Then Olympe told me to come closer, and whispered that in exchange I could watch the bride from a vantage point where I wouldn't be seen. I couldn't resist the opportunity to finally look on this beauty I'd heard so much about.

I had to climb up on the kitchen hearth and peer through a small gap between the lava stones of the wall. It was a perilous undertaking, involving moving the fire and my pot filled to the brim with bubbling stew, sweeping up the embers so they didn't burn my feet, then climbing on to the raised stone. I hoped this woman's beauty would be worth the risk.

Olympe was right: through this hole, you could see as well as through a window. The opening was just the right size. How had she known it existed? Was this how she observed what I cooked and managed to copy all my dishes down to the last ingredient? I decided I'd confront her about that later. The door from the house opened and the young bride appeared.

Against the black and grey cobblestones, her feet looked almost luminous. My friend had not exaggerated: the woman was incredibly, almost alarmingly pale. She looked as if she might be ill. Her slender arms hung from angular shoulders. Olympe opened the woman's shawl to reveal oval breasts that pointed slightly downwards, with large brown areolas. They resembled two newly-carved pestles. I couldn't stop a picture appearing in my head of a pair of men's hands resting on them, squeezing them, before being replaced by a different pair of hands. Tamu's words still rang in my ears: 'Don't forget that she was already no longer a girl when you married her.' Did this woman still love her previous husband? Was that why she couldn't accept her new one? Was it grief that had made her so pale?

The rest of the woman's body was silhouetted in the fading light. She was thin and slight. Her veil was removed and her head appeared, concealed by a mass of black hair, gathered at the nape of her neck into a coiled braid. She sat down before I could see her face, which she kept lowered. Olympe poured the first jug of water, and I watched as it trickled over the rosy yellow skin. The woman's back was perfectly smooth, without a single blemish. She uncoiled her hair, and that famous waterfall from the island of Mwali cascaded past her shoulders before coming to rest on the stone where she was sitting. An image came to me unbidden, of Fundi Ahmad tangling his fingers in her hair, drowning her nose and mouth in it. I quickly banished it. Olympe plunged the jug into the bucket again and poured water down the woman's right side. At this point she half-turned, in the way people do when they sense someone's watching them, and out of contempt or provocation, want it to be known that they're aware. Her face remained in shadow.

There was no one behind her in the courtyard. I was watching her through a hidden gap in the black stone wall, and the sun had just set; it was impossible for her to have seen me. Calmed by this thought, I continued to stare at her back and the hair that hung down it, hypnotised by the spectacle of water trickling through wavy locks.

As the fourth pitcher of water was poured though, something happened that disturbed every fibre of my being: the woman turned and locked eyes with me.

I was so disconcerted by the precision with which she did this, while Olympe continued to pour water over her, that I didn't realise at first. Then I saw.

It was her.

Her gaze was steady. My eyes widened. My heart began to thump unnaturally, high in my chest. I couldn't seem to take in enough air. I opened my mouth to shout, but no sound came out. Only my mind managed to whisper her name, as she gazed at me, unperturbed; a slight smile playing at the corners of her lips, whether hopeful or bitter I couldn't say. She seemed sad, but also determined to let me stare at her, so I could confirm I wasn't mistaken, to offer up that beautiful face that had been lost to me for so long.

Halima.

I'd planned to make *futra* that evening; I'd already made the dough of flour and coconut milk and left it to prove under cover in the heat of the sun. Now and again, as was my nature, I lifted the lid to check on it, despite my mother's warnings that doing so could ruin the whole endeavour. I couldn't help it—my desire to know was always too strong. I enjoyed watching the bubbles rising slowly to the surface, making the dough bulge grotesquely, then bursting like angry lava, leaving a crater that would soon swell up again. Perhaps it was the repetition that fascinated me; it made me think of life endlessly renewing itself before our bewildered eyes, until death finally came along to cook us. The *futra* was the perfect representation of that cycle, right up to the moment it was baked on the charcoal stove: you scooped up salt water in the palm of your hand, threw it into the cast-iron pan, then watched, entranced, as the drops scattered in all directions across the burning surface, like a damned people trying to escape divine wrath. Then you took a little dough in your hand and dropped it on to the pan before the last drop of water evaporated. You sprinkled sesame seeds over it before it set. Once the bottom of the dough had hardened, you flipped the pan over. The top of the dough, still liquid, rushed to obey gravity and flow downwards, but the heat of the embers stopped it dead in its tracks, and the fire licked off the parts it was able to reach, blackening them. The pan was then turned back over and the *futra* peeled off. The result never ceased to impress me: it looked like a mountain range, white and dotted with sesame seeds, but instead of its peaks being capped with snow, they were either golden or charred, their crispiness contrasting with the softness inside. The *futra* was the story of our lives: imprisoned always between fire and embers, running in all directions to escape the fragility of our bodies and souls, sometimes tempted to put an end to ourselves in an impetuous rush towards oblivion. Then seized, frozen in place. Living, I thought, was a tortuous journey and would always remain so.

I was absorbed in these reflections when I heard a *'hodi!'* from behind the metal door of the kitchen, which opened straight to the outside. A little girl had been sent by Olympe to collect some embers. As I placed the glowing sticks into her hollowed-out coconut, the girl put her face close to mine and whispered, in a voice that still held the delicate warmth of a child's alongside the sweetness of a more mature timbre, 'Olympe says her mistress wants to see you this evening, at bath time.'

I nearly overbalanced and spilled my ladleful of embers on the child's skinny fingers. The girl had a knowing little smile on her face, overjoyed at having been given a secret mission, excited by the intuition that, for reasons she didn't understand, she held in her hands something hotter than a hollowed-out coconut full of smouldering ash. I nodded, a little too quickly; a little too obediently too, as if this little girl had the power to take back what she'd just said if I didn't answer immediately.

She added my agreement to her embers, then ran off, one or two sparks flying from her hands, like the small splinters of my heart that she carried back to her mistress.

Nothing combined enchantment and terror quite like the narrow paths and stone walls of Itsandra after dark. The grey tones of the houses and flagstones, the chunky balustrades, the wide staircases without handrails embraced the half-light and gave it a palpable, pulsating life. The dimness infiltrated even the lanterns on verandahs and terraces and the doorways of houses; it found its way inside, hushing voices and silencing cries. At night, we didn't speak, we whispered: greetings, conversations, arguments all took place in a solemn murmur, as if we were wary of that half-light, sensed it might leap on us and devour us if it heard our raised voices. It was the time for the gentle muttering that accompanied the clicking of rosary beads; that sent lucky children off to bed or, in places where there was no room for luck, gave the order to stay quiet or to enter a room in secret: 'Come here, my boy; come here, my lovely girl…'

Two huge elephant tusks barred the carved wooden door of Fundi Ahmad's house. The *fundi's* grandfather, Sheikh Sadr, was said to have been an elephant hunter in his youth. He sold the tusks to the sultans from Oman who came to conquer the islands off Tanzania. The sultans mounted them on their doors as a warning to enemies seeking to enter their walls with hostile intentions. Their homes were entered through the women's door, to the left. This door was decorated with lattice work: when the sun shone through it, a dappled pattern was cast on the courtyard floor beyond. The men's door, to the right, was embellished with domes or spikes and remained forever closed.

Olympe met me at the women's door. Her *leso* was wrapped round her chest and tied at her left shoulder. Unlike me, Olympe wore her hair short, accentuating her prominent cheekbones and large, slightly slanted eyes. Normally those eyes expressed playfulness, but when her full lips twisted in sadness, melancholy could inhabit them just as easily. At those times all you wanted to do was take her in your arms. Olympe was like me in this, though: she always wriggled away from attempts to comfort her. It was as if she couldn't let herself fall into the arms of a compassionate soul in case a river of tears flowed out of her and never dried up. As long as no one showed us compassion, we could accept our condition, turn a blind eye to all that we lacked.

Nothing was worse for the poor, I thought, than compassion: it burst the bubbles of tranquillity we created and subsisted in. It offered us a mirror, while insisting, 'You need help. See how much better my life is than yours? I'm going to help you!' But did we ask to be helped? Compassion was voyeurism disguised as charity, because without poverty there would be no need for it. Even if it was sincere, it was of no use to those to whom it was directed: it fed on misery as much as misery fed on it. Who was more in need of pity, the poor soul or the compassionate one?

Inside our bubble, Olympe and I were sisters. With a

simple glance, we understood each other. I could see in her eyes that something was wrong.

'The mistress can't see you tonight,' Olympe breathed. Her irises shone in the moonless dark. 'She's ill. Come back tomorrow night, after the *isha* meditation. She should be better by then.'

I opened my mouth to ask what was wrong, if it was serious, if the mistress was in pain, if there was anything I could do, but Olympe closed the gate before I could utter a word. Or perhaps I'd stood there for so long, paralysed and bewildered, that she'd concluded I had nothing to say.

I was deeply disappointed, though I'd had no right to expect anything from Halima. She owed me nothing; it was I who needed to see her, and she was doing me the favour of inviting me into her home. Still, I knew I wouldn't be able to sleep that night. The moon was invisible, the shining beetles of the stars had hidden themselves away under their white quilt. I hated cloudy nights; they forced me to contemplate the darkness, and I could find no source of light in my heart. I began to chant the *surah* of sunrise. It soothed me, but I stumbled over the words, forgot every third verse, as if someone were distracting me by whispering inscrutable messages in my ear. Finally, exasperated, I let out a moan that didn't relieve my tension as much as I wanted it to, and which I quickly stifled, because shouting was forbidden.

I lay down on the mat beside Tamu, my heart in my throat. She greeted me in a sleepy voice.

'*Ewoyi ndawe*? Is that you?'

'Yes,' I replied dully.

'I left you some manioc and *madaba* in the *sinia*. Aren't

you hungry?'

'No,' I said, in the same tone. 'I'm going to sleep.'

'What happened?' she asked, an edge of fear in her voice. 'Did someone touch you?'

'No, no, Mother, don't panic. No one touched me. I'm just not in the mood to eat.'

Her voice calmed a little, but her vigilance remained. Our mothers were so used to the limitless power of the masters that when a young girl suddenly went silent, they always suspected the worst.

'*Yee*,' said Tamu. 'You'll eat your rice tomorrow morning before you go to work, unless you want to faint in the kitchen. Then something really could happen to you.'

I gave an 'mmm' of assent. I was about to lie down on my stomach when I heard footsteps on the gravel three steps from the house, followed by a loud *'hooodi!'* Tamu hadn't heard; she was already snoring. The *'hooodi'* came again. I recognised Fundi Ahmad's voice. I welcomed his arrival as one would welcome a saviour. My day wasn't lost after all. I reached out and gently shook my mother by the shoulder.

'What?' She lifted her head. 'What's the matter with you today?'

'It's Fundi, he's here!' I almost shouted. This irritated her even more than my late arrival had.

'Speak softly, magpie beak! He might go away again!'

I closed my mouth and sat up in bed. I realised I didn't know my *surah.* I was torn between the fear of being asked to recite it in front of Fundi and the joy of seeing him again. This jumble of feelings was not unfamiliar to me; I experienced it every time he visited, with varying degrees of intensity depending on how well I'd mastered the *surah*.

But tonight there was another feeling too. I didn't yet know what to call it, but it was as if my heart had been plunged into a boiling cauldron. It was a pain I'd never known before: blistering, eviscerating. It persisted even after Fundi had stepped inside to join my mother. It spoiled the pleasure of seeing him, and no matter how hard I searched for it, the cause eluded me.

When their loud, breathless conversation began, my mother's face, which I sometimes pictured pressed against the *fundi's*, was replaced with another in my mind—Halima's. That was when the pain reached its peak and I fainted.

The hour of *isha* was still a long way off. Each time I noticed the sun had advanced a little across the sky, my legs would start to tremble as if there was an earthquake beneath me. If the day didn't end soon, I feared I might explode, spewing lava like the Karthala volcano. In fact it was one of the longest and most trying days of the year: the day of the *mauvé,* the purple vanilla. I plunged my arms up to the elbows into the boiling water to submerge the jute bag in which we'd placed the ripe, yellow pods, took them out and plunged them back in again, beneath the incredulous gazes of my friends. Why, they demanded, did I not hold my bag by its edges, so only my fingertips touched the water? When I made no reply, they all started to shout at once:

'Come on, Hardie, you really don't feel anything? It doesn't burn you?'

'You're insane! What's wrong with you?'

'Have you completely lost your marbles?'

'Have you gone deaf as well?'

Then they sucked the air between their teeth, a choral hiss of disapproval and saliva spray, before returning to their own work, trying to ignore me but shaking their heads from time to time and casting reproachful glances in my direction.

I didn't feel a thing. However long I held the bag

underwater, however often I plunged my arms into the fiery heat, all I could think about was the hot water that had been placed underneath Halima, and how long she'd had to sit there on that bench. I wanted to take her in my arms, to stroke her neck, to whisper soothing words in her ear. Then I'd think of Fundi Ahmad, of everything he did for me, and my heart would swell until it pressed against my ribs and threatened to break them.

Oh, Halima.

'It's here!' came a sudden shout from the other end of the line of women. I spread out the edges of my jute bag and there it was. The *mauvé*. The pods had turned from a dull yellow to a purple that gleamed in the midday sun. They'd puffed up, straining their seams, promising thousands of fragrant beans. I loved the special scent of the vanilla at that first stage of processing: warm, earthy, as fresh as milk straight from the animal, still scented with its body and slightly metallic on the tongue. It was time to carry our bags all the way up the narrow kitchen stairs to the roof.

The roof was flat, so when we spread out the pods they were evenly exposed to the sun. We emptied our bags, then bent down to separate the pods and place them one beside another. Bent over like this, we resembled worshippers in a mosque. In fact only two of our number prayed five times a day: Sahiba, who'd adopted that first name to please her master, and Rabi'a, who'd chosen the name of a mystical Persian or Arab goddess from ancient times. The rest of us were not sufficiently steeped in the religion of our masters to care about such things. Some of us believed that the masters were naturally closer to God than we were, since sacred blood flowed in their veins. They were able to access some higher state of mind, far removed from our trivial everyday concerns. Others amongst us thought that, given all the work we had to get through in a day, pausing five times to chat to the father of creation was hardly practical. 'He should talk to us for a change,' said one. For me and a few of the others, the father of creation was actually a mother. We weren't sure why we believed that, except that we'd been born with it, just as our own mothers had. Our Queen Abé had never demanded anything of us in terms of prayer.

At last, sunset came. We'd worked outside all day. On other days, we finished at *asr* time, as the shadows started to lengthen under the waning sun, then moved on to our household chores, but the vanilla had claimed more of our time. *Maghrib*, the hour before *isha*, was already approaching.

Oh, Halima.

I said goodbye to my friends, who still couldn't believe my performance with the hot water—'*Pvala*, what was up with you earlier?'—took the stairs down from the roof and ran to my mother's house. Tamu still wasn't home. I scrubbed myself with the *pindo* until its coconut fibres scraped my knuckles. I took a jar from under my bed, extracted two of last year's vanilla pods, dry but still full of their tiny seeds, and rubbed them on my wrists, in the crooks of my elbows, around my neck and behind my ears. My heart was thumping: I could've counted every beat if I hadn't been too busy preparing. This time, I'd decided, whatever Halima's state, I was going to force my way into the house. If Olympe blocked my way, I'd push her over: I was much taller and stronger than she was. She'd probably be angry with me for two or three days, then she'd forgive me. I wasn't completely sure about the last part, but I didn't care.

Oh, Halima.

I applied coconut oil to my hair, just enough so the smell wasn't overpowering, and parted it in the centre before flattening it with the palms of my hands so it framed my face. I looked at myself in Tamu's mirror. The call to *isha* prayer reverberated off the city walls, while my ears rang with a completely different call, a different name, a different melody.

Oh, Halima…

*

Olympe put up no resistance. Her lips even stretched into a teasing smile when she saw me, all oiled up and perfumed, wearing my yellow *leso* with the hibiscus flowers around the chest and with my hair styled as if I was going to a wedding. She let me inside, then released the laugh she'd been suppressing.

'*Pvanu*, have you just met Soulé?'

By way of reply, I pinched her on the arm. This amused her even more.

'He's got nothing to do with it, Olympe,' I mumbled, trying to hide my smile. 'So, can I see her today?'

Suddenly I felt awkward. Why had I dolled myself up

like this rather than just come as I had the day before, looking ordinary? Would Halima have gone to so much trouble? Of course not. She'd probably find me ridiculous.

We walked across the dark courtyard, watched by two guards who took their attention off me once they registered that Olympe was with me. Then we had to cross the *baraza* terrace, passing under the great archway that marked its entrance and past the stone benches reserved for the men. Olympe stopped in front of the imposing mahogany front door. The door frame, as in all the masters' houses, was wide and decorated with engravings. Spirals wound up the sides, punctuated with raised dots. The design entranced me, though I couldn't remember what it signified. Along the top, the spirals snaked either side of a verse from the Qur'an. The light from the lanterns in the wall nooks was too dim for me to make out the words, which were already hard to decipher because of their intertwined and superimposed letters. Only '*basmala*', 'In the name of Allah, the origin of all, the ordainer', was recognisable.

Olympe suddenly turned to me, guilt and uncertainty on her face.

'I'm sorry, Hardie.'

Thinking she was about to forbid me from entering again, I pulled myself up to my full height.

'Don't tell me that—'

I was on the verge of exploding, my heart about to burst from my chest and fly off in search of Halima. There was nothing else in my mind: my thoughts screamed her name, my blood beat out the rhythm of the word: Ha-li-ma!

I didn't have time to finish my threat; in one swift movement, Olympe grabbed my head and pressed her *leso* firmly against my nose, before releasing the pressure slightly, while still keeping hold of me. She had a strength I'd never suspected. In the shock of the moment, I took a sharp breath in. Dense fumes scented with clove and ginger rose up my nostrils and tickled my sinuses. The last thing I saw was Olympe's face; her kind eyes, her lips pressed together in concentration. Then the flavours of wild thyme, beach rose, laurel and ylang-ylang made their way to the back of my nose and throat, and I was plunged into darkness.

For the first few days, I refused to look at him. I'd never left the house I grew up in; the beloved stone house that held my last memories of my mother. He'd taken me from it without even consulting me.

My father had a house built for me and my husband to live in, as is customary. It was in Itsandra. My husband allowed me to get used to his presence, making no attempt to come near me. When his sisters, my sisters, or the women who ran the house asked if he found me to his liking, he always said the same thing: 'What happens behind my bedroom door concerns only my wife and me. All you need to know is that I'm happy.'

When they asked him if I was pregnant yet, he told them his heir would come when the time was right, just like the child of the prophet Zachariah, who'd waited for God's decree before appearing.

I never heard my husband complain about me.

I got used to him clearing his throat before he entered the house, loudly enough for me to hear him. It was his way of signalling his arrival so I could react as I wished. If I didn't want to see him, I'd retire to the bedroom, behind the gauze curtain he'd had hung across the middle of our bed. If I felt like company, I'd stay in the living room. If he found me there, a smile lit up his face, but he made no comment. He simply ordered that dinner be served.

After a year of living like this, my husband came home exhausted one evening. A fight had taken place between his boss, a wealthy Indian trader, and a customer. The Indian traders all lived in the *medina* in Moroni, in the two or three storey houses that faced each other across the cobbled streets. A bridge often connected the roofs of the houses. If the daughters of the families wanted to go from house to house, they were required to use the bridge. It meant they could cross the street without being subjected to the impertinent gaze of Comorian men, who no Indian wanted for a son-in-law. Such were the ways of my people: individuals lived alongside each other and interacted with civility, provided no-one tried to mix their blood.

The daughter of my husband's boss had broken that rule. Out of sheer curiosity, she'd asked one of the house boys to show her the town's street and its inhabitants. She'd swapped her sari for a coarse-knit *leso* and toured the *medina* with him, keeping her face down so as not to be recognised. But a child spotted the light-skinned foot under her long dress and identified the delicate, elaborate henna designs used by the Indian women. He pointed it out to his mother, who hurried the young woman home. Someone spotted her and informed her father, who took it out on the messenger, calling him a liar. Fists flew, followed by a frying pan and a ladle. Both men suffered minor injuries. My husband had to separate them and repair the damage in the shop.

It was one of my maids who told me all this.

I sensed my husband's weariness as he collapsed on his wooden seat to my left, in front of his plate of green bananas, meat and coconut milk. I couldn't help but feel for him. The words escaped my mouth unbidden.

'You must be exhausted.'

He froze. Those were the first words I'd spoken to him since we got married. He turned to me. I didn't dare look at him, but the expression I caught on his face from the corner of my eye seemed like relief. I was touched.

'Yes,' he said after a moment's pause. 'I am. It's been a difficult day.'

'Some days are more difficult than others, that's true.'

He straightened up in his seat. I couldn't have refreshed him more if I'd offered him an infusion of my young blood. He chewed slowly on his food.

'You're right,' he replied, dumbfounded.

A short silence followed. Noises filtered through from the kitchen: a pan lid falling with a metallic clang, the song of it swirling against the stone before it stilled on the floor. As if coaxing a bird he'd long been pursuing, my husband continued to speak to me.

'Have you heard what happened at Mohandas' place?'

'Yes,' I replied. 'A fight?'

'That's right, a fight.'

His voice became more and more animated as he

told me the details, which I already knew. We hadn't exchanged more than two words since our wedding day; now we were having a conversation.

'Indians don't like their daughters mixing with Comorian boys,' he concluded.

'I've heard that too. Comorians don't like their daughters mixing with Comorian boys either.'

He nodded enthusiastically.

'Yes, exactly! We're a mixed-race people who don't like mixing. We only get what we deserve.'

'One day, that will change.'

He looked at me, intrigued.

'What makes you think that?'

I recited my favourite verse from the Qur'an: '*We have made you into nations and tribes, so that you may know one another.*'

He seemed impressed.

'Fair enough. But once people from each group have got to know one another, and their group has grown larger, don't they then need to go and meet other groups?'

'Just as God changes shape with every moment, so do nations. The nation of yesterday does not have the same composition as the nation of today, nor does it reflect the nation of tomorrow.'

This time he stopped eating completely and studied me carefully. Despite myself, I smiled beneath my veil. He brought his face closer to mine, while still keeping a respectful distance. All I could see were his lips stretched into a wide smile.

'Tell me,' he whispered. 'Why do you keep that veil on in my presence?'

*

His name was Fadili. His features suggested an alliance between Africa and the Orient. His complexion was dark brown, his jaw broad and square, his nose angular. His slightly full lips often smiled at the challenges the day threw up. He had lively eyes, with irises as brown as the pod of a pigeon pea plant and crow's feet at the corners when he smiled. A mass of black curls framed his face, sometimes dropping over his forehead when he'd neglected to trim them. His arms were lean and toned from tilling the fields after work. His legs were as firm as stone. I knew he watched me while I slept. Sometimes I heard the rustle as he lifted the curtain that hung between us. After a few moments of silence, interrupted only by our breathing, he let it fall again.

That famous evening, when we had our first conversation, I agreed to take off my veil. He stared into my eyes. A maid came in to clear the mat in front of us. He pretended not to see her and continued to look at me. Frozen, I didn't realise that my hands were sliding towards his until I felt his soft, moist palm meet my own. How bold I was! How I loved this new freedom. 'I mean you no harm,' he whispered. 'When she was on her deathbed, my mother told me her only wish was that I should marry the daughter of an educated man, that I should shower her with honour and love, and that I should give her a child. I wanted to pay homage to my mother. Your father is a respectable man. But you're more than someone's daughter. You're more than a promise made to a mother.'

*

My father. Respectable, of course, in public. Ambiguous with me. He taught me the Qur'an, encouraged me to learn as much as I could about it, but declined to use it to liberate me. He rejected all my interpretations of the holy books if they leaned towards any idea of women possessing power.

One of our disagreements concerned a verse which, according to the scholars, had ushered in the ascendancy of men over women.

'Father,' I asked innocently one evening, 'Could you translate this verse for me?'

'It says, "Men have superiority over women, for they have been favoured over them". We have the strength to protect you, you see? That's why we're superior to you, and we know better than you what's good for you.'

'Father, the word *qawwamûn*, which you translated as 'superior', comes from the root *qm*, which also gives us the word 'base', doesn't it?'

'Yes,' he replied, absent-mindedly, absorbed in his reading of the Treasure of Grammar.

'But then, Father, couldn't we say that men are more

like women's base, their foundation?'

'Yes, yes.'

'And isn't the sentence containing *fadhala*, 'to favour', a bit ambiguous, since it doesn't specify whether it means the men or the women are favoured?'

'It means the men, my daughter.'

'But what it says is, "because of the favour given to some of those over the others".'

He turned, visibly irritated, and locked eyes with me.

'Exactly, daughter of Zuleika Burahim. Some of the men.'

'But Father, in Arabic grammar the masculine takes precedence over the feminine. What if 'some' referred to both men and women? What if—'

He raised a threatening finger at me. I was surprised to hear a tremor in his voice.

'Your Qur'anic master is wrong to beat you so rarely, and so am I. You are nothing, do you hear me? Nothing! When I married your poor mother, may Allah light her resting place, no one welcomed me into her family. All of her uncles were mad, and the women in her family were penniless. I had to grow up on my own, in my own home, when I should have been brought up by your uncles, as is our tradition. Even they can't do anything for you. Without me, you're nothing! Nothing! Now get out of my sight, wretch, or the next dress I give you will be made of *ndjeni* leaves!'

He raised his hand and left it suspended in the air, while his wild eyes shot lightning bolts at me. I didn't wait for him to strike; I jumped to my feet and fled.

That was the first and last time I pushed my argument so far in front of my father.

*

Fadili wanted the opposite. He sensed I was keeping my opinions to myself. Even when I didn't speak to him, he still recounted for me the sermons he heard at the mosque on Fridays. He noticed that my shoulders tensed whenever an exclusively feminine obligation was mentioned, such as the duty never to refuse your husband.

The evening I took off my veil, he told me he wanted to know what I thought. I hesitated, but he encouraged me. I ended up telling him everything. I could tell from his dilated pupils that he was captivated by my ideas. In the days that followed, we explored all the avenues I'd been forbidden from exploring before. We re-read verses of the holy book together, and Fadili agreed with my provocative interpretations, encouraged them, pushed me to censor nothing when I spoke to him.

'What if a servant's listening?' I said anxiously. 'I'm not sure the world's ready to hear what I have to say.'

'The world is never ready to be challenged,' said Fadili. 'But one day, when you're ready, your words will break through these walls.'

I was a child when Fadili married me, and he treated me like one until I became a woman. In time, I began to love every inch of his skin. He was a new territory I could explore further every night. I'd never hated him; it was my destiny I'd hated. Now it seemed rosier because of him. He never demanded more than I wanted to give him. When I needed a friend, he was there. When my body cried out for a masculine presence, he answered my call, with all the tenderness that distinguished his character.

For the first time in my life, I felt grateful to my father.

Yet there were nights when I still dreamed about his hand hovering in the air above me. In the dreams, it came down, connecting with my cheek, and its impact scorched me like a dry-season sun.

*

Fadili had good judgement and knew a thousand different paths that led to my heart. I repaid him a hundredfold: he'd turned me into a woman who smouldered with desire, a tigress who doubled as a good *dimku* who let herself be caressed beneath the sheets.

Few people travelled for pleasure, so people were surprised to see us on our sedan chair, Fadili wearing a caftan and me covered from head to foot, on our way to visit some distant farm. There I would drink the milk that the farmer had milked that morning, uncover my shoulders and climb to the top of the flower-carpeted hills to breathe the fresh air. At night, we made love. In those isolated places, there was no need for me to stifle my cries of pleasure.

Ten years passed in a bliss that few clouds obscured. But this happiness, like everything else in the world, had to end. It happened in a way that was as unexpected as it was painful.

*

It was all so sudden, I didn't have time to react. Even today, when I think back on it, I feel petrified.

That day, Fadili came home early from the mosque. As soon as I saw him I had a feeling of foreboding. All day I'd been hearing alarming news from the city. The maids were saying the Wazungu, the new masters of our island, had arrived to collect the taxes, and that the town chief had refused to hand over the money he'd got from his citizens. Because of this, we had to deliver several tonnes of corn as compensation and provide all the copra soap we produced for free. All men would be requisitioned for the week to help with the corn harvest. The colonial administrators had also taken the opportunity to demand that men bring their wives to them. I was terrified that would happen to me. I'd already been given once to a man, and although I'd come to love him, I couldn't stand the thought of being passed from his arms into someone else's like a sack of rice.

I was pacing up and down in the living room when Fadili walked in. He was livid. His eyes, usually obscured by his heavy lids, flashed like glowing moons. Blue lines streaked across his beige skin. Two raindrops glistened in his dark beard. I couldn't help admiring his face, as well as the elegance of his *kandu,* perfectly uncreased even at the end of a long day.

I got us some tea with milk and cardamom and *kuskuma* pancakes with a vegetable sauce. He ate in silence. This alarmed me even more. My heart was beating so quickly I couldn't swallow. I cleared away the mat. Fadili drank his glass of water in one gulp, then exhaled slowly. He put the glass down and turned to me.

'Halima, I've got something to tell you. Something serious has happened.'

My first thought was for my father. His health had been poor for some time. After he hadn't come to see me for a fortnight, I'd gone to visit him and found him bedridden. He'd started praying at the mosque again, but he didn't stay to chat with his peers, preferring to go straight home. Perhaps he needed to take a wife.

I was running through all the possible scenarios in my mind. But the one Fadili was about to outline was worse than anything I could have imagined.

*

Ever since we'd married, a cloud had hung over our happiness: the cloud of dishonour. My father was a respectable man; he'd been a judge and then the chief of the city, an important link between the citizens and the colonial administrators.

But my marriage, while it had pleased his community, had in fact never been complete. A man of my father's standing was required to marry his daughter according to the custom: a week of festivities, with food distributed throughout the town on the first day, money sent to young single men on the second day so they could accompany the groom to his bride, and generous meals every day to give the young people the strength to perform the ceremonial dances in the evenings. It was never too late to do the right thing: ten, twenty or thirty years after the marriage, the union was still considered unofficial if these requirements hadn't been met, and the bride and groom would not be invited to any of their friends' weddings. Even if it took several years to raise the money needed to organise the customary celebrations, everyone was expected to do so, all the more if they came from a family of noble descent like mine. This was the law of the *'ada,* the wedding feast.

Fadili was a thinking man who was repelled by this kind of pomp. He prized simplicity. After prayers, he didn't sit outside the mosque with the other men discussing the city's past glory and setting the world to rights. He mingled a little with those who played the *mraha,* then came back to join me at home.

For Fadili, these types of festivities were a way of trying to emulate the sultans, whose influence was already in decline. Nothing was more abhorrent to him than a king. Of course the dances were beautiful—they reminded us of our Arab origins and celebrated our antecedents—but they required astronomical expenditure, the sole purpose of which was to show off by spending more money than other families had. Fadili preferred to invest in our daily lives, in the futures of the children he hoped we'd have.

My father had been unable to persuade him to change his mind. He'd tried going through me, demanding I reason with my husband, even suggesting I blackmail him. At first I didn't love my husband and didn't care what people said about my marriage. Once I did love him, I had new reasons not to care. Each year, as the customary wedding month approached, my father would raise the subject again. Of course people gossiped: our resistance intrigued them.

That year, my father had renewed his request, arguing that he'd left us alone for ten years, that he was getting old, and that he couldn't bear for Allah to take his soul before he'd had the joy of marrying his daughter according to the custom. Fadili had remained unmoved, my father had became enraged, and soon he was seen less at the mosque than before.

When the marriage month arrived, a man called Ahmad, a Qur'anic master who'd trained in Tanzania, announced his decision to take a wife. He was said to be a descendant of the prophet and one of few people who knew Islamic jurisprudence inside out. His arrival in Itsandra caused a stir. Every father in the town went to visit him to offer the hand of his daughter. The man already had two wives; one in Bandamadj, the other in Itsandra.

One day, I went to visit my father to take him some ointment for his joint pain that Fadili had brought me from work. I found Master Ahmad already there. He was a tall, thin man with a dark complexion. He wore a white turban, the symbol of the descendants of the prophet, and a long pink *djuba* coat over his white *kandu*. He sat with his hand resting on the knob of his walking stick and stared at me. I hated the look on his face, as well as the way he was dressed—the classic costume of the pious man—rosary beads dangling from his fingers, lips moving constantly, an affected piercing gaze. Who did these scholars think they were? Didn't they know that even the servants who worshipped trees and spirits had a faith deeper than their own?

Master Ahmad, on the other hand, expressed great pleasure on seeing me. He examined my face closely before turning to my father.

'Brother, I had no idea you had a daughter!'

His voice was deep and cool. It seemed to come from one of those caverns said to be inhabited by *jinns*. I got up to get two cups from the acacia wood sideboard. I breathed in its dry, sweet smell. I brought back the filled teapots a servant had handed me.

I placed the pots on the round side tables next to each man's seat, then swivelled the cup-holders out from beneath the tabletops and placed the cups in them. Then I filled them with herbal tea. As I poured the translucent brown liquid, the scent of lemongrass wafted through the air, followed by an array of other fragrances, bittersweet and pungent: ginger, cloves, bay leaves, wild thyme, cinnamon and cardamom. A drop escaped from the spout of the teapot and landed on the Persian carpet that Fadili had brought for my father from a trip to Oman.

'Yes, I do have a daughter,' my father said. He sounded almost resentful.

'And is it true what they say? That her husband doesn't afford you your rightful place?'

'There's nothing incorrect in what you've heard, brother,' my father sighed. He shook his head sadly and gave a tight smile of resignation.

Ahmad straightened up, puffing out his chest.

'How unfortunate! Such cruelty to impose something like that on a man like you. Neither respectful of your stature, nor benevolent towards your advanced age.'

I couldn't bear to hear any more. I took my leave.

Unmarrying was common in my town, as were alliances 'by exchange', in which a man gave his sister in marriage to his brother-in-law. But there had to be a valid reason for separating two spouses. My father thought he'd found it: not only had Fadili refused to give me a sufficiently ostentatious wedding, in which the men paraded around in sultan's robes and the women sprinkled perfume on their feet, but the dowry he'd given was two gold *louis* coins and an illuminated copy of the Qur'an. In my father's opinion, that wasn't a high enough purchase price.

All Master Ahmad had to do was wait until the

pressure on my father's fragile shoulders was so great he'd do anything to relieve it.

As the rumours began to circulate more widely, he offered my father more than double my previous price.

*

On the morning of the month of *Asorotan*, my father went to the Mosque of the Key, where Fadili usually lingered after the dawn prayer to perform his own prayer cycles and meditation. My father entered the space, which was empty and still fresh from the morning breeze. The sun streamed in through the square holes in the wall, drawing trapezoids of light on the raffia mats.

The man I loved was sitting on his heels in the middle of the room, running the beads of an imaginary rosary through his long, slender fingers while moving his full, well-defined lips. What a pity, my father must have thought, to be so handsome and yet not be of noble blood. An even greater pity that a son of such fortunate birth should refuse to submit to the rules of society.

Still, my father had determined that it must be done. He sat down to the left of my dear husband. According to the religious books, the left is the position from which subversion is best practised.

'*Kwezi*, my father,' whispered Fadili. 'I'm glad to see you back at the mosque.'

'*Mbona*, my son,' replied my father. I'm here because I need to talk to you.'

'I hear and obey, my father.'

'Don't speak too soon, my son. Remember that Abraham, the father of us all, said the same thing to God before he discovered the Lord wanted him to slaughter his own son.'

'Does my father intend to demand such a sacrifice from me?' asked Fadili, suddenly alert.

My father remained silent for a few moments. Time for a crow to caw, for an eagle to swoop down on pieces of meat left to dry on a roof.

Then he took a deep breath. His legs began to tremble. The doubt that had nagged at him until then became pressing. He hiccuped.

My father had achieved what every man on earth dreams of: he'd had a daughter and had married her off rich. Yet he thought he heard cries of indignation coming from the depths of his family tomb; from his own father, it seemed. The sound of this cry echoed inside him; it caused him to wake up panting and sweating; made his mornings feel empty and hopeless. It was the howl of a father who'd died too soon, betrayed by a son who'd tried his whole life to succeed, but in the end had failed to marry his daughter to a descendant of the prophet.

Perjury! Treachery! Defilement! My father had given his daughter to a man of ordinary blood, a man who had not been granted the divine cloth or the secrets buried inside every letter of the Qur'an, like treasure chests in the sand. A man of noble character, perhaps; but not of noble blood. What sacrilege!

This was the cry that tore my father apart every night, and which he was about to confide to my husband.

My father's mouth was dry and he suddenly felt extremely hot. But he was a strong man, and determined to do anything, even something absurd, to get what he wanted. He pulled himself together: the cry coming from his father's tomb was loud enough to drown out any personal doubts or what scruples he might have had.

Fadili waited patiently, his hands resting on his knees, his eyes half closed; the posture of the wise man who submits to the world's demands.

My father took the plunge. 'My son,' he said, 'The sacrifice I'm asking you to make is as difficult as that demanded of Abraham by God. It stems from the same elemental need: that we heed the divine messages and obey what they tell us to do.'

Increasingly intrigued, Fadili asked, 'Father, what is it I can do for you?'

The silence that followed was excruciating for both of them.

Finally, my father said, 'Imagine, my son, that I am Abraham, and that God has just asked me to slit my own son's throat.'

Fadili listened in horror as my father outlined his discussion with Ahmad, and concluded his speech with his preposterous request.

'I've come to ask you to give up what you love most. The most generous believers are those who relinquish what they love more than anything in the world, what they look on as their lifeblood. I've come to ask you to accept a fate as terrible as that of Ishmael, when his father, Abraham, my ancestor, came to tell him he'd been ordered to slit his throat to fulfil the sublime and terrible destiny of God's messengers.'

Fadili stared at my father like a newly-plucked cock: stunned and desperate. But he continued trying to understand.

'I don't see your meaning, Father. I have no child to sacrifice.'

'Come on, Fadili, we're adults!' my father exclaimed, exasperated. 'Stop your pretence. I've come to ask you to divorce my daughter.'

*

Fadili wished his father-in-law good night and, with a rustle of linen, left the mosque without another word. My father remained motionless.

Fadili trudged through the deserted streets of the city, under the watchful gaze of the full moon. Reluctantly, he let his footsteps lead him back to our house, and to me.

As he told the story, I began to feel unsteady, as if the ground were giving way beneath my feet. I couldn't speak. Panic began to dig its claws deeper and deeper into me. Imaginary ants climbed up my arms and legs, crawled all over my face with a thousand tiny legs, making me shudder. My whole body turned cold and numb.

'I'm going to have to summon your father to the

court of the *cadi,*' Fadili said.

He turned to me, put a hand on my shoulder, then let it drop heavily.

'I have to do it, Halima. He can't force me to leave you. But he's threatening our peace. And my honour.'

I only heard snatches of what Fadili was saying. Force… leave… tranquillity. His voice seemed muffled, as if wrapped in clouds, while my head floated, high up in the sky. Was I a titbit being squabbled over by two roosters?

'Halima?'

Gradually, my swirling thoughts began to settle. I filed each of them away in a corner of my mind, scrupulously assessing and analysing the facts in front of me, as if I'd been asked to make a mathematical calculation.

'Halima? Sweetheart?'

'Summon my father,' I said.

*

My husband set off, tall as a minaret, his back as straight as a spike, for the *cadi's* office.

I knew this office: it was my father who'd had it built. There was a table made of lychee wood, with intricate floral carvings around its edges and in its centre, the kind that adorned the tables, beds and doorways of the very rich. Among the *sharifs*, the supposed descendants of the prophet, these engravings were accompanied by verses from the Qur'an, into which molten gold was sometimes poured. There were other symbols too, evoking ancestral beliefs that weren't spoken of.

I paced up and down in the house all morning, at a loss for what to do to calm my frayed nerves. No matter how much I tried to keep myself busy, time refused to pass. I sat down at Fadili's desk and picked up the *calamus* and the box of ink he'd brought me from Oman. I tried to sketch something, but my hand was trembling so much I couldn't even get the tip of the *calamus* to meet the paper. My stomach felt as if it was infested with carnivorous insects.

When the door finally opened, I felt as if a tidal wave was rising in my chest, sweeping up all the fear that had been stagnating there. It died in a seething foam at my toes.

Fadili stood in the doorway. His face evoked not victory or reprieve, but anger. The pulsating vein of rage on his forehead looked ready to burst. I could tell his fists were clenched from the tension in the muscles of his forearms beneath the sleeves of his *kandu*.

'What happened, my love?'

He didn't look at me. His eyes were searching the room for something. He walked over to the bed, crouched down and reached his arm under it. My heart pounded. When he found the bag, the vein on his forehead began to throb again. He flung the bag violently on to the bed, then threw open the trunk that held his clothes.

Realising the situation was serious, I lost all restraint. I ran to him and grabbed his arm.

'What are you doing, Fadili?' He reached for the green *djuba* he wore over his clothes. How many times had I taken that *djuba* from him? How many times had I held him against me, still wearing that *djuba*? How many times had my desire wriggled its way beneath that green cloak?

His hand hung suspended over his clothes, just as I hung suspended waiting for him to speak. Without moving the hand, he finally opened his mouth. His voice was ragged, his words interspersed with gasps of breath. His eyes were clouded.

'What am I doing?' he asked, 'I've done everything. I've taken care of my wife. I've avoided all contact between her and my family, in accordance with the agreement we made. I've loved her as no one can love a woman. And now…'

He stopped to take a breath. He tilted his head, as if resting it on an imaginary shoulder. I felt as if I was swimming in a stormy sea. He breathed in once more, then continued.

'I wasn't surprised when your father came to see me and asked me to leave you. It's the sort of thing I'd expect from him. But what he did to me today, Halima, is unacceptable. It's… no, I can't do it!'

'What can't you do?'

Finally he looked at me. A tear rolled down his cheek and died on his *kandu*, in the middle of his chest. I wanted to lick it off, to lick up all the tears he shed, now and forever.

'I can't stay,' he said with difficulty. 'I can't stay with

you after what he did to me.'

'But what did he do to you? I've got a right to know what's keeping you from me!'

He turned to me, his eyes red. In a trembling voice, he recounted his meeting with my father and the *cadi*.

'The *cadi* began by explaining to your father that a union blessed by Allah could not be undone by anyone other than the two spouses. And your father… he asked him to open the book of ablutions and to read the page on dry ablutions. You know what that page says, don't you?'

'That when you can't find water to purify yourself, you can perform your ablutions with sand,' I stammered.

I looked away and said no more. Fundi nodded, satisfied that I understood: sand was the default choice until the preferred option of water came along. I knew my father could twist the rules, overstep the lines, bend convention to his will. All I could hope for was that something would stop his hand before it came down on me. My hope was weak, though, in the face of my father's will.

Fadili's next words hit me like a slap in the face.

'That's what your father told the man who loves his daughter more than his own life. That he was just a pile of sand, a clod of earth.'

*

Time stood still around us.

There was a leaden silence. It was as if all the bustling

activity of life had been paused. We'd been plucked up by a rare wind, and I knew that at any moment the stillness would give way to a violent tornado. With my eyes, I begged Fadili, 'Hold me safe in your gaze, just for one more moment. At the eye of this cyclone that our lives have become, let's claim this stillness as ours. Let's at least have that.'

Fadili's eyes were moist, his lips trembling. He gripped the edge of his *kandu* tightly in his fist. I reached out to him, my fingers brushed his face, and I found myself sinking into a strange hallucination.

At first it was as if I floated on the crest of a wave, then my whole mind was submerged. Images started to flash before my eyes at random, then came thick and fast. Faces, hands, mouths, staring eyes. Bodies draped in ancient fabrics, clothes that no-one had worn since antiquity. A vision of a distant, unknown past possessed me. There were mountains, the scent of olives, men and women who seemed larger than life and shone brighter than the sun. In the midst of it all, I saw myself, draped in red cotton cloth embroidered with mirrors. My face was thinner, my waist more slender, but it was me. At my feet, inert, lay a man. I looked down at him in horror. He didn't have the same dark eyes or hair, but in the depths of his lifeless gaze, I recognised Fadili.

There was another man behind me. He was gripping me by the waist. It felt it as tightly and painfully as if I were trapped in a vice. That man was Fundi Ahmad.

I cringed before this awful vision. Suddenly I was snapped back to reality. Fadili was looking at me with his pitch black eyes. His cheeks were wet with tears. His voice was as dry and heavy as a millstone.

'I'm sorry, my pearl of Arabia. I'm sorry.'

Halima had faithfully reproduced Fadili's tone. Her words hung in the air, as harsh as they were desperate.

It was hard for me to believe that anyone could leave a woman like Halima. How long had we been sitting next to each other on this low wall? As she talked, she'd arranged some pebbles into perfect rows in the space between us. She picked one of them up and put it down next to me. The tiny, hollow sound it made echoed in the space between us.

I told her I thought someone would have to be mad to abandon a woman like her. She looked at me with eyes that held both kindness and pain.

'You abandoned me, didn't you?'

It was like a knife in the gut. I had abandoned her. But what else could I have done? I was constrained by so many forces she had no understanding of. I gazed at her nose, so small and narrow I wondered how she managed to breathe through it. My fingers itched to reach out and trace her jawline. A thought crossed my mind. I quickly suppressed it, but not before it triggered a wave that washed through me, leaving me soaked like the sand at the shore.

In one of the tales told to discourage servants and masters from mixing, a young princess called Bibi took advantage of her parents' absence to ask her maid to take her out of the house. She'd never set foot in the outside world. There were so many new things to see: grass, flowers, butterflies… every time Bibi demanded to know what the things were called, the maid asked for one of the girl's accessories in exchange. Bibi handed over her bracelet, her gold chain and her earrings. Finally, the two exchanged dresses, and the child learned the name of the blue expanse with white patches in it that stretched above her head.

Wearing the girl's dress, the maid presented herself as the princess to a neighbouring king, and the princess became the maid. When the deception was discovered, the false princess was imprisoned in a bag which was placed on the ground at the entrance to the palace. Anyone entering the palace had to step on the bag, and hear the squealing noise it made.

The moral was that servants are inevitably deceitful and deserve the harshest punishment, while the children of masters are innocent and good, open to deception unless society remains vigilant.

'Is that why you made Olympe put me to sleep?'

'Oh, Hardie, I'm sorry about that.'

Halima's cheeks flushed. It was like watching two hibiscus flowers blossom under her skin. I'd never seen that happen to someone's face before: my own embarrassment, like that of my friends, was perfectly concealed by our darker colouring. Halima was nothing like us.

'Listen,' she said, 'Fundi Ahmad doesn't want anyone to visit me. If he found out anyone had been here, I don't know what he'd do. I put you to sleep so you didn't see any of the corridors that led you to me. That way there's no risk you might let something slip by mistake.'

'But I'm the *fundi's* favourite pupil!'

'He'd take it all the harder if he learned his favourite pupil had flouted his authority.'

A silence settled over us. The small room we were in contained nothing but the low wall we were sitting on and a brown rope bed beneath a rectangular window. A moonbeam shone through the window, bathing the bed and half of Halima's body in its blue glow. Parts of me were also illuminated. Halima was staring at me.

'Is he… kind with you?' I asked her.

She didn't understand what I was alluding to. 'Fundi? Yes, he shops for me at the market, asks me what I want to eat, makes sure I have everything I need.'

'No, I mean… is he… gentle with you?' I insisted.

'Oh, that.'

She squirmed on the low wall, tugged at a knot in her *hami*. Her face hardened and she spoke vehemently.

'I'm not there when it happens. It's my body he's doing things to. My heart is with Fadili.'

I was silent. What Fundi had told my mother was true; Halima was resisting him. He insisted, and she took refuge somewhere else. I'd already heard from my friend Mlima that it was possible to escape in your mind like that: she'd done it when her master wanted to use her body. She'd disappeared in her mind and taken refuge in the arms of her father, who'd died the year before.

I changed the subject.

'And Fadili, was he gentle with you?'

'Not very.' She turned to me, a mischievous smile on her lips. 'But I didn't want him to be!'

We both burst out laughing.

'I'd like to experience a love like you had with Fadili with a man,' I said after a silence.

'You will one day.'

'I very much doubt it. Love's not permitted for people like us. My own mother didn't want me, so…'

'But Tamu loves you like a mother. I don't even know what a mother is. You're so lucky you have Tamu.'

'Didn't your mother bring you up?'

'I never knew her. She died giving birth to me.'

'Oh!'

'But she's with me, watching over me. I feel her presence.'

'If she was watching over you, she wouldn't have left you in the hands of Fundi Ahmad!'

'You don't know that.'

'Halima, the woman who bore me disowned me. Tamu took pity on me. Why did the woman who should have protected me try to kill me?'

We were silent for a moment. Then Halima took my hand. 'Come,' she said, 'I've got something to show you.'

I followed her down a winding passageway that led to another, then another. The further we went, the narrower the passageways and the lower the ceilings. By the time we got to the third one, we had to stoop. My back began to ache. Part of me wanted to turn back, but I couldn't face the thought of going back through all those corridors again. Finally we stopped in front of a carved wooden door. It must have been a third of my height and half Halima's height. The frame was decorated with spirals like those Tamu sometimes traced in the sand, out of Fundi's sight, while mumbling words I didn't understand. Verses from the Qur'an were engraved at the top of the frame. I wondered why the door was so small.

'It's to slow down the enemy,' said Halima. 'When they come in—'

She didn't finish her sentence, but opened the door and stepped through. I saw that it led into a huge room. As I bent down to enter, Halima's warm hand grabbed the back of my neck.

'I've killed you!' She shouted, then burst out laughing. 'See—that's what the low corridors and the tiny door are for: as soon as the enemy's in, they're knocked out!'

A cool breeze alerted me to the fact that I'd been mistaken: this was not a room but a vast open-air atrium. It had a floor of black and white flagstones and was surrounded by high walls.

In the centre of the space rose an incredible structure. It was shaped like a triangle, with one perpendicular wall and two that sloped. The two sloping walls were linked by a staircase that seemed to reach right to the sky.

It was an observatory.

Fundi had told me about the stargazing observatories built by astronomers in India, Persia and other places renowned for their knowledge. This was the first time I'd seen one in real life. It was made of huge triangles and spheres of red and yellow stone, with that dizzying staircase at its centre. There was an enormous pole with an iron bar fixed to it at an angle, and a semi-circular piece that could move along its axis. As the sun cast its shadows, Halima would teach me later, this contraption allowed for the marking of time. It was more beautiful than anything I could have imagined.

*

Halima reached out her hand to me. A childlike smile illuminated her face. I took it, even as I chided myself for my servility.

She led me up the stairs. At the very top of the building was a stone platform wide enough for two people. In the centre of the platform was a rectangular pit filled with fine sand. I noticed small hillocks on it, in a regular pattern: someone had been trailing their fingers across it.

I was bursting to know what this was, but I'd been taught not to ask questions.

Halima untied a knot in her *hami* that she'd made at her hip and brought out several black pebbles. She placed them on the floor one by one.

'*Al Jafr*,' she murmured. 'The Sand of Knowledge. Fundi Ahmad has me studying time reading.'

'What's time reading?'

She looked at me.

'It's the knowledge of what has been, what is, and what will be for any soul. You can read the destiny of every soul. Look.'

She moved two pebbles to the centre, then placed two more on either side. Then she placed two more pebbles below the first pair, two more at the side. When she'd finished, there were seven pairs of pebbles in all, arranged in two rhombuses, one above the other.

I couldn't make sense of it, but the harmony of what she'd built told me there must be some logic behind it, something Halima was trying to teach me. She took a slow breath before speaking. Her voice cut through the still darkness like a gleaming blade. Above us, the stars seemed to form an even more immense canopy than usual. Paradoxically, though I'd never looked at them from so high up, they'd never seemed so far away. Halima's voice accompanied the gentle breeze.

'In every situation in our lives, there's a force that's hidden. Beneath the chaos, there's order. Beneath everything that pains us, there's a reason beyond ourselves.'

She placed two fingers around the pebbles in the centre and picked them up.

'You were born of a mother and a father, even if you never knew them.'

She picked up the two pairs of pebbles that flanked the first.

'You can feel all the rage in the world towards them; you can resent them for abandoning you to the point of killing them again and again in your anguished thoughts, but your rage will be vain and useless. Whatever you blame them for, it will be of no help to you: your destiny was to be alone at that point in your life. Whatever their reasons for abandoning you, it was the only thing they could do. Whether our parents are with us or not, sooner or later the time comes when we have to seek the strength inside ourselves. In the plan of the universe, nothing comes too early or too late. Every stone has its place.'

She lifted two more of the stones.

'You'll find helpers along the way. But the one and only person who can change things is you. If you're suspicious by nature, your allies will be torn from you; you'll learn to rely only on yourself.'

There was just one pair of pebbles left.

'I'm as alone as you are, Hardie. Let's unite our solitudes, as we tried to do once before. If you help me, I'll help you. My heart tells me we're going to move forward together.'

My own heart was beating at a speed I didn't know it was capable of. At the same time, I felt a blanket of calm wrapping me: it rested at my chest, in the place where my breasts should have been. The pain was still there, but for the first time since I'd had my breasts ripped from me, I felt it ease a little. Somewhere inside me, things were beginning to make sense: I knew there was an order, even if I couldn't decipher it.

I looked at Halima. She met my gaze. Our faces were so close, I could feel her breath tickling the place between my nose and my upper lip. I wanted to lose myself in the darkness of her eyes; to drown in that night-time ocean, drop down to the very bottom and gather up the full moon that lay there. She'd said 'together'. A thought was forming in my mind. I didn't want to look at it, because it threatened to break me, but it slipped from my lips unbidden. My voice shook as I said, 'What if… the time comes for us to part again?'

I lifted one of the remaining pebbles from the ground. Halima snatched it out of my hand.

'Two stones, two people,' I protested. 'If there are two stones, they can be separated.'

'No,' she said, 'You and I are one and the same stone.' She

placed the pebble back down again. 'One and the same soul.'

A soft, soothing sensation flooded my chest. One and the same soul.

'Yes,' she said, reading my thoughts. 'And now you must go. The last star has just appeared in the sky.'

I looked up. The last star, Al Marrikh, had indeed appeared in the queen's long train. It was recognisable by its reddish hue. It signalled the final service at the mosque; soon the men would finish praying and go outside to sit on the steps and chat for a while before returning home.

I leapt to my feet. I hesitated on the stairs.

'Don't be afraid; it'll make you fall,' Halima teased.

It wasn't fear of heights, but the question I hadn't had a chance to ask that was making me pause. Halima pretended to give me a push.

'Go! We'll meet again soon, in five days' time, when the moon's full. He always stays longer at the mosque when the moon's full.'

I paused for another second, then pelted down the endless staircase. Halima hadn't really explained what the observatory was for or what it was doing there. There was still so much to be said. When I reached the low doorway, I turned back.

'Don't send the same child to me again,' I called to her. 'Just tell me the time and I'll come.'

'All right, then. Come at the same time.'

'And also…' I was about to ask her not to knock me out at the gate again. She anticipated my request and interrupted me. Her smile was gentle, but her tone was firm.

'Aren't you making enough demands? You'll be put to sleep, Hardie. For your own protection.'

I stooped down and made my way out into the narrow passageway. I felt the heat rise in my cheeks when Halima hissed, 'Don't forget: no more separations now. We're together!'

My heart moved as if in time with her words, as if to anchor them inside me.

*

When I arrived home, Tamu wasn't sitting outside the front door as usual. I assumed she must be inside, going over the invocations she'd just learned from Fundi Ahmad: 33 *istighfar*, 33 *tasbih* and 33 *lutuf*. Thirty-three was the sacred number.

Inside, though, I found Ramla, Mlima, Ramla's aunt and another woman. Some of them were busying themselves around a pot in the middle of the main room, others were rummaging through our bedrooms, lifting our mattresses and shaking out our sheets. There was no sign of Tamu.

When Ramla saw me, she leapt down my throat. '*Bo Gailla*! You disappeared off somewhere, and now your mother's been kidnapped!'

HAWWAZ

My dream dissipated in a greenish haze. I forced my eyes open. A pale blue glow was filtering through the shutters, patterning my mat and the sheet that covered me with small rectangles. The air smelled of incense and burnt wood.

I propped myself up on my forearms and stretched myself awake. I noticed an odd sensation; something I'd never experienced before. Beneath my body was softness. It was not a mat I was lying on, but a mattress.

The events of the previous day returned to me in flashes. Halima's face as she demanded I be given a mattress. The *fundi's* face, insisting I come and stay with them. 'I'll take care of you,' he'd said. Why had he said that?

The rest came flooding back.

Tamu's face.

Tamu had disappeared.

*

Nobody had seen her come home from work. According to Ramla's mother, she'd left with two *hamis* she was going to dye for the *fundi's* young wife. She'd headed off towards the beach at Hatov, where she washed her fabrics before soaking them in the plant dyes that she left in large black buckets beside the rocks.

People had seen her leave, but no one had seen her come back.

When I heard the news, I pretended I wanted to go and look for her in Ahmad's Wood, where she sometimes collected branches before coming home.

Everyone believed me.

The next day, the men from the neighbourhood who'd been out to search for Tamu came home empty-handed. I cried all the tears my body could produce.

Tamu had never made me feel I owed her anything. She'd never opposed my desire to explore the world, to the limited extent that our circumstances allowed. She'd just say, 'You're so unusual, my daughter,' with a sadness in her eyes.

She wanted a better world for me than the one we lived in: one in which curiosity wasn't frowned upon, in which I'd be allowed to sit up all night counting the stars.

She'd taken me under her wing when my real mother had failed me.

Now I had no way of rescuing her.

Two, three, then four days passed with no news of Tamu. Soon, two weeks had elapsed.

I'd searched the forest with a fine-tooth comb. I'd swum through deep waters to places where even the boldest fishermen never ventured. The salt had traced channels in my skin; some of them had even bled, so relentless was my swimming. I'd searched all the caves that lined the beach. I'd found nothing.

The full moon continued to shine down on me, as if encouraging me to persevere. Yet I could feel myself tiring. The moon shined even brighter then, urging me not to give up.

Suddenly, I became enraged with it. As if from the depths of the earth, a wave of anger rose up from my battered, bleeding feet, climbed my body and lodged in my chest, choking and cruel. It rolled over me like a thousand rampant waves. My arms felt as if they were burning. They itched for movement, so I flung them in the air above my head and released the wave of rage in a monstrous howl.

I screamed at the moon for demanding everything from my people, yet doing nothing for us. I called it by name. 'Mawu, you've betrayed us! You were Tamu's goddess. She loved you with all her heart, sacrificed her hen in front of the house for you, spilled its blood in your name. Her only fault was wanting her child to better herself, to learn the language and religion of the masters. Do you blame her for that? Are you really so blind, or so cruel?'

This rant wasn't enough to dispel my rage. I turned away from the moon's pitted face and grabbed the first rock I could find. It was a huge boulder, the kind that forms part of a border the length of the beach, fruit of the union between the sacred fire, which rises up from the ground in the mountain of Kathala, and Mother Earth, whose arms encompass everything. My hands came to rest on the jagged surface of the rock, and I felt its sharp edge.

I called out to the fire god, 'Mantis! You heard my lament, and you remained silent! Yet so many times you've given your fire to those who wished us harm! If Tamu is dead, if it's because of someone with malicious intent, I swear on her flesh that I'll find your hiding place and pluck you from the heart of the earth!'

I grabbed hold of the rock, as if I could lift it and throw it, despite its size. I pulled at it with all my might.

Then it moved.

Beneath my clutching fingers, the rock severed. A huge piece detached itself and seemed to rise to meet my hands. My veins felt as if they were filled with burning liquid, my body went numb. An inexplicable force drove me. I lifted the piece of rock towards the sky and held it above my head, screaming at Mawu and Mantis in a voice like metal shearing under a blacksmith's hammer. Then I hurled the rock violently at the ground, where it smashed into a thousand sparkling black pieces.

Something had taken possession of my will.

These were the actions of a different me: stronger, angrier, more free.

Gradually, the torrent in my veins calmed. Breathless, my eyes burning, I looked back at the moon. Its otherworldly glow was fainter now: it had donned its coppery nightclothes and was preparing to sink into sleep at the edge of the sea.

Between the rows of palm trees, I thought I saw two lights piercing the darkness, then a third, lower down, swaying gently back and forth. I shouted wildly, 'Who's there? If you're a *jinn*, come out, I'm not afraid of you!'

The lights disappeared. I was too disturbed and exhausted to pursue them.

I looked down at the fragments of rock, dark stars against the immaculate white of the sand. Suddenly, seized with fear, I ran.

*

I ran full pelt until I got to the edge of Ahmad's Wood, where I collapsed on a tree stump. The tears came then; a steady stream interspersed with crashing cascades.

A hand came to rest on my shoulder and gently squeezed it.

I looked up, expecting to see one of the men from the nearby town who roamed the fields looking for some poor girl they could take advantage of. Still reeling from what had happened on the beach, I prepared myself to fight, clenching my fists and summoning back my fury.

But it was Fundi Ahmad's face I saw looking down at me. The setting sun gave his lean figure a burnished hue. In his white *kandu* and golden *kofia*, which stood out strongly against his dark skin, he could have passed for the angel Gabriel grasping Mohammed's shoulder as he revealed the sacred book.

I smiled wryly to myself: in the religion of our masters, there were no prophetesses, especially not black ones. According to the *fundi*, believing in them was sacrilege. The role of women was simply to bear new believers in their bodies; If they were among the fortunate few, they might bear a descendant of the illustrious divine messengers.

After what had happened to me on the beach, I felt a little less awe before the *fundi*. I was still stunned and bewildered. It could've been a hallucination. But it felt as if the river that had made its bed in me was still flowing through my veins.

'You must be tired, my child.' Fundi frowned.

I made no reply, but dipped my head to let him know he

was right. He looked at me for a long time. I was afraid that if I looked at him again, he might guess something had happened. After a short silence, accompanied by the chirping of crickets, he took a deep breath and looked around for something to sit on. There was nothing but branches, henna bushes and nettles. Above us, the trees loomed, their foliage ever denser, as dark as a warning.

'Come with me,' the *fundi* finally said.

I did so; slouching, trailing my feet, holding his hand like a child who's just had her favourite sweet snatched away.

A few moments later, we were sitting on the low wall beside the big tamarind tree, facing the cemetery. I sometimes met my friends there if we finished work at the same time. Our masters didn't treat us like employees. Some of us were available to them at all hours of the day; a lucky few were sometimes given one evening off each week. The others would steal a few moments between the preparation of the evening meal and the return of their master from the mosque.

Whenever we met, we'd share the sweets our mothers had prepared: rice cake, pieces of caramel, a doughnut sprinkled with sugar. Tamu knew the doughnut was my favourite, and that I liked it big, brown and crispy at the edges.

A huge burden had begun to weigh on my shoulders. I felt like crying again, but the presence of the *fundi* forced me to be brave.

He gave a deep sigh.

'Listen, I've always thought of you as my child. You're not like the others. You learn in a different way, and you have a true relationship with the sacred text. That's not the case for everyone, and believe me, not even some of the greatest scholars can read the Qur'an with the attention that you show. In fact, attention is not the word. You seem *inhabited* by the Qur'an. You're this close—he pointed to the space between his index and middle fingers—to understanding its full meaning.

He remained silent, as if to let his words sink in. In the silence of the night, I could hear the whisper of the beads of his rosary clicking together. I looked down at his hands. They were streaked with veins, and his dark skin made his fingers look like solid, gnarled twigs of teak.

He continued, lowering his voice a little, 'At the moment, though, you have too many worries. Being a girl, and a servant's daughter at that, is preventing you from reaching your full potential. I realise that now: if you're still a bit slow, it's because I didn't understand it earlier. So I'd like to welcome you into my home.'

He paused. I struggled to grasp the bizarre statement I'd just heard him make.

'But there's one thing I must impress on you first.'

My heart leapt. I knew what was coming. My skin crawled with a shameful feeling. There were conversations I should never have overheard, others I should never have had. 'This will backfire on you,' Ramla had said. She'd been right to warn me.

'If you come to my house, you must promise not to try to have contact with my wife.'

I made the mistake of feigning ignorance.

'Which wife, esteemed Fundi?'

He snorted the way he did at *shioni* when we claimed we hadn't had time to revise our verses.

'Listen,' he said, trying to control his irritation 'Halima is not a woman of good influence. She… has strange ideas in her head, put there by her former husband, a scoundrel from Moroni. They distract her from her duties as a wife and her destiny as a proper Muslim. Do you remember the passage I taught you regarding the roles of women and men?'

I opened my mouth with difficulty. The passage he was referring to was painful to me. It made me think of the day Ramla's mother had placed the hot banana skins on my chest.

I began to mumble the sentences Fundi was expecting.

'Allah took a rib from Adam and from it he fashioned his wife. Inside, the woman remained curved like a rib. Because she is curved, it is her husband's duty to… to…'

I couldn't help it—my voice dried up. The words rolled behind my teeth and shoved each other to the back of my throat.

'What are you waiting for? Carry on!'

I took a deep breath and imagined I was the *fundi*, reciting the *hadith*.

'It is her husband's duty to straighten her as best he can. He must do this gently and with patience, because not only will she resist, but if he forces her to stand up straight, she will break. Woman is by nature a crippled creature who must be tamed with indulgence, for she alone can protect man from his perversions and carry humanity inside her.'

By the end of the last sentence, I was breathless. I'd run the final words together, like a last spasm before vomiting bile.

A memory came to me. Tamu was lying beside Fundi in the bedroom. Only the thin curtain separated them from me. Fundi had just recited this quote, attributed to the prophet, while they were debating a subject he thought Tamu was ill-placed to understand. She'd laughed in his face. When he asked her why she was laughing, she replied, 'My grandmother used to tell my mother that a man was only a rough draft of a woman, and that his only use was to satisfy his wife so that from her enjoyment the rivers and streams of life could flow. Granted that's not very flattering to you, but couldn't you find a better way of restoring your dignity than just reversing the roles?'

Though it was said in jest, I detected a hint of sadness in Tamu's voice; the melancholy of the defeated.

A long silence followed. Fundi was upset. Shortly afterwards, he got dressed, put on his shoes and left without saying goodbye.

As for me, that passage was engraved in my memory. I'd learned all of Fundi's teachings by heart, but part of me reproached myself for knowing all the words that insulted women in the *hadiths* he'd taught us, and which we repeated with fervour.

The only thing that really connected me to the *fundi* was the Qur'an. We were both madly in love with it. Its poetry, its melodies, which were one with the meanings of its words. The slippery consonants of the word 'sea', *bahr*, carried me with them across the waves. Those of the word *riyâh*, 'wind', propelled me over the hills of my island, sitting on a cloud. My favourite was the word for 'to guide' or 'to change'. It sounded like a sigh, the exhalation of a being longing for an encounter that would change its life. *Mh*.

Fundi had guessed at my love affair with the sacred book. He knew the way he and I felt about those words was not something he could teach to others without undermining his credibility. When we were alone, he alluded to it, but not without taking a thousand precautions to ensure I didn't denounce him for heresy.

I was very fond of Fundi at that time. He had a nasal voice that often oscillated between low and high pitches, but it had the effect on me of pure water drunk after days of thirst. Although I felt repelled by some of his beliefs about women, he was still the *fundi*, my master, the person who brought me closer to the stars.

Yet I deplored the fact that my long talks with Halima, when we sat perched on the platform of her starry observatory in front of her tray of sand, might henceforth be banned.

'My wife is strange,' the *fundi* continued. 'She's... not like other women. She's too excited, too thirsty for... ah, I don't even know what she's thirsty for! She spends her nights wandering, or lost in her papers. Sometimes I forbid her from going into my office, in case she rummages through my books and finds some sentence or other that she can reinterpret as she pleases. She doubts certain sayings of our prophet, and questions the exegesis of the Qur'an. Associating with her could destroy your relationship with the sacred scriptures. That's why I implore you to stay away from her. If you disobey me, I'll be forced to have you removed from the house. Do you understand?'

I took a deep breath. In the air that entered my nostrils I sensed the scent of the sea, so special to me, associated with the day I first met Halima. I clutched the corner of my *leso*. I'd kept the object she'd entrusted to me there beside me all this time. I conjured up Halima's dreamy gaze, her laughter, the ideas she'd shared with me in hushed tones. I imagined her teaching me how to handle the black stones and the *jafr*. I saw myself telling her the stories Tamu had told me.

Tamu who was gone.

My joy dulled and my excitement deserted me as soon as I remembered its source. Halima had a father and a husband. However tyrannical they were, they were poised to protect her. I had no one.

'Yes esteemed Fundi,' I answered. 'I understand, *kwezi*.'

I summoned the strength to stand, and my shoulder supported by Fundi's warm palm, I walked with him towards his stone house.

*

It was Halima who'd insisted I be given this padded mattress. It was strange not to feel the slight twinge in my joints after spending a night on the floor, not having to stretch out my neck so much because it had been supported by a pillow. Strange, too, to have my own room with a place to sleep in it and a place to keep my things—a tin trunk, which I could lock with a padlock.

I got up with disconcerting ease and found my way to the place where I could do my ablutions.

The room I'd been given was the one reserved for midwives. It opened onto a passageway that wasn't as small as those I'd gone down with Halima, but still low enough that I had to stoop. Along its length, small rectangles had been cut out to let in daylight. No daylight was yet entering, though, so I returned to my bedroom to get the lantern from my chest.

I came out again, my flame swinging back and forth as I walked. My back was beginning to ache, and I was cursing this life of privilege that forced me to walk hunched over through endless corridors, when Olympe appeared in front of me. I could neither pass her nor turn back. We were stuck. It was odd to be standing in front of her in the house she'd only allowed me to enter after drugging me. As soon as she saw me, her face, which had been fixed in an expression of exasperation, softened.

'Hardie, dear Hardie! How are you feeling?'

I hadn't attended the funeral organised by members of the community for Tamu, because I was outraged by their assumption she was dead. While my other friends had said things like 'You're only hurting yourself', and 'You should accept Allah's will, which no one can change,' Olympe had supported me. As there was no body, they'd buried Tamu's *saluva*, the one with the interlocking squares. I felt pained that they were burying that fabric: it contained ancient knowledge, inherited from our ancestors, represented by the squares. Tamu had promised she'd pass that knowledge on to me as soon as I'd completed my education with the *fundi*. She hadn't planned to disappear before that happened.

In the flickering light of our lanterns, through the shadows, I could just make out Olympe's scar. I'd seen it so often since I'd known her that usually I didn't notice it. Long ago, when we were children, Olympe had told me how she got it. The image of her as a little girl suddenly came to my mind: she was sitting in front of a pot of corn porridge and bashing the top of her banana stalk with a stone, trying to get hair for her doll. Her mother turned round to pick up a bottle of milk to pour into the bubbling pot. Olympe became angry at her banana stalk for not relinquishing its fibres and hurled her stone at the pot, which her mother hadn't had time to close. Then the splash, the howl and the permanent scar.

'I'm fine, Olympe,' I reassured her. 'I'm trying to comply with Allah's decree. How are you?'

'Stop it, you can't do that to me,' she retorted with a smile. 'I know you're suffering. I don't know what to do to make you feel better. Do you know I dreamed about Tamu last night?'

'Did you?' I asked, with the eagerness of a hungry man hoping for food.

'Yes. She was sitting in front of a huge, gleaming palace, all dressed up in her precious *zari* dress.'

I closed my eyes and tried to picture Tamu in her *zari*, feasting in the afterlife. The image wouldn't come.

'Try to calm your heart, Hardie. Your mother's happy where she is. A palace! That means she already had a good relationship with Allah, and now she's in a good place, with Him.'

'Her place was with me, not with Allah,' I wanted to say. I held back for fear of being accused of blasphemy. Even Olympe was careful about that sort of thing.

'Thank you, Olympe. It does me good to know she's at peace,' I lied.

'If you want to wash, you can use the toilets right behind your bedroom. They're reserved for new mothers. I sometimes go to them to fetch water for my mistress.'

So I turned back, Olympe following behind me. Had she emphasised the word 'mistress' to remind me of my rank?

In any case, Olympe's kindness put me at ease for the rest of the day. I cooked with her, helped her fetch water, then went with her to Qur'anic school, where we met up with our three friends. Ramla hugged me for a long time; Mlima caressed my cheek; M'maka kept her hand in mine for a while.

As we were well into our apprenticeship, we were also required to teach the younger children. Ramla and I were both about to memorise the last *surah* of the Qur'an, after which we'd have the right to study the magic hidden behind the letters of the sacred book. The others still had three or four particularly difficult *surahs* to read, and we had to help them too.

After listening to each child, we all read the last ten *surahs* of the Qur'an together, to help the younger pupils memorise them. Short and rhythmic, these verses sometimes inspired the children to do funny dances: we'd done the same at their age. The verses of the *inshirah*, the overture, all ended the same way, in '*ak*', and consisted of two sentences of the same length. Despite the ban on singing the Qur'an and dancing to its melodies, even the most serious child found it difficult not to bounce to this as if it were a nursery rhyme. Fundi didn't like to see us dancing—he said it was an art form inspired by the devil—so we had to content ourselves with remaining seated, raising our arms in the air and swaying them from side to side.

Alam nashrah-laka sadrak
Wa wadha'nâ—laka wizrak
Alladhi an-qadha dhahrak
Wa rafa'na laka dhikrak
Fa inna ma'a l'usri-yusrâ
Inna ma'al usri—yusra
Fa idhâ faraghta—fansab
Wa ilâ rabbika—farhab!

Most of us recited these verses without having the slightest idea of what they meant. We had no clue whether they described something good or bad, and we didn't much care. The important thing was not to know the meaning of the words, but to commit them to memory in place of the pagan litanies of our ancestors. That was something I learned later. Back then, I just enjoyed the children's enthusiasm. At the end of the dancing *surah*, we all burst out laughing. Fundi pretended to lunge at us with his stick, but did no more.

That day, just as we were getting ready to read—or rather, sing, may Allah forgive us—the *inshirah*, a woman around the age of our mothers appeared in the doorway. I'd just lifted the stick to start the children off, and had to raise it again to stop them reciting.

'Come in,' I told her.

'I enter with gratitude,' she replied. She walked over to the *fundi* and placed the back of her right hand on her left palm to show her respect. The *fundi* placed his right hand on the woman's right palm.

'Mother of Hussam!' he exclaimed, not hiding his astonishment.

'Father of all the children!' she replied, holding his gaze.

'So you've come to learn at last?'

'Yes, Fundi.'

'Your husband has finally granted you the right to learn your religion?'

'Yes, Fundi. I insisted, and you know how I insist.'

Fundi gave a knowing chuckle.

'Very good, Ma Hussam. You're welcome. My five wise women will teach you everything you need to know.'

The woman walked towards us and took her place in the circle of children. Teaching a woman old enough to be our mother was strange. We didn't sing the Qur'an that day. But I thought I saw one or two dancing arms in the children's circle. Ma Hussam glared at them, then gave us a disapproving look.

'I don't think I'm going to like this one,' Olympe whispered to me.

She came to me at nightfall.

As soon as she opened the door, the room filled with her scent: coconut milk and jasmine. It's hard to describe what I felt when I saw her. It was as if my heart was swelling, straining to escape my ribcage. There was a tickling sensation deep in my belly. My legs started twitching, wanting to run, who knows where. Fear rippled through my guts. My mouth half opened and remained that way. I gulped for the air that suddenly felt too thin.

Petrified, I locked eyes with her. I opened my mouth wider, but still failed to produce a sound. I wanted to say, 'Get away from me. The *fundi* said I mustn't see you. He was very clear. If you stay here, you're signing my death warrant.'

Another voice inside me was saying, 'Who cares if I die, as long as I can see you, even if it's for the last time.'

She shone in her white *hami*. Her skin, gilded by the light of the lanterns, glowed like the skin of the ripe guava I held in my hand. I'd just taken a bite.

She carried a double incense burner made of fired clay, decorated with white patterns. The air began to take on the perfumes of myrrh and sandalwood. It grew dense, loaded with a promise I struggled to define.

If I hadn't been feeling so helpless, so embittered, I might've been able to appreciate Halima's presence in my room. It was often this way between us; my preoccupations intruding into the time we had together.

'How are you finding your new bed?' she asked me.

She'd sat down on my mattress of guinea fowl feathers and kapok.

'It's fine,' I said, through pursed lips.

Her mouth twitched with the hint of a smile. She placed the incense holder on the floor; it made a hollow sound on the flagstones. A few small sparks escaped, speckling the darkness with orange. Beside the door, my candle sputtered, its wick close to being consumed.

Halima sighed. I sensed her discomfort. The shadow of her husband hovered over us, ready to pounce.

I realised that only made her presence in my room more exciting.

She didn't seem to know where to start, so I spoke first. 'I dreamed about Tamu last night.'

Halima lowered her head. She fiddled with the small metal ring on the side of the incense holder.

'What was she doing?' she asked.

'She was dressed like a married woman. She looked so beautiful.'

My throat constricted. My voice faltered. Halima placed her hand on my arm. It felt soft, and as warm as the smooth paving stones at sunset prayer time.

'I know what you're feeling, Hardie. I mean… I can imagine it. I've never known a mother's love like you have. It must be ten times worse for you to have had her, then lost her.'

Conscious of my own egotism, I tried to compose myself. How could I cry for a mother I'd known for years when Halima had only the vaguest memory of hers? We'd both lost our blood mothers, but for Halima no one had filled that place. She'd had to navigate life with just an authoritarian father who showed her little affection.

'My father loves me,' she said, reading my thoughts, as always. 'He might be blunt, but he does love me. Before I was married, he used to go to the market for me. He got my dresses mended when they were torn, or he bought me new ones. He curled my hair.'

I didn't like to hear her speaking deferentially of the father who'd invaded her privacy and destroyed her marriage. Instead of saying so, I found myself telling her the story Tamu had told me; of how Islam first came to our island.

'Before we all became Muslim brothers, there was a marriage rite here. It consisted of both parties saying, 'Love me, and let me love you.' It was a practice inherited from our ancestors who lived across the sea, in those places where the islands are as big as oceans. Tamu's grandfather had a miniature bow, carved from an animal horn, and tiny arrows. When he caught sight of the woman he wanted to marry, running between the rocks of their sandy land, he did as tradition dictated and fired one of his little arrows right into her left buttock. They got to know each other, and their families agreed to their request to be married. So they could be joined, they each spoke the words, 'Love me, and let me love you.'

We carried on that tradition, even after they brought

us here.

Then one day, two men heard talk of the new religion. They were sent by their master to Mecca to learn about it.

When they came back, they abolished the old marriage rite and started a new one, which required neither the presence nor the agreement of the woman. One of these men was nicknamed Mtswahindza, 'the man who no longer knows how to love'.

But we followed his rules. That's how we became undesirables in our own land.'

Halima swallowed. There was a pause before she replied.

'Fadili always used to say that the message should be separated from its bearer. An idea can be great; it can change the world. But if the wrong person has the job of explaining it to others, the idea can lose its heart, its spirit, its meaning. That's what's happened to us: the wrong people have spread false interpretations, they've suppressed beliefs that aren't even excluded by the Qur'an, and they've privileged their personal interests over everything else, because they're greedy men.'

I felt like arguing: I remained convinced we'd been robbed of our heritage, our story, had it supplanted by something else. I was filled with rage. It was as if her disappearance had revealed who my real master had been all along: it was never the *fundi*, it was Tamu.

'If those people misinterpreted anything, it was that they didn't hold the truth: we did. We're the ones who named the constellations! They merely attached their own words, so well that now we don't even remember the original names. They're thieves of knowledge!'

'Who exactly do you mean by "they"?'

'The Arabs, the Persians, the Indians.'

I bit my lip. Halima's light skin came from her Sharif ancestors, descendants of the prophet, Arabs. Her father and forefathers were proud of those origins. To insult them was to insult Halima.

She turned her face from me and stared at the wall. The candle guttered out, plunging us into darkness. I groped to find the spare one I kept beside my pillow.

'No need,' Halima muttered drily, 'I can walk that corridor with my eyes closed. I'm leaving now. I'll spare you the sight of my criminal features.'

She stood. I wanted to stop her, to grab hold of her *hami*, but my body, wracked with pain at the disappearance of Tamu, refused to obey. It compelled me to be loyal to my mother, despite all that simmered inside me for Halima.

She moved to the door, then stopped.

'You see,' she said, without turning, 'I spend my life between these walls. All my life, all I've seen is walls. But in my mind I've created windows, and I've looked at the sun. I understand that it has many rays. You can go outside every day, and you don't even bother to observe this spectacle. You're too busy defending your own personal ray, just like the masters do with their religion. No ray is more important than any other. Sleep well, Hardie.'

She left by the small door.

I couldn't finish my guava. A portion of the fruit had remained in my throat the whole time. Now it descended, slowly and painfully.

That was our second separation.

I remembered my *hitima*, the day I'd finished reading the entire Qur'an. For the children of nobles, this day was marked with a feast: the pupils were all invited to eat goat's meat and rice in a sauce of curdled milk and honey. Cardamom biscuits, coconut milk rice cakes, caramel sweets, coconut sweets, tamarind juice and just-ripe mango were all devoured. Before the meal, the teacher would read *Yâ Sin*, the *surah* to cure all ills and grant all wishes. It was the one recited when someone needed to find a lost object, and the longest text children had to learn. Then the feasting would begin.

My *hitima* was celebrated at home, with Tamu and my four friends. It was the same for them. Though we hadn't expected him, and he wasn't supposed to come, as we were not of the same rank, Fundi had also been there. He'd brought the curdled milk and honey, and Ramla's mother had made the cardamom biscuits. At the end of the meal, Fundi had taken a vial filled with black liquid from the pocket of his robe. It was charcoal mixed with coconut oil. He asked for a steel dish, which I hurried to bring him. On it, he inscribed the first verses of the most powerful *surahs* in the holy book.

'This way,' he said, 'When I teach you their secrets, they'll find their way more easily into your mind.'

He poured water into the dish, and we watched as the

letters slowly dissolved. He collected the dark liquid in a glass.

'This is your first *azaïma*,' he said, handing me the glass. 'Drink it and reach the highest pinnacles of wisdom, my daughter.'

My daughter. I knew that Tamu, who stood behind me, was trembling with emotion. I was trembling too, moved that there should be a man in this world who saw me as something more than prey. I took the glass from Fundi's hand, a little too eagerly.

'Careful,' he growled, 'You mustn't spill a single drop!'

That was more like the Fundi I knew.

I drank the liquid slowly. The charcoal gave the water a slightly bitter taste. It felt as if something hot was coursing through my limbs, but it wasn't unpleasant. Fundi was looking intently at me, as if impatient for me to finish. He was mumbling something. I realised he was praying. When I'd swallowed the last drop, he inhaled, to gather all the incantations he'd been muttering, then breathed out over me, directing them into my mind.

The glow of well-being started in my head and spread down my neck, to my shoulders and through my whole body.

I'd been blessed.

*

Fundi had summoned the five of us to the foot of the mango tree at the edge of the land that bordered his stone palace. Seeing him sitting there on the grass, a stick in one hand and a rosary in the other, wiry from age and the long meditative walks he took, inspired both respect and tenderness in me.

Despite everything I might have thought about the Arabs and their followers, Fundi was the closest to a father I'd ever had.

The fresh trade wind was blowing in from the west. The rainy season was over; the fruit season had arrived. The air was thick with the scent of ripening lychees, mangoes and bananas. Soon, all the maids would be squeezing the pulp between their hands to make fresh juices for the masters.

I hadn't told my friends about the fire that had sprung from my hands. I'd decided to keep it secret, partly so as not to arouse their jealousy, but mostly—though I was loathe to admit it to myself—because I was paralysed by fear.

When we reached the fruit-laden mango tree, we saw that Fundi was surrounded by various objects. I counted six rosaries, five books, five bundles of incense sticks and some wooden dice the size of a thumb.

The salute to the master was always a solemn moment. You placed your right hand on top of your left, palms up, and held them out to him, murmuring the customary submissive greeting, '*kwezi*'. The master would then place his right palm over your hands and respond with a blessing, '*mbona*'.

Each of us performed the greeting, then we stood there, unsure what the master wanted us to do. We'd never seen Fundi in this setting. The walls and raffia mats of the Qur'anic school were the only context in which we knew how to place him. In this sun-drenched place beneath the mango tree, surrounded by tall grasses and feeding butterflies, he looked more like one of the dark-skinned sorcerers we were forbidden from mentioning. He also seemed more serene than usual.

'Well,' he chided us with a smile, 'Are you going to sit down or not?' He lifted his shoulders in a questioning shrug.

I sat on Fundi's right, Ramla on his left, and the others in front of him. The objects lay between us. I savoured the caress of the wind on my cheek.

'*Pvanu,*' he said, 'There's something you need to know. You live in a world dominated by foreigners: it's the Indians and the Arabs who rule us. You see me as your master, but in fact I'm a slave just like you are. The ideals of brotherhood that were handed down to us don't exist in the minds of the people who taught us this religion.'

He turned to spit out saliva yellowed by the tobacco leaves he was chewing, then continued.

'But I'll tell you one thing: Islam is an incredible religion. It can save your life. Learn its language and its laws, and you'll be able to bend some of these people to your will. You'll be able to make them respect you; perhaps only a little, but that's already a lot. That's why I've decided to share with all of you, my daughters, my undesirables, the knowledge hidden in the sacred book.'

He brought out a Qur'an he'd been keeping behind his back and placed it on his lap.

'Well,' he said irritably, shrugging his shoulders again, 'What are you waiting for? Get your books out.'

We complied, clumsily, pulling our copies of the Qur'an from our rice sacks.

'Now. In this book, each chapter is a key to a world we never knew existed. This key opens both the inner door, that of the soul, and the outer door, that of the body and the world. Those who know the secrets of each letter will be among the *ulul-albab*. Do you know what an *ulul-albab* is?'

We all shook our heads apart from Mlima, the group's storyteller, who nodded. Mlima always knew everything before the rest of us.

'Enlighten us, Mlima.'

'*Ulul-albab* is the one who knows the secrets of each letter and so knows all the levels of reading in the Qur'an, Master.'

Fundi smiled warmly at her. I thought I saw a hint of disappointment in his eyes, but it must have been a figment of my imagination; he'd never taught us this before, so we couldn't be expected to know it, and he had no reason to be disappointed in us. I gave a quiet sigh of relief.

'Correct, but incomplete,' said Fundi, in his time-honoured way. 'An *ulul-albab* is a person who, through the secrets of the letters, has access to the knowledge of the entire divine message, from the time of the polytheists up until Islam.'

'But polytheists are ignorant, Fundi,' protested Ramla, the rebel of the group. 'That's what you taught us.'

Fundi shook his head.

'Knowledge is the only thing you can steal without being punished, and all humans are wells of knowledge. Even the polytheists. Some people just don't know that they are. Those people need a guide who can draw out the knowledge they have buried deep in their souls. That's what our prophet did for one part of humanity. It's what the polytheistic priests did for their people. And it's what I'm doing for you.'

I inhaled deeply, as if to breathe in his words.

'Each letter contains a secret,' Fundi continued. 'We'll

start with the individual letters. As you know, almost every chapter of the Qur'an begins with a whole sentence. But some of them begin with groups of single letters, of varying lengths. Who can recite for me the list of single letters that begin a chapter? We've learned them.'

We all answered at the same time, '*Qaf! Nûn! Hâ, mim! Yâ, sîn! Kaf, hâ, yâ!*'

'Well, well, *djayyid*,' Fundi laughed, 'I see you've forgotten nothing. Now I will tell you their secrets.'

He leaned towards us, a mysterious smile on his lips, and we realised this was an important moment.

He picked up one of the wooden dice and held it up for us to see. It gave off a powerful scent of eucalyptus. The strength of the scent—minty, slightly peppery—suggested the die had been carved from a young trunk, barely taller than me.

Tamu would not have approved: she hated it when a living tree was cut down. For her, it was nothing less than murder. 'When we collect wood,' she said, 'We clear the forest of its dead branches, so other plants can grow freely. And they believe that their sacred book gives them the right to kill living beings!'

'There's a blessing that can only be found in youth,' murmured the *fundi*, glancing at me.

I looked down. Had he read my mind? Or just noticed a glint of anger in my eyes? I felt his inquisitive gaze on me for a moment longer, then he turned to the others. 'Take a good look at this die and the characters on it.'

A letter had been engraved on four of the sides. We recited them in chorus, one after the other, then put them all together: *sîn, aïn, fâ, sâd. Sa'fas.*

The master moved the stones away from the ground by his feet to create a small area of sand. He used the die to write the first letters of the Arabic alphabet.

د خ ح ج ث ت ب ا

Alif. Bâ. Tâ. Jîm. Hâ. Khâ.

'How many letters are there between *bâ* and *jîm*?'

We counted.

'Two, Master.'

'Good. And between *jîm* and *dâl*?'

'Two, Master,' we replied.

'Good. *Alif, bâ*: one and two. *Jîm* is the fifth letter. *Dâl* is the eighth letter. Which gives us this number.'

On the sand, using a corner of the wooden die, he drew the number 1258 in Arabic, taking care to separate the digits.

He circled the 1.

'This is the unit. In the beginning, we were alone on this island. We didn't have Islam. We were masters of nature, but we lacked the final message that would allow us to accomplish our mission on earth.'

He circled the 2.

'This is duality. Our mission came to us, carried by Islam. But it brought violence and subjugation with it.

He circled the 5.

'This is freedom. Soon the time will come when we will no longer be at the mercy of the Indians and the Arabs.'

He circled the 8.

'This is power. When we have achieved freedom, our time will come to reign again. We will be the holders of knowledge.'

He spoke in the monotone of a man possessed. We all had our eyes fixed on him. I was about to ask him what he meant by 'freedom' and 'power', but Olympe spoke first.

'Master,' she asked, 'How will we know when the time has come?'

He looked at her. 'Which time, my daughter? The time to be free or the time to reign? Always be precise in your questions; God doesn't like vagueness.'

'The time to reign, Master.'

I couldn't believe how quickly Olympe had accepted this idea. I looked at my other friends. Apart from Mlima, the storyteller, none of them seemed to share my concern. Was that a warrior flame shining in the master's eye?

'The time to reign has already begun, my children. Can't you see? I'm a child of servitude and today I'm teaching those who were the masters of my ancestors.'

'She'd never say so, but she misses you. You should go and see her.'

I was talking to Olympe in a corridor of the stone house. The five of us had left early that day to collect branches from Ahmad's Wood. All the way there, all we could talk about was the master's mysterious and disturbing words. At least, two of us found them disturbing; the other three were as bouncy as fleas.

'The *fundi* said loud and clear what we hardly dare think secretly to ourselves!' M'maka said.

Back at the *fundi's* house, Olympe and I both let our gaze drift towards the windows of Halima's rooms.

'She's not been feeling well the last few days. And tonight Fundi's going to visit his first wife.'

'I'm not allowed to see her, you know that. And anyway, what can I do to make her feel better? I'm not a healer. I'm not her husband. I'm just a poor, powerless servant.'

Olympe rolled her eyes.

'Stop talking rubbish, Hardie. You know perfectly well the place you hold in her heart. And don't make fun of me. I'm the powerless servant who can't do anything to help her. You're the beloved. Not many of us can claim that.'

I lowered my eyes. I wanted to apologise, but Olympe was already turning away, a bundle of wet clothes on her head.

*

That evening, I took advantage of the *fundi's* absence to go to Halima's room. It was in disarray. The bed had been overturned and a wooden chair lay on its side on the floor. Halima's raffia prayer mat was unrolled in a corner, a Qur'an splayed carelessly on top of it. I rushed over and picked up the Qur'an, inhaled the scent of its pages and placed it gently on a small, carved wooden table.

At the centre of this chaotic scene, Halima was on her knees, hands pressed to the floor, head bowed. At first I thought she was crying. I approached her slowly and put my hand on her back. She immediately shook me off. Stung, I started to walked away. But she murmured, 'I'm almost finished.'

I approached her again and saw that she wasn't crying or sulking at my presence, but leaning over her tray of fine sand. There were three stones on it. She traced a dotted pattern around two of the stones, then removed the other one from the tray.

She sat up, cross-legged in front of the tray, her chin nestled in the palm of her hand, deep in thought.

I sat beside her, almost against my better judgement, as was usually the case when I was with Halima. My tongue tingled to ask her the questions that were filling my head: why was the room smaller than last time and no longer open to the sky? Where had the observatory gone? How could all these rearrangements have happened without me hearing anything?

Was Fundi working with *jinns*, as King Solomon had when he engaged them to build his monuments?

Instead, I remained silent. Halima turned to me, her eyes sharp and piercing. 'Do you have it with you?'

At this question, the memory of the morning we met came flooding back, followed by the memory of our final outing to the forest. The wind playing with the hems of our dresses, Halima's hair flying out behind her, mine resisting. Our laughter every time one of us stumbled. Our terror, too, of being discovered; its bittersweet taste.

Then the mysterious object, the dark look in her eyes as she pressed it into my hand. The fear in her voice when she entreated me never to unwrap it.

It had been difficult carrying that secret with me every day, tied up in the corner of my *leso*, with no idea what the thing even was. My friends used that place to stash cakes, pieces of toffee, or the ginger sweets we sucked to soothe our throats after long readings of the Qur'an. I'd never seen anyone else hiding a strange cubic object in there. When my friends asked me what I had inside the knot at the corner of my cloth I made no reply. They'd concluded it was just some everyday talisman.

At home, in the evenings, it was hard to keep my promise to Halima. I'd take the parcel out and stroke it, close my eyes and feel under the cloth for rough areas. Then I'd put it away again: according to Fundi, broken promises were one of the devil's favourite foods.

'Give me back what I entrusted to you.'

I was speechless. After all the years I'd spent with it, I

couldn't imagine no longer feeling that object at my side. It had been my proof of my bond with Halima; of the fact that, despite the many barriers between us, I was more to her than a *mshendzi*.

Slowly, I untied the knot. The paisley pattern of my *leso* gave way to immaculate white muslin. I'd often wondered how this muslin managed to retain its dazzling whiteness while my *lesos* were constantly staining.

Halima was watching my hands, her eyes bright with anticipation. When she raised them to mine, she saw my fear, and the glow faded a little.

'Don't worry, Hardie,' she said. 'I'm not going anywhere without you.'

I didn't understand what she meant, but her tone reassured me. I held out the object to her. She stopped me with a pink palm.

'Unwrap it,' she said quietly.

With trembling fingers, I obeyed. I untucked a corner of the muslin. The fabric slipped through my fingers, as if it were playing with me. I untucked the second corner, then the third, then the final one.

At last, the object revealed itself to me.

It was a wooden die, crudely cut. Its edges were rounded, its surface rough. The most surprising thing about it was its smell. As a child, I'd often thought I detected a particular scent, an unidentified type of tree, as we went about our work in Ahmad's Wood. When I mentioned it to my friends, they said they couldn't smell anything unusual. Later, I'd asked Tamu about it, and she'd responded with a string of questions I found difficult to answer: what other fragrances did this remind me of? Was it like the sea breeze at dusk? Was it mildly irritating to the nose? Did inhaling it have an instant calming effect? And the last question, which I'd brushed off with an embarrassed grunt: had I felt myself overcome with desire when I smelled it?

To my indignation, Tamu had concluded that I'd just come across an ordinary tree. We'd forgotten all about it.

Now I had my answer to the final question. I glanced at Halima. Her answering gaze inflamed me. I looked quickly back down at the die.

'This is called an *abjad*,' Halima said in a whisper. 'It's a cube carved from the trunk of a sacred tree. But that's not its greatest virtue. Look.'

She turned the die over between her fingers. On its faces were letters of the Arabic alphabet: *Alif, bâ, jîm, dâl*. It looked like the dice Fundi had shown us as we sat under the mango tree, but I sensed there was something different about this one. It seemed to emanate a powerful, even frightening aura.

'I know you're wondering what happened to the observatory and everything else,' Halima whispered. 'You'll soon find out. I just need you to trust me. Do you trust me, Hardie?'

Did I trust her? I had no idea. All I knew was that I would've followed her anywhere, done anything for her. I told her so. 'You're the essence of my wood. I don't have goals; people like me aren't supposed to. When you entrusted me with this die a few years ago, you gave meaning to my life. So I'm ready to follow you anywhere.'

She smiled, but there was a firmness in her look. She

stopped spinning the die between her fingers, clenched it in her fist and locked eyes with me.

'Gratitude is a double-edged sword. It manifests itself in each of us in different ways. People who think they're inferior try to use other people's gratitude as a weapon to dominate them. People who think we're all equal use it as a crutch to help them in the service of humanity. I am in no way superior to you; one day I could become useless, even harmful, to your cause. So try to be in the second category.'

The days passed. I despaired of ever seeing Tamu again. My time was spent helping Olympe to do the housework in the mornings and having lessons with Fundi in the afternoons.

Fundi's house was huge. It had ten rooms: three bedrooms and seven sitting rooms, each with its own function. The toilets and kitchen were in the courtyard, as in other homes. In the first sitting room, Fundi received the city's dignitaries: the judge, the men who'd won the right to decide on the city's future because they'd married off their daughters, the ministers and the sultan's men. All came to ask him to pray for their plans to come to fruition. Fundi didn't always know the details of these plans; he was content to be told their general aims. Was it the acquisition of a new estate, the marriage of a daughter, the departure of a son for religious studies, or an affair of state?

Whatever the case, he listened patiently to the man's plea, then sat him down on a prayer mat facing towards Mecca. He took his place behind the man on the *fitako*, his dark wooden seat, with a copy of the Qur'an in his hand. He lit incense and placed the holder on the ground. The men coughed at the dry, acrid smoke, while Fundi chanted *surahs* and verses of the Qur'an at dizzying speed. From time to time, he would pronounce the man's first name, the one associated not with their father's name but their mother's, as is the custom when praying for the dead.

One day, during one of our lessons beneath the mango tree, Fundi explained that in Islam, the mother was God's substitute for her child, and that it was therefore to her that he should refer if the divine answer to a prayer was slow in coming. 'Our real surname is our mother's first name,' he told us. I asked him why, then, people were called by their father's first name. He pretended not to hear my question.

Halima had already provided me with her own answer during one of our secret meetings. 'Men decided to emphasise their paternity to reassure themselves,' she said with disdain. 'The men in the time of the prophet were no different from Muslim men today: scared to death of women. I believe this fear was heightened when Mohammed revealed himself first and foremost as a messenger for women, whose aim was to put women and men back on an equal footing, to give us back our power.'

Obviously I hadn't said any of this to the *fundi*: he'd have known immediately where it came from.

The second sitting room was reserved for audiences with women. They came discreetly, draped in black *bwibwi* that they fastened under their chins with two small straps. The dark fabric separated in places to reveal the shimmering colours of their *lesos*. Their business was always so secret that Fundi demanded I put down the teapot, cups and rice cakes as quickly as possible and leave. When I tried to eavesdrop, all I could hear were whispers, sometimes suppressed sobs, followed by reassuring murmurs from Fundi. In Itsandra, the business of men was conducted in the open; anything to do with women behind closed doors.

In the third room, a variety of ordinary citizens came to present their requests to the *fundi*. Some sought a reassuring explanation for a strange dream; others came to ask for a prayer to address a particular problem.

One day, as I was preparing the afternoon tea, one of the town's doctors, who'd trained in Damascus, came to see the *fundi*. He had an anxious air about him. He'd married a young woman from Itsandra, but after three years of fruitless attempts to conceive a child, he'd left her. The town gossips said she was obviously barren and he'd been right to leave her. The woman's father, however, had not accepted the separation. One evening, as the doctor was returning from the mosque, he felt a hand rest briefly on his head. He turned round and saw a man walking swiftly away from him, furtive as a thief. He recognised his former father-in-law. At the mention of the man's name, Fundi shuddered, but continued to listen, head bowed. I stood with the teapot in one hand, waiting to be instructed to pour.

The doctor then told Fundi about his second marriage, to a young girl from the neighbouring town of Tsudjini, and their concern because, after three years of marriage, no children had been born.

Fundi nodded slowly.

'I know your father-in-law,' he said, breathing slowly to regain his composure. 'He's a *fundi* too, but of the worst kind: the kind who uses his knowledge to do harm. He concocts spells by twisting Qur'anic verses. He utters curses by turning his palms downwards instead of towards the sky. The hand he placed on your head was one he'd just cursed. He intended to remove your chance of ever having an heir. But I'm going to free you, my son.'

The young doctor listened, wide-eyed with terror, then nodded vigorously.

Fundi asked for a steel plate and inscribed verses from the Qur'an on it using a calamus and charcoal-based ink. He poured water from the Zamzam spring over the dish, and the letters formed into black blobs that danced around each other. Then, using a coconut-shell spoon, Fundi decanted the water into two glass bottles.

'On Tuesday night, after the *laesha* prayer, drink the contents of this bottle and get your wife to drink the other one. You won't just have one child; Allah willing, you'll have a whole tribe of them.'

Whether thanks to the *fundi's* concoction or not, a few months later the doctor's wife was said to be pregnant.

That night I dreamed about Tamu. We were sitting outside our tin house, my head resting on her lap. She was stroking my hair and telling me the sagas of the stars.

'That's the pointed ladle of the water goddess. There, just to the left of the moon, are the three lost sisters. You're still too young for me to tell you their story.'

'You always say that!' I protested.

'I'm sorry, darling. Oh, here's one I can tell you. There, just below the pointed ladle.'

It was a hunter with his bow. He'd been chasing a zebra across the sky since the dawn of time. Those who simply repeated the stories said he was hunting it for its meat, which was said to confer superhuman strength. But the real storytellers, those who were not afraid to invent because they knew invention was part of creation, told a different tale.

On one of his journeys, a prince from the East stopped in the middle of the desert, exhausted from hunger and thirst. This desert was the hottest on earth: it was called the *Kaa la hari*, the 'Fire Within', because it was an emanation of the fire of hell that burns at the centre of the earth.

The prince had dragged himself to a small shrub with sparse leaves, in the hope of benefiting from a semblance of shade.

He fell asleep. When he woke, the shrub had disappeared; in its place were three huge tubers oozing a whitish sap. Without thinking, driven only by hunger, he grabbed one of the tubers and was about to bite into it, when a cry rose up from behind a dry bush.

Whipping his head round, he saw a short, sinewy man with apricot-coloured skin. He wore nothing but a leather thong over his sex. A bow hung from his muscular shoulder. The hunter stepped forward, one hand outstretched in warning, but the prince understood nothing of what he was saying. The hunter grabbed the second tuber, broke a piece off and held it above the prince's head. Instinctively, the prince tipped back his head to drink the sap that flowed from it. A slightly acidic but incredibly refreshing taste filled his mouth. The liquid slid down his throat. The hunter then took the fruit the prince was holding and handed him his own. Perplexed but thirsty, the prince grabbed the tuber offered by the hunter, pressed his mouth to it and drank greedily, like a newborn suckling at its mother's breast. As he drank, he felt his strength returning; his muscles re-invigorating and the blood flowing back into his legs. He picked up the third tuber and put it in his mouth, after offering half to the hunter, who shook his head in refusal. When the prince had finished drinking the sap from this one, the hunter spoke again. This time, to the prince's astonishment, he could understand the hunter's language.

'You fell asleep under the traveller's shrub,' explained the hunter. 'The first fruit you ate is the one that provides us with drink. The second one you ate is the one used to understand our language. Health and language are the two indispensable forces for any man who wishes to survive in our country.'

The prince nodded. Even more surprisingly, he then began to speak in the language of the hunter. It was a language that sounded like clicks, as if he were beckoning his horse. Where was his horse anyway? He looked around him, suddenly panicked—how would he ever get home without his horse?

'Don't worry,' said the hunter, sensing his thoughts. 'Your horse is safe. It needs to regain its strength. And it's no coincidence that you arrived in this place. I have some things to teach you.'

'And the first fruit, the one you stopped me from eating?' asked the prince, who was still hungry.

'That fruit is there to remind you never to eat to your heart's content. You must leave it there. That's your first lesson: learn to trust in the generosity of nature. She will provide you with everything you need, so there's no need to rush to eat everything she has to offer.'

The prince stayed with the hunter for several days. He learned to track giraffes, to overcome cheetahs through cunning, to capture elks and hartebeests—huge goats with horns that pointed straight up in the air. He and the hunter grew fond of each other and became increasingly inseparable. Their whispered conversations by the fire began to cause a stir in the hunter's community, who were suspicious of two males being so close.

One day, one of the young men in the community insulted the hunter. Hurt, and unable to acknowledge to himself his love for the prince, the hunter insulted the idiot back. The prince decided it was time for him to leave. Mounting his horse, he galloped back to the place where he'd first met the hunter. The hunter came after him. Curiously, the third tuber was still there, intact, fresh white sap still oozing from its skin. The prince grabbed it.

'No!' cried the hunter.

'If you don't tell me the truth about this tuber, I'm going to eat it.'

'It's there for…'

'Don't give me that nonsense about nature's abundant gifts.'

'That's not what I was going to say. This fruit can make you unhappy if you're not honest with yourself. If you eat it while your intentions are clouded, if you betray your heart and your instincts, it will lead you to unhappiness. If you eat it with clear and honest intentions, it won't solve your problems, but it will give you the courage to face them.'

'I know exactly what my heart wants,' retorted the prince, trembling with emotion because he knew he was lying. 'It wants me to return to my country, where I'm needed. I've stayed here too long. I've caused you trouble. It's time for us to go our separate ways.'

The hunter reached out his hand to prevent his beloved from eating the fruit, but to no avail. The prince took a bite.

He was immediately transformed into a zebra. The transformation was a horrifying sight, and caused the hunter to howl in pain. The prince was horrified by what had happened to him; he began to stagger around, screaming. Finally, consumed with shame, he fled. Without thinking, the hunter mounted his horse and set off in pursuit of his beloved.

'Since then,' concluded Tamu, 'The hunter has been chasing his prince across the firmament. Until he catches up with him, they won't be united in the sky. But it will happen one day. All those who love one other end up as one in Queen Abé's kingdom.'

'I want to be united with you in that kingdom,' I said.

'You will be, my daughter. As soon as death takes my soul, I'll unite with you. My body will give you unimaginable strength, and you'll be queen of the world, an heir to Queen Abé.'

*

I woke with a start, drenched in a sweat infused with the blend of jasmine and thyme that was Tamu's scent. I broke down in tears.

When my tears had dried, I realised I'd made a decision: I was going to go and look for Tamu, so that one day we could be reunited among the stars.

*

She was waiting for me. She knew I would come. She was sitting with her back to the door, manipulating something in front of her. I approached her slowly, giving her time to register the sound of my sandals on the flagstones. She turned her head slightly but didn't look at me.

I crouched beside her. I closed my eyes and inhaled her perfume. It was a rare variety of jasmine with flowers that only opened on the nights of the full moon.

'I've come to ask for your help. I need to find Tamu.'

She was silent for a moment. Then she picked up a calabash that sat beside her and poured me a drink from the ornately-carved coconut shell.

'I'll tell you where the observatory is,' she replied.

She stood up and pointed at the wall that now stood in the place where the huge building had once been.

'It's all on the other side,' she murmured.

'Which side are you talking about?'

My sentence faded, as did my vision: Halima became increasingly blurred. A cloud of smoke swept me away, into nothingness.

*

'God's quilt is infested with bedbugs.'

The voice I hear is not Halima's. My eyes remain closed. I open them, but still I cannot see: darkness has swallowed everything. My numb body seems to be hovering in the air, or bobbing on water; I can't tell.

The voice repeats itself. '*E dara ya mgu nkunguni*. God's quilt is infested with bedbugs.'

I know that phrase. It's a *ndzinyo*. I'm in total darkness somewhere and a voice is asking me a riddle. Am I dead? I remember Fundi's lesson about the terrible ordeal of the grave. When a loved one dies, the family and villagers bury the corpse, wrapped only in a shroud, which has a hole at the right ear. The body is placed on its right side, so this ear touches the ground. The *surah* of oneness is then read three times, the headstone is put in place and aloes planted on the grave, and the dead person is left to commence their journey of no return. This journey begins at night, once the cemetery is deserted. Two angels, Munkar and Nakir, place themselves beneath the right ear. In their heavenly voices, they ask the dead person three questions: 'What is your name?', 'Who is your God?' and 'What is your religion?'

If the person answers all three questions correctly—'My name is Such-and-such', 'Allah is my God', 'Islam is my religion'—a door opens on to a garden of eternal delights; rivers of milk and honey, huge and beautiful flowers. If one of the answers is wrong, a trapdoor opens beneath the dead person and they begin an endless descent through the flames of regret and despair.

As I teeter on the edge of the unknown, I begin to think Fundi must have got it wrong: the angels aren't asking important questions, but speaking in the kinds of riddles we exchange in the evenings before going to sleep. This amuses me, and I answer, suppressing a laugh, 'The sky and the stars.'

Immediately my vision clears. The first thing I see is Halima—I like this paradise already—but the man standing next to her is old and nothing like the ewer-bearing youths we were promised.

'You can get off the boat now.'

Halima takes my hand and we step out of a boat. Then darkness returns.

Suddenly I'm awake. I'm lying on hot, stony ground. It's as if I've been thrown on a blazing fire. I roll on to my side. My muscles somehow feel stronger than usual. I can feel them sheathing my body, encasing it in a firm grip. It's a new sensation, so surprising I almost lose my balance. I put one foot on the ground, and stare at it in shock: my foot is pale and streaked with veins. It's enclosed in a soft, leather sandal. The hem of some sort of robe brushes my ankle. Panicked, I explore my body. I'm wearing a beige *kandu*, dusty with sand. My hands are broad, my fingers pudgy.

I shield my eyes with one hand and scrutinise my surroundings. Sand, swirling dust, mud huts in the distance.

The most disconcerting, extraordinary thing of all is what I feel between my legs: the intimate fullness, the sense of having another world hidden inside me, has been replaced by a protuberance. My most secret part is now exposed for all to see.

I'm a man!

*

I'm sitting on a pile of stones beside a square house built from the same kind of stones. A man with a full beard and shining eyes is walking towards me. Instinctively, I recoil, as I always do when men approach me.

He sits down beside me.

Other men run up, as if responding to a signal. Some sit at my feet, others on the stones. They greet me in Arabic, then wait, their eyes fixed on me. The deference in their expressions confuses me.

The first man puts a hand on my shoulder, then brings his face close to mine. He gives me a smile of infinite benevolence.

'It's me, Hardie. Don't be frightened; just go with it. Trust me.'

Incredible as it seems, I recognise him, or rather her. It's Halima. I want to ask her what's happening to us, what she means by 'just go with it', but there's no time. A powerful shudder suddenly runs down my spine, my mouth opens without me controlling it, a huge amount of air rushes forcefully down my throat, like a wave rippling through me. I close my eyes in shock, but also, without understanding why, to let this breath infuse me. I feel as if I've been sitting here for longer than it seems, have been thinking about something for a while and now, in a moment of illumination, I have the answer. Images form behind my closed eyelids; blurred at first, then increasingly clear. Some are frightening, others soothing. I open my eyes.

The men around me obviously understand what's happening better than I do. They're paying close attention, their gazes intense, their lips trembling with emotion. Some hold calamus pens filled with ink; on their knees are animal skins, flat bones or parchment, ready to write on.

I wonder what they're waiting for, then suddenly I

understand. They're waiting for me to speak. Their fervour is the same as that I've seen in in the eyes of some of the *fundi's* disciples.

My heart races. I turn to Halima, or rather to the man who speaks like Halima. He gives me a knowing look and a tiny nod—yes, you've understood correctly, no, you're not dreaming, yes, you are him.

Instead of reassuring me, this increases my fear. The man who is Halima doesn't give me time to get used to the idea before he says, 'Come on, tell us what you see.'

'Yes, tell us!' the other men chorus.

I close my eyes again. I see a star shining in the centre of a daytime sky. A pain stabs through my head, like a blade piercing my temple and trying to reach the other side. A cry, like the predatory call of an eagle, chills my heart and makes me tremble. Something compresses my chest, gently at first, then harder. The sensation spreads to my arms and legs: I feel like I'm imploding, as if my whole body is being pushed, or squeezed into a narrow tube.

Just as I'm starting to feel breathless, the pressure suddenly stops. I expand again, like a piece of bread dipped in tea. I keep my eyes closed, more to avoid the gaze of the men around me than to experience what I'm going through more fully. My whole being now seems to unfold, as if I'm becoming taller, broader and rounder. I'm lighter too, like a cloud dissipating but without losing density, stretching to cover the whole sky.

Only then do the words come to me. Clear as water, they flow from my mouth and settle in droplets around me, liquid treasures floating on the warm air:

I see the earth shaking.
I see the mountains colliding.
Together, we rush
Towards an oasis.
You are divided into three groups, running in pairs.
There are people to my right; who are these people?
Others to my left; who are these people?
Some of you are far ahead,
Closer to the blessed place,
The garden where life flourishes.
Many of these people belong to ancient tribes.
Only a few of them are ours.

When I open my eyes again, the men are all leaning forward, scribbling frantically on their pieces of wood, animal shoulder blades and skins, or cloth stretched across wooden frames.

They finish recording the words I've spoken. I feel as if I've just woken from a long sleep. If I could, I would've stayed wherever I was for longer, but something beyond my control has dragged me back.

A short, stocky man is coming towards us. He walks briskly, his sandals ploughing through the sand as if he's trying to dig a furrow. He stops in front of me, his head bobbing from side to side, his eyes narrowed, a slightly mocking smile on his lips. I can tell he aims to throw me off balance. He's savouring his triumph in advance.

'So, tell me,' he says. 'You claim to have travelled across the vast world, then ascended into the heavens, all in one night?'

I nod, astonished both by his question and my immediate answer, which springs to mind just as the words I spoke earlier did.

'In fact, the vast world and the heavens are part of the same realm, and are within our reach,' I reply.

'And you say you also stopped off at the shrine in Jerusalem?'

'Yes. I did two cycles of meditation there with the most beautiful souls of our species.'

'Ah! Jesus, Joseph, Moses, Noah, Jethro, Joshua and Adam? All in the same room?'

'Yes, and many others whose names don't appear in the gospel, but are mentioned in older works.'

He stares at me for a moment, perhaps tempted to believe me. Then he lifts his chin and fires me a challenging look.

'I don't believe a word of it. Prove to me that you've been there. What do the four sides of the shrine look like as you approach?'

I swallow. No shrine materialises before my eyes. I know I didn't actually enter it, but found myself inside, without having to walk the path to approach it. How can I describe its four faces? The man bursts out laughing.

'You see?' he shouts to the group. 'He doesn't even know what the shrine looks like! And he expects us to believe that he prayed there? My friends, we must execute this charlatan!'

I turn to Halima, my heart thumping in terror. To my surprise, she—he—smiles. Already there's a clamour around us, but he tells me calmly, 'Concentrate. Go back to where you were, because I believe you were there. Look straight ahead and you'll see it.'

I do as I'm told. At first, nothing comes to me. I decide to imagine I'm walking barefoot towards the holy city. I see an expanse of sand, the sea of this land: it slips between my toes like foam before retreating, leaving just a few grains clinging to me. There are tufts of grass here and there. Memories flood into my head. They're not mine, and I understand they belong to the man whose body I'm occupying. This man has lost several members of his family. I feel dizzy thinking about my mother in this world, who's dead; my father, who I never knew; my grandfather, who died before I reached the age of reason. A feeling of profound solitude grips me. I try to soothe myself by imagining each sparse tuft of grass is one of their footprints: they're few and far between, you might not notice them if you didn't think to look, but they're there. I cling to this thought. Gradually, the terrain changes; the ground starts to feel rocky. The moon is full and there's no sound except that of my feet against the stones. The rough grass grows more abundantly here. Suddenly, the temple looms before me, bathed in blue light.

Halima's male voice seems to come from far away as it whispers, 'Describe what you see.'

I do so.

'The shrine is not a building. It lost its façade a long time ago. It's just a wall; the remains of a temple from the past that was destroyed by human greed. The wall is made of solid blocks of stone, selected for their sturdiness. Painted on it are scenes of the battles our ancestors fought against invaders. This place will be the focus of the deadliest wars of our time. It will be occupied by men who believe they have access to the whole truth and who will kill each other in its name, men who've forgotten the essential: that we are one, wherever we are, wherever we come from, whoever we follow, whatever we believe. Every one of us is searching for the same thing, and all of us are fallible. Our differences are simply the notches that allow us to slot together to form this unity that is humanity; the cuts in the wooden framework that allow the beams to be inserted and the building erected.'

When I open my eyes again, the man who challenged me is kneeling at my feet, tears streaming from his eyes. I can't tell whether they're of rage, sadness or joy, and he doesn't give me time to find out. He stands up, turns on his heels and walks away, his shoulders stooped.

The assembly sits transfixed. Some of the other men's eyes are also clouded with tears. I sweep my gaze over the group and see no women or children. I feel their absence like a dagger to the heart, reminding me what an orphan I am in this place.

'Where are your wives?' I ask them, suddenly finding an authoritative tone. 'Where are the women who gave birth to you, and those who support you every day? Where are—'

I'm interrupted by a couple making their way towards the group. The man is pulling the woman along by the side of her headscarf, shouting at her to stop whining. When they reach us, my friend calls out to the angry husband, 'Brother, what's the matter?'

'O Sidiq, it's been several days now since I pledged allegiance to your friend and joined his faith. This woman has followed me, like the obedient wife she is.'

He gives the woman a sidelong glance.

'Or rather *was*! For a fortnight now, she's refused to

give herself to me. No matter how gently I seduce her, she won't offer up her body. Didn't the messenger'—at this point he gestures at me with his chin—'say that our women were fields for us to plough? Didn't he say we were each other's garments? Why will she not clothe me?'

As Halima—or rather Sidiq—tries to reason with the young woman, I look discreetly at her. She has the body of a barely-pubescent girl. Lustrous strands of black hair escape from her headscarf, which is embroidered with gold thread and tiny mirrors.

Her face holds such sweetness that I wonder how anyone can even cast a disparaging glance in her direction.

'My sister,' murmurs Sidiq, 'You are your husband's treasure. You are the cloak that protects his body from its urges, so they can be directed at no one but you. Isn't that an honourable role?'

The women looks at us from beneath her eyelashes. No, it's not a look; it's a harpoon. Her eyes shine with distress, but behind the curtain of fear is a glimmer of defiance. It points to a fierce resistance, a 'no' that seems to come from deep inside her. I meet her gaze; she immediately lowers her eyes.

Not before the fire in them has ignited something in me.

At that moment, I understand the reason for my presence in this place. I've seen this look of refusal, this resistance, in the eyes of some of my friends. Each of them was the student of another man before becoming a disciple of the *fundi*. Each of them had to undress at least once before the feverish eyes of her master. Each of them shuddered when his hands rested on her back, and felt a dull humiliation when he whispered, in a hoarse voice, 'Well, help yourself to food and drink.'

And at night, as they fell asleep, they felt a deep disgust for themselves slowly taking root in their being. Fundi rescued them, one by one, from the hell to which life had condemned them; the same hell from which Tamu rescued me.

I know Sidiq is doing his best. I know they're all doing their best, that they've turned away from their old beliefs to follow me where I've offered to lead them. I know their intentions are pure. Yet they're about to treat my message as law, and that would kill it for good.

Sidiq's words have rekindled a fire that was slumbering in my veins. I feel a white-hot rage. If I don't restrain myself, I might grab hold of the stones we're sitting on and crumble them in my hands.

A roar rises up from within me. I bellow out the word 'NO!'

The men gape at me. Sidiq and the husband must have noticed the anger in my eyes, because they look frightened. I'm panting, exhaling noisily, like a bull trying to tear free of its tether.

Words fly to my lips and pour out of me in an uncontrollable stream.

'Lovers are a garment for each other, yes. But a garment is a piece of cloth that caresses only one body: yours. Your spouses are the conduit through which you learn to love one being in particular, your true love: yourself.

'You, my brother, are the loom on which your wife learns to weave love. In time, she will learn to direct this love towards herself. It's the same for you: you learn to appreciate her qualities and tolerate her faults, weaving a garment of tolerance and indulgence with which you will be able to clothe yourself. Only when you're able to love yourselves can you live in peace with one another. This is one of the meanings of this revelation; this is what I understand of it today. If, one day, any of you have a deeper understanding of it, even after my death, you must hasten to share it. For now, meditate on this.'

'My brother, perhaps your wife has already learned to love herself. She no longer wants to be the bone on which your desire is written. She wants complete desire, a desire that doesn't see her as an object. You should let her cover herself in love before you demand it back from her.'

The entire group stares at me, dumbfounded. I turn to Sidiq, frightened by what I've just said, horrified to have uttered these shocking words that don't belong to me. I expect to see anger and resentment in his eyes, but he looks at me with admiration, a hopeful smile on his lips.

*

When I came to, Halima's face above me was like a breath of fresh air. She was staring at me with her piercing yet benevolent gaze, a gaze I felt was undressing me and loving what I had hidden inside me.

'Were we men?' I asked her.

She smiled tenderly at me. 'Men, women… to me, you're just you.'

In a voice as soft as a trade wind waking up at dawn, that delicate whisper that heralded the coming gust of wind, she breathed, 'Hardie…'

I'm not sure exactly what happened next, but before I knew it, my hand was on her cheek, then on the nape of her neck, and I was drawing her confidently towards me. She let herself be guided to my lips.

Neither of us uttered a sound. All we did was make trembling, impulsive gestures. In an instant, my cloak was under me, spread out like a calm sea; hers covered us, soft and floating. My lips sought her neck, her hands explored my hips, my thighs, moved towards my secret parts.

She found me, and I found her, in the wild intertwining of our bodies. It was as if the moon itself had taken up residence in the depths of my being. I joined my sighs to hers, and with one voice our ecstasy rose like a prayer to heaven.

We remained there for a long time, lost together in the folds of our cloaks, inhaling each other's skin: breathless, exhausted, complete.

'If Tamu's still alive, it will be very hard to find her.'

Olympe and I were sitting on the stone helping Halima take her shower. Olympe poured water over her from a jug, while I rubbed her skin with soap. Fundi Ahmad had been with his first wife for the last few days, meaning I'd been free to come and go between my room and Halima's. Olympe knew what was going on, at least partially. She was unaware of the extent of our feelings, or that desire had crept in. If she ever found out, there were two possibilities: either her affection for me would save us, or she'd be too scandalised, would reveal our secret, and Halima and I would both be ruined.

Olympe emptied out a full jug of water. The foam slid over Halima's slender body before trickling away between the pebbles.

'If she is alive,' Halima continued, 'It's because she's been sold. Traders from Zenj are still coming here with trunks full of spices. They don't mind a slave or two to boost their profits.'

'That's true, mistress,' said Olympe. 'It happened to my Aunt Sulwe. Her forest *jinn* were no match for the eel *jinns* on the island of Ndzuani. She was taken there with her two sons. Now she has to grow tomatoes, and perhaps children in her womb for her master.'

'And it's not just the selling that's worrying,' Halima continued. 'Two days ago, Fundi told me a lady had disappeared. Someone you teach the Qur'an to.'

Olympe turned to me, her eyes wide.

'Is that…' I began. 'Are you talking about Ma Hussam?'

Halima frowned.

'The name sounds vaguely familiar, yes… she was definitely a mother. She went to the market and never came home. The strangest thing was that her masters didn't want to part with her. They'd even given her a piece of land on their estate. You don't do that for a slave you want to sell!'

'You think her disappearance is suspicious?'

Halima stood up, signalling that her bath was finished.

'Yes. I think slaves are being kidnapped. And I'm afraid for you, my dear ones.'

She couldn't help but let her gaze linger on me. She turned to Olympe too, to balance things out. Suddenly, her eyes lit up with a defiant gleam.

'What if we investigated these disappearances? What if we went looking for these people ourselves?'

Olympe was as intrigued as I was. 'What do you mean, mistress?'

Halima looked at us again with her piercing, inscrutable gaze. She took our hands. Her voice became serious.

'You're going to go to the market disguised as sellers. No one really knows who all the different sellers are, whereas I, with my skin colour and rank, would be spotted immediately. You'll ask the other sellers questions about the disappearances.'

'But, Mistress!'

We'd both shouted at the same time, so terrifying was the idea.

'What if someone recognises us?'

'You'll just say your mistress sent you to sell fruit from her estate. What could be more plausible than that?'

Halima gave a sly smile. Her eyes sparkled, as if she was about to have the most wonderful adventure, through us.

'We're going to be like the investigators of King Haroun, who ruled in the land of my ancestors. He used to disguise himself as a merchant and wander the streets. I've always dreamed of doing that! Come and see me tomorrow morning and I'll show you how to do it.'

She hurried off to her room. I followed in her footsteps.

'And if Tamu is still alive?'

Halima stopped walking. When she turned round, her expression had changed. She looked thoughtful and slightly stern. She weighed her words carefully.

'Then I'll help you to get her back.'

*

The fruit and vegetable seller didn't want to answer our questions; she was too busy trying to offload the ripest oranges and tomatoes on the most credulous passers-by. Nor did the man selling spices brought by the Arabs, who thought we were too curious. 'What do you care about that?' he said, 'Aren't you grateful you still belong to the same master?'

In the fabric aisle, we found Mlima, our storyteller.

A few months earlier, she'd been sold to a rich merchant.

Fundi was one of his most loyal customers, so the merchant let Mlima continue coming to Fundi's lessons. He'd decided to sell some of the fabrics she dyed to foreigners, so Mlima now spent a lot of her time at the market.

It was strange to see her outside our usual context, as if we'd all been transported to another planet. I thought she looked as if she'd put on weight. She sat at the back of a stall hung with brightly coloured sheets, her generous posterior planted amongst heaps of golden silk thread and rolls of white cotton. She was sewing *kandu*. Some were still incomplete, loose threads hanging off them. Others, with elaborately embroidered necklines, were carefully folded at her feet. Mlima loved sewing as much as she loved telling stories. She always embroidered spirals in tight rows, that ended up getting unpicked so they didn't take up all the space on the fabric.

I greeted her casually, as if we didn't know each other, indicating one of the hanging robes.

'Sister, how much for this *kandu*?'

'Which master do you want to buy it for?' she asked, playing along.

'My master, the one who taught you how to speak like the Arabs,' I replied.

She whistled through her teeth.

'Who are you? A dead woman come to settle a debt?'

'No, a living person come to pay off a debt.'

She burst out laughing. She beckoned Olympe and me to come closer. We made our way to the back of the stall, careful not to get tangled in the swathes of fabric that brushed against us. I savoured the whispering sounds they made, different depending on the fabric: the hoarse voice of linen, the soft murmur of satin, and the slightly metallic laugh of *hudhrung*, the fabric of the rich landowners.

When we reached her, Mlima asked us if we were thirsty, then clapped her hands without waiting for an answer. A girl of about seven or eight, one of those usually sent to fetch fire, appeared, her head bowed. Mlima ordered her to go and boil some milk, cinnamon, cardamom, vanilla and black tea, and to bring us three cups of it once the liquid had turned golden.

'It's a new recipe from Ceylon,' Mlima murmured, licking her lips. 'So, tell me the news! What brings you here? Did the princess of pretension send you?'

That had been Halima's epithet in our neighbourhood ever since it had become widely known that she resisted Fundi's amorous advances. My cheeks burned. Fortunately, my dark skin hid it.

'Mlima, something strange has been happening,' Olympe said. 'Servants have started to disappear. Ma Hussam, for example. There's been no news of her since—'

'Shut up, idiot!' cut in Mlima, her eyes wild. 'Maybe she's busy. Do you think everyone spends their nights out wandering the streets like you do?'

When Mlima tried to sweep a subject under the carpet, it meant she knew something about it.

'Mlima, please, tell us what you know,' I begged.

Mlima rolled her eyes and turned to Olympe.

'You still putting up with this one?'

'I'm surviving,' replied Olympe, turning her eyes heavenwards.

'It's not like you've got a choice,' I retorted. 'You should've been born lighter-skinned. Mlima, I'm waiting. My master's worried. He wants to know what's going on.'

She sighed, gathered up the sides of her *mkumi*. It was the green of a dry season forest, with yellow stripes around the edges. The main pattern was a large grid with a jasmine flower in the centre of each square. The green was far too dull for Mlima's dark skin, but I didn't say so —she'd have sulked and not given me the answers I needed. As I didn't want to lie, I complimented her on her *maqbadhi* instead.

'Those sandals suit you beautifully.'

'What's beautiful?' she grumbled, shooting me an irritated glance. 'Certainly not these cracked heels and these toes that can't seem to point in the same direction. I feel like I've been rubbing lime into my skin!'

I said nothing. It was customary amongst maids to play down one's beauty. It was a way of warding off the jealousy that the masters' wives might feel towards us; also a way of saving our skins. The habit had begun with the *suriya*, the concubines, then spread to the other women. If one of our master's wife's friends happened to be passing by and overheard our conversation, she'd be quick to report it to the wife. It was best for us if they both laughed at our ugliness.

Mlima looked around to make sure she wasn't being overheard. Then she gave us a serious look, the kind she used to give us when she was younger and was about to launch into a story. That was how Mlima was: to her, everything, from an ordinary saying to the gravest insult, could be explained through a story.

She began, in a barely audible whisper:

'Many years ago, before all of us were born, a man arrived in Itsandra by boat. His ship had run aground on the coast. He was the *qarân*, the scribe of the king of some country of light-skinned people with strange ways, people like your friend the princess of pretension. So, when this *qarân* arrived, he was given a royal welcome by the town's nobles, because the chief was afraid that other ships might follow, and these ones might be full of mercenaries: brutes who burn down houses, kidnap children to take to their sandy lands, or to our neighbours in the kingdom of Zenj, where they're castrated and put to work for the nobles.'

I noticed Olympe shudder. I didn't like this story much either, but at the same time I was drawn to it. It gave me a sense of reliving forgotten moments, buried deep in my memory. Mlima continued, still in a whisper, 'So it was in the people's interests to welcome the *qarân* and show deference towards him. They served him tea and cardamom rice cake. They provided him with lodgings while he waited for his ship to be repaired. In exchange, he organised a huge prayer session, where he taught the people of the town to read the Qur'an, rid themselves of savagery and embrace the holy religion of Mohammed, bringing them safety in this world and in the hereafter.

'He ended up staying for several years. When merchants from his home country arrived, he persuaded them not to burn down the town of Itsandra, because it was now populated with good Muslims. In gratitude for this, the town offered him the ultimate treasure: a wife from its noblest family.

Her name was Mwandziwa. The *qarân* had her baptised as Faïda, meaning 'the reward'. She was said to have been overjoyed to be chosen, and to have aroused the jealousy of her sisters and friends. Once in the *qarân*'s room though, she screamed so loudly, people wondered whether the man was about to slit her throat. She gave birth to two children. Their descendants became the two great families of Itsandra: the Hassan Sharifs and the Sharif Mohameds. Your friend, the princess of pretension, belongs to the latter.

'So, in the house where Faïda lived, there was a little boy called Mohoro. He was in charge of all the household chores in the bridal bedroom. When the *qarân* announced he was going back to his dusty homeland, Mohoro's father suggested he take the boy with him, so he could learn the civilised ways of the Arabs. The child followed the *qarân* and stayed in his country, where he grew up to marry a slave and have several children, who had children of their own. One of these children then returned here as an adult and started his own family.

'What does all of this have to do with us? Well, my sisters, it so happens that the descendants of the *qarân* want to go back into business. There's a shortage of slaves in the kingdom of Zenj. All the slaves they have there are already being used in the sugar cane and clove fields. The masters want to build bigger cities in the land of their ancestors, and Zenj no longer provides them with enough labour. The houses of their rich citizens need maids and servants too, but they don't want just any old servants: they want civilised ones who know how to make tea and recite from the Qur'an like performing monkeys.'

The little girl reappeared in the doorway, a tray in her hands. She set it down beside Mlima, then disappeared immediately. Mlima smiled; satisfied, it seemed, that she too had a maid. Ever since she'd been bought by the rich market trader, she'd tried to adopt his aristocratic ways. She passed us our cups.

'Taste this marvel. They call it *chai*; I call it the milk of the rich. After this, you'll be coming back every day, begging me to give you some before you die of thirst.'

I took a sip of the chai, thinking of the little girl. It tasted sweet and just a little bitter, with the signature flavours of vanilla, cinnamon, cardamom and ginger all infused in a long-steeped black tea.

'So obviously it's women who are most in demand as house slaves. For reasons you're no doubt familiar with: they're more docile, they can learn to cook quickly, they can help the wives give birth. And sometimes they can give birth to new servants themselves.'

Olympe and I shuddered.

'My friends, I think Ma Hussam has been kidnapped. And she's not the only one.'

As she said this, she gave me a sympathetic look. Before I could ask a question, Mlima stood up to attend to a potential customer.

'Yes, what would you like, master? A stole for your wife? *Hami*? A dress? Ah, it's for a wedding? Well, we've just received these magnificent red stoles with gold and yellow stripes. They've come straight from Abyssinia…'

As we walked home, Olympe shook her head.

'It can't be true! Could we be snatched in the street, just like that? It can't be true, and yet it sounds true… we're finished, Hardie, wretches that we are! Oh no… I hope at least that, if we're captured, it's by good Muslims…'

I hardly heard her. Ever since Mlima had given me that look, my blood had been boiling. When it was time to go back to Halima, I signalled to Olympe that she should go without me. I told her I absolutely had to wash my *hami* in the sea, it was so dirty. She let me go.

I ran down the hill to the shoreline, branches whipping me, brambles scratching my legs. I didn't stop until I was standing in front of the jagged, black rock. The rage was flowing through me with such force that I knew if I cut my finger on the rock, my blood would gush like a spring from the depths of the earth. I grabbed a piece of the rock and made the gesture of lifting it. An entire section responded to my touch. Underneath, the rock was molten: I was staring straight at glowing lava. I lifted the huge piece of burning stone up to the sky.

'I asked you to spare Tamu, and now I hear that you've handed her over to the demons! I hate you, *Mawu! Mawu*! I hate you!'

I smashed the rock on the ground. The sand solidified on contact into a carpet of smoking embers. Despite the heat, I sat down on the sand and burst into tears.

*

Halima was standing in the centre of her room waiting for me. Today she was wearing a green robe secured at her breast by a gold brooch. The green complemented her burnished skin and jet-black hair. I was dressed in a robe that was white in name only.

Halima's eyes sparkled. 'I'm going to show you something,' she said mischievously.

She was so beautiful, I could've melted at the sight of her.

But I was impatient: I needed her to help me find Tamu.

She must have guessed my thoughts: her smile vanished and her expression became serious.

'This is something that will help you find Tamu. Come with me.'

She gave me her hand, then immediately snatched it away again, giving me a look of confusion. She motioned for me to follow her.

I walked behind her, my heart pounding so hard in my chest that it made my arms ache. She stopped at the wall opposite the entrance to her room.

'Tell me, Hardie,' she said in a whisper. 'Has anything strange been happening to your body recently?'

I wasn't sure what she meant.

'When I touched you, your hand was burning, as if you were holding embers.'

I made no reply.

'Don't be afraid. I know it's strange, but you can tell me what happened; I promise I won't tell anyone. Something happened just before you came to see me, didn't it? If you tell me, I'll take you to Tamu.'

That was all it took to convince me. I'd have done anything to find Tamu; my sympathetic ear, my shoulder to cry on. She couldn't solve all my problems, but she'd always been able to soothe me, to make my dark thoughts disappear.

I told Halima everything. About the fire, the moon, the hot river in my veins, the stone lifting beneath my touch. She listened attentively, sometimes raising an eyebrow. Her nose, aquiline and with a ridge at its tip, wrinkled when I mentioned the still pool of lava beneath the rock. When I'd finished, she gave a broad smile, revealing her teeth—all in a neat row with the exception of her right incisor, which protruded slightly, intensifying her charm.

She laid a hand on my shoulder and whispered simply, 'Thank you.'

I'd expected her to be frightened, or not to believe me. It was hard to imagine she'd actually taken me seriously. I'd told no one about this, hoping that as time passed, the memory would fade and I might decide I'd been dreaming. Lulled by the repetitive rhythm of my days in the stone house, I'd almost started to convince myself I had been.

But Halima thought it was real.

She scrutinised me, a look on her face that was part concern, part fascination. Then she turned to the wall and placed her hand on it. Something extraordinary happened. At the place Halima had touched, water began to seep between the blocks of stone, tiny trickles at first. Halima watched it with a frown. Her chest rose and fell rapidly, her half-open mouth emitted increasingly hoarse breaths. Without turning round, she asked me in an urgent tone, 'Do you know this proverb, Hardie? A wall built by a liar always lets in the rain. I'm the rain, and I live enclosed inside walls of lies. But one day, all of this will crumble.'

A crack echoed through the room, followed by another, louder. Water began to gush from every gap between the stones. I barely had time to grab Halima's hand and drag her away before the stones began to crash down, the sound deafening, until they were all piled up in front of our feet.

I pulled Halima to me and we huddled together in the corner of the room. She covered me with her arm, as if her frail body could protect my larger one. Despite everything, I closed my eyes and snuggled up to her, my nose in her neck, breathing in her scent of jasmine.

When the sound had stopped, Halima disentangled herself gently. She took my face in her hands.

'Look,' she said.

I opened my eyes and turned towards where the wall had been. I couldn't believe what I saw.

The wall seemed to have been reduced to a pile of volcanic sand.

That wasn't the most surprising thing, though. Beyond the pile of sand was an immense open courtyard, paved with small stones.

At the far end of it, rearing up like an immovable peak, was the observatory.

The building was as imposing as ever. A perfect triangle, soaring towards the sky from a base that seemed planted in the earth. The staircase was there, intact. Only the top had changed: above the sandy plateau there was now a kind of gazebo topped with a small dome. I glanced to my left: the room was still there, it was just missing a wall, and yet some sort of barrier seemed to be separating the room from this improbable structure.

I was bewildered.

Halima was striding towards the building, poised and proud. I followed her, my legs wobbly. I didn't know what to make of any of it. Was the way she'd touched the wall similar to how I'd touched the rock, without even knowing what I was doing? What was happening to us? And why was there an observatory hidden behind Halima's bedroom?

None of it made sense. I closed my eyes and bit my tongue, wondering if I was dreaming. But my eyes reopened on the same scene.

Halima had put one foot on the first step and was waiting for me to join her. Her *hami* fluttered in the light breeze.

I stood behind her. My ears were burning, my jaw ached from clenching my teeth, and I felt as if the ground was giving way beneath me. Halima began to climb the steps. As I followed her, I had the sensation that everything I'd known or learned up until then in my life, from the *surahs* Fundi made me repeat, to the burning banana peel on my budding breasts, to Tamu's stories, was taking on new meaning that was still indecipherable to me, while at the same time losing any meaning it had had before.

My world would never be the same again.

*

The sandy plateau was half covered by the shadow of the dome. There were two small benches, one on either side of the gazebo, between its pillars. Halima sat down on one of them and invited me to sit opposite her. The benches were low, allowing easy access to the sand. Halima placed a splayed palm on the sand and whispered, '*bismillah*'. Then she began to slowly trace patterns with her fingers. As she did so, she said, 'Hardie, what do you want most in the world?'

'To find Tamu,' I said quickly; perhaps too quickly.

Halima remained silent, as if to let my words sink in. Then she nodded and continued, 'We both want the same thing. To be reunited with someone we love.'

I thought I saw a tear roll down her cheek. She'd been together once with someone she'd loved deeply, someone who'd opened her eyes to so many things that her new husband couldn't bear it. She'd been torn away from that love by a father who respected only the alleged nobility of bloodlines.

Absorbed in my own pain, I'd forgotten that my beloved also suffered. The intensity of my feelings for her had blinded me to the fact there was someone else in her heart.

I suppressed a grimace of pain. I hid it as best I could, but Halima's words had bruised me. The pain was gradual rather than immediate: I felt sorry for her before I felt hurt, then hurt because I felt sorry for her, and because I meant so little to her—so little to myself. It was as if she were slowly pushing a *kofia* embroidery needle into my heart, a needle made from a fish bone thick and strong enough to create an eye in the fabric, so that golden flower petals could be embroidered around its edges. The deeper the needle went, the more my pain increased.

But I could embroider the sun's rays around my wound.

Halima had looked away from me. She was still tracing shapes in the sand.

When she finished, a small smile of satisfaction played on her lips.

She'd drawn an ever-narrowing spiral. Several lines converged towards the centre, barely touching. She placed small stones in different parts of the spiral. The blue moonlight made them shine like gems. It was then that I noticed something that had escaped me the first time I'd seen these stones: they had inscriptions engraved on them; Arabic words. On one,

I managed to read '*sa'fas*'. As I discreetly tried to decipher what was written on the other stones, I heard the same word, '*sa'fas*', come from Halima's mouth, followed by other words, whispered very softly:

Sa'fas, qarshat, hawwaz, hutti...

'Give me your hand, Hardie, now!'

She took my hand in hers. Her hand was warm and soft. Our fingers entwined tightly. I barely had time to see the object she'd just taken from her *leso*. It was the wooden die.

'*Abjad*!' she cried, throwing the cube into the centre of the spiral.

A swirl of sand rose up between us, enveloping our hands.

Everything vanished.

At first, there's nothing but darkness. Wherever I turn, all I see is deep black, as if the darkness has become a blindfold that not only covers my eyes but penetrates deep into my corneas. Slowly, my vision acclimatises, and I begin to make out the pale silhouette of Halima. She's standing in front of me. I can't tell what she's doing. I see the glow of her eyes, but I can't tell if it's her mouth moving or her chin. I think it's her mouth. It seems she's talking to me, trying to convey something important. Then a cavernous sound echoes behind me: it's the hoarse, raspy voice of a man who sounds as if he hasn't slept for a long time.

'Who are you?' he barks.

I turn round and come face to face with the same old man as last time, his half-length beard trimmed in a neat semicircle. He's dressed in white from head to toe; a long, gleaming robe and a cotton *keffiyeh* that falls elegantly on either side of his face. His skin is almost as dark as mine. His expression is inscrutable, neither smile nor frown.

'I said who are you?' he repeats.

He's speaking a language I haven't heard for a long time; the guttural, consonant-rich tongue of Tamu's people. I manage to dredge up enough words to introduce myself.

'I'm Hardie, daughter of Tamu.'

He looks at me. Behind me, I feel Halima's hot, quick breath on my neck. She's worried for me.

'What are you looking for?'

'Someone I've lost. My mother.'

His forehead creases.

'Your mother?

'I mean Tamu. My adoptive mother.'

His brow relaxes.

'You may come aboard if you can answer my riddle. Are you ready?'

'Yes,' I stammer.

'God's staff is knotted all over.'

Halima's hand rests on my shoulder. 'Hurry up, Hardie,' her fingers say. I think quickly: a sweet taste suggests itself, followed by a stringy texture and the sound of hard skin being peeled off. I suddenly shout, 'Sugar cane!'

My voice echoes strangely in the silence of the night.

The man smiles.

'You may pass,' he says warmly.

He disappears. So does everything else.

*

Two ships are sailing through a fog. It's so dense it's hard to make out the shapes of the sailors, but you only have to hear the cries of alarm all along our deck to realise danger is imminent.

I'm standing on deck, gripping the rail with my right hand. I raise my left arm and am surprised at how heavy it is, how awkward it feels to raise it so high. I'm wearing a man's long-sleeved shirt. I've never worn anything that covers my arms before, but my body seems used to it.

Time is short: there are ten pairs of eyes in front of me; ten men waiting for my order. I hear myself shout, 'Arm the guns!'

The sailors comply, rushing to relay the order and get to work.

My clothing makes a metallic clink as I move. I realise I know the names of all the things I'm wearing. I have tight-fitting breeches and boots of the finest leather, studded at the toes. My chest is encased in a silver armour plate. I'm wearing a neck plate and shoulder plates too; the neck plate hits against my chin when I lower my head. The object that restricts my arm as I try to lift it is a thick, wide red armband.

A deafening blast echoes through the mist. The cannonballs tear holes through the other ship. Its gigantic silhouette fragments, revealing black, smoky sky between its entrails.

'What now, Captain?'

Again, several pairs of eyes turn to me. The men are hanging on my decision. I consider. Thoughts of a kind I've never had before dance inside my head in an organised, calculated choreography. After what seems like an interminable amount of time, a decision takes shape: we must check whether we can still see the second ship, and attack it without delay. If it's a friendly ship, we'll bring its passengers aboard. If it's a pirate ship, we'll sink it.

I look around me, wondering where Halima is, so she can explain where we are. The other ship is moving in our direction. I wait until its bow is a mile and a half from ours, then shout again, 'Arm the guns!'

My men take their posts in one fluid movement. I hear the

crackle of fire creeping along fuses, a sound that's surprisingly familiar. Then the thud of the cannonballs exploding from the gun. I contemplate their flight through the fog. I don't flinch, but rejoice as I hear two cannonballs exploding on the other ship's deck. The ship is now close enough for some of its passengers to board ours. They waste no time. Hearing them speak, I realise we've shot down a Turkish galley. My men cross swords with the foreigners, and I launch myself into their midst. I don't know how to fight, yet my hand pulls the sabre strapped to my waist from its scabbard, and my arm begins to perform movements of parrying, attack and defence that I've never learned.

It's much more elaborate than the dance at the *tari* party we have at rich people's weddings on my island, in which noble grooms pretend to cross swords with their enemies.

It's more risky, too: with every screech of metal against metal I sense the threat to my life. But I carry on. My sabre pierces the belly of more than one sailor. We're well on the way to wiping them out, when a voice shouts from the midst of the enemy troops, '*Español, Español!*'

I order my men to stop the attack. We've killed all the Turkish sailors. The only men left are Spanish galley slaves. It's not hard to tell them apart: their trousers hang off them in tatters and their torsos are streaked with lashes. As they stand in front of me, drained, I see before my eyes, as if in a dream, the image of a row of galley slaves chained to benches, eating and relieving themselves where they sit, always rowing frantically. My heart aches for them.

My sailors round them up and bring them before me.

Their rags must have been breeches at some point in the

past: you can still just about make out the colours. I expect their condition of servitude to prompt the men to lower their eyes in my presence; instead, they look straight at me, an urgency in their gaze. I understand that they want to talk to me alone. With a wave of my hand, I dismiss my men. They obey, but not without grumbling. Once back at their posts, they keep a close eye on us.

One of the galley slaves steps forward. He's one of the few who still sports a shirt. It's untucked from his trousers, but the cotton fabric is skilfully woven. I guess he must be a fallen captain, a man whose ship was hijacked by Barbary pirates. There's pride in his eyes, the residue of a dignity that his companions have lost through mistreatment.

When he opens his mouth, his distinguished diction in Spanish confirms my intuition. 'God rewards magnanimous people like you, Captain. On behalf of my compatriots, I would like to thank you.'

I nod. 'The Turks have a saying for this kind of situation: you don't thank someone who's only done his duty. I only did my duty, gentlemen. Protecting my ship and offering asylum to my brothers.'

He looks at me for a long time. Something in his eyes reminds me of someone. But my heart tells me it's not Halima. It couldn't be her: she would've given me some sort of sign. Where is she anyway? Have I lost her? Where am I?

'I have a feeling you're not from here, Sir,' says the spokesman for the galley slaves, with a slight smirk. 'May I ask where you are from?'

I open my mouth, hesitating. Should I say I come from an island called Ngazidja? They'd never believe that. That I came here without knowing how? They'd believe that even less. Fortunately, my tongue and lips respond without me having to tell them what to do. 'I'm Spanish,' I say. 'My name is Captain Miguel de Cervantes. Our fleet is flying the English flag to deceive our enemies. But you're not our enemies, are you?'

'Even if we wanted to be, we couldn't afford to. I'm Federico Ricared, at your service.'

He bows. When he looks up at me, I'm intrigued to again recognise someone else in his features. I've met him in the distant past, and he always smirks when he sees me. I know him, but from where?

I offer to take the galley slaves home once we've anchored in Algeria to trade weapons for spices. They accept.

*

The next day, the sky clears. A brisk, invigorating wind fills our sails. I grab the railing, lift my chin and inhale the sea air. I can't stop wondering where Halima is. Admittedly, it's partly because without her I have no idea how to get home, but if I didn't feel the way I do about her, I might not even care about that. The adventures of the day before seem to have injected me with fresh blood. Everything is fascinating and new: the strength in my arms, the lick of the wind and the salt in my hair and on my skin. Skin that's as white as milk, muscles that are dense and powerful.

The question in my mind gradually becomes a statement.

It must be the best thing on this earth to be a man the colour of milk. Wherever they go, milk-coloured men are welcomed as the descendants of the prophet, even as celestial beings.

The lighter their skin, the more they're adored, respected and venerated. Their wives are carefully protected inside houses like treasure chests. An enviable position, though not a very stimulating one, if Halima's experience is anything to go by. For my part, if Queen Abé, our creator, had allowed me to choose what kind of life I wanted to be born into, I'd have chosen to be a man the colour of milk, free to sail the seas as a lord, to live off the fruits of my labour, to enjoy the favours of every woman who crossed my path. Unfettered. I could visit the islands, as the Persians and the Arabs did, but instead of enslaving their inhabitants, I'd try to find out how their world worked. I'd help Tamu return home to her land of red sand. I'd listen to Mlima's tales all day long. I…

'Captain! Captain! Captain!'

The voice seems to be coming from far away, but the sailor is right beside me. I turn to look at him. His eyes are desperate, his mouth wide open and gasping.

'Good Lord, Sancho, what's the matter with you?'

'Captain, why didn't you answer? We're under attack from Barbary pirates!'

I turn quickly towards the deck. The sailors are loading the cannons in a panic. Two ships are boarding us, port and starboard. The oars protruding from their bellies indicate the presence of galley slaves. The power with which they push back the waves suggests they're newly captured; men still strong enough to move the ship forward, who don't yet need to be whipped to force them to work.

I'm about to give an order when I spot the captain of the other boat.

Across the ever-decreasing space between us, I can see

his eyes shining like two sharp diamonds, piercing through the mist. He wears a richly-decorated caftan and has a long turban wrapped around his head. His ferocious gaze is fixed on the sailors. Then his eyes meet mine, and he gives me a look of pure hatred. I falter. Never, in my life as Hardie, did I provoke such a strong feeling in anyone. There's something intoxicating about it.

Sancho speaks to me again. 'Captain, I had to give the order to fire.'

'What?' I say in a faint voice, as if waking from a dream.

'You didn't answer, so I didn't have the ch—'

A whistling sound interrupts my second in command. Suddenly, the tip of a sabre appears between Sancho and me. The blade has pierced him, and its bloody tip seems to be looking at me, also desperate, also surprised to be there, instead of being melted into a more useful instrument; a cooking pot, perhaps, or a kitchen knife.

Horrified, I watch as Sancho collapses at my feet, his sentence still hanging in the air. When I look up, the last thing I see is the face of Federico, the leader of the Spanish galley slaves. He holds a black canvas bag over my head. I don't have time to speak.

'Sorry, Captain,' he murmurs in Spanish, 'But the Barbaries are the winning side here.'

I'm plunged into darkness again.

*

'Hey, wake up!'

I'm in a room with dark, grubby walls. A stench

permeates the space; a mixture of sweat, piss and excrement. Instinctively, I move back towards the wall. I feel a bulge beneath my buttocks. A hand lands on my back and violently pushes me forward.

'Get away, you!'

I straighten up and wait for my eyes to get used to the dim light. When things come back into focus, I see a man with a scar on his face, shaggy hair and beard. He's dressed in a long, dirty white robe. Despite the scar, his features are harmonious: he was handsome once.

'I'm sorry,' I stammer.

'So you should be,' he retorts gruffly. 'If you were at least a beautiful girl, or a eunuch, we could've worked something out. But you stink of semen. I prefer people who know how to be discreet.'

I sit back down and cower, a little ashamed.

'Where am I?' I ask him.

He stares at me for a moment, then holds out a piece of bread.

'Want some?'

I hesitate. Where the man I am comes from, accepting a meal from a stranger is frowned upon. Still, I reach out and grab the bread. I devour it in one bite. I was starving.

'You're in Algiers, my friend,' he continues. 'Do you know what happens in Algiers?'

I shake my head slowly, just an attempt to put off the inevitable: I think I know what he's about to tell me.

'Algiers is hell. You take what you're offered or you die. Are you a Christian?'

I nod.

'Then it's purgatory and hell for you. You're in enemy country. Prepare for the whip and servitude to the death.'

*

We're served sticky semolina floating in whey. I sniff my bowl and wince. From our cell, we can hear the insistent whistling of the wind, the neverending music of the dunes. I have no idea if it's day or night. My cellmate calmly dips his fingers into the slop and brings it to his mouth delicately, as if he were enjoying a plate of steaming *camarónes*. He eats dutifully, savouring every mouthful. The smell disgusts me too much to do the same. I scrutinise him more closely. His gentle, almost youthful features contrast with his broad, square jaw: he seems like a child forced by circumstance to grow up too quickly. His half-closed eyes give him the air of a jaded man; yet a few hours earlier, when he looked at me and told me where we were, I'd noticed an intensity and gravity to his regard, like that of a teacher.

This thought brings Fundi Ahmad to mind. A wave of panic crashes over me. Is it already daylight on my island? Has my absence been noticed? Good Queen Abé, what if I've been here for two or three days? What am I going to do when I get back? How will I explain such a long absence to the *fundi*?

Without looking up, my cellmate addresses me, putting a stop to the mad rush of my thoughts.

'If you don't eat, you die. If you don't get any love, you die. So eat everything you can, and eat it with love. That's the key to not vomiting. When you've been here long enough, you'll know what I'm talking about.'

I stare at the slop. My stomach growls with hunger. I do as he instructs me, plunging my fingers into the soggy semolina, rolling it into grainy pellets in the palm of my hand, then bringing them to my lips. The mixture is acidic and sticky, but it doesn't taste as bad as I expected. The texture of whey mixed with semolina reminds me of bits of banana soaked in coconut milk for hours—a dish Tamu excelled at. Her name, after all, meant 'the exquisite'.

I devour the dish quickly, before it can get cold. Outside, a prayer call sounds. I ask my cellmate which prayer the faithful are being called to.

'*Maghrib*, the sunset prayer. The time when the locals say devils are chained and the heavens are moved by human suffering.'

We listen in silence. The chant of the *muezzin* sounds like a lament, the notes rising and falling with a mournful tremor that lends them a special solemnity. My cellmate has closed his eyes. I do the same. I've never pondered the *muezzin's* call before. Back in my home, it's only the men who hurry to mosque at the sound of the call. The women go and do their ablutions; maids, like me, hold the jug and pour water over their hands. Sitting here like this is the first time I've been able to listen to the musical qualities of the chant.

After the prayer, the whole citadel falls asleep. The only sounds are the snores of the guards and the breathing of the other prisoners. I can't sleep. My mattress is a hessian sack stuffed with straw: pieces poke through the holes of the sack and into my skin.

I sit up slowly. A whitish glow penetrates through a small opening in the prison wall. I need something to occupy my mind. In my jacket pocket, I find my notebook and pen. I hold them up to the light. Some ink has dried on the tip of my pen; if I press down a little it will be enough for me to sketch with.

I leaf through my notebook. It's filled with my travel observations. My handwriting is delicate and small, difficult to read in such low light.

I press the tip of my pen on to a blank page. The first thing that comes to mind is the letter *waw*. Clinging to this vivid memory of my life as Hardie, I trace its shape.

The scratching of my pen on the paper attracts the attention of my neighbour.

'Have you got a wife?' he asks.

I shake my head.

'So who are you writing to? Your father, to get you out of this mess?'

He chuckles to himself, then straightens up.

I show him the page I've just written on. He takes the notebook from me and scrutinises the letter. In the next cell, someone is reciting the Throne Verse of the Qur'an. My companion raises an astonished eyebrow.

'You can write Arabic?'

'I think so,' I reply.

'What do you mean, you think so? Can you or can't you?'

'I think I can only remember this letter,' I say. I try to remember the others, without success.

'It looks like a backwards six,' he says, looking more closely at my *waw.* 'When I first came to Algiers, I met a young sailor from here. He told me he came from a long line of spiritual leaders whose group name was something like sifa… sifi…'

'Sufi?'

It's the reciter of the Qur'an who's spoken.

'Hey, are you eavesdropping, Abdelatif? Go back to your gibberish!'

'I'm not going to let you mangle the sacred words of my religion,' retorts the other man. 'I must correct you. Would you like it if I misspelled the name of your virgin?'

'Leave my virgin out of this, idiot!'

'You see.'

'Well, since you're butting in, you can help us. What's the meaning of this letter… what is it?'

'*Waw*,' I say.

'*Waw*. My Sufi friend said that each letter in your Qur'an has a particular meaning. He also said something about numbers; I can't remember what.'

The Qur'an reader speaks again. For some reason, what he says surprises me.

'*Waw* is the most important letter for anyone who wants to get closer to God. It's the symbol of man's union with God. It is also the number six, but I can't remember what that number signifies.'

Union with God. Why, in my life as Hardie, would I be in search of that?

'Thank you,' I say simply to both men.

'Don't thank me, go to sleep,' replies my cellmate.

I think back to the look in the eyes of the man who took me prisoner, then to the look in the eyes of the woman who accompanied me into this reality. At the mere thought of her, my male body ignites. I look down and contemplate my taut, muscular, arms. Between my strong legs, I can feel my third limb, the one the men back home use to strip young maids of their dignity. Sometimes they give them false hope to soften the blow, sometimes they just take what they feel like taking, while the women are too stunned to fight back. I'm on the other side now; one of them.

My neighbour's voice breaks the silence, sounding sleepy, but echoing clearly between the stone walls of the cell.

'I know where you come from. But do you know why you're here?'

'My name is Captain Miguel Cervantes. I was on a mission for the queen and my crew were captured by Barbary pirates. I'll get out of here soon and go home to my country.'

'Of course,' he says, as he inserts a sliver of wood between his teeth. 'And I'm the King of Italy. I know where you're from, boy. You're not from here. *Not from here at all.*'

My heartbeat quickens, pounding at my temples. My ears feel hot. What does he mean? Does he really know where I come from? Does the man I am have some sort of shadowy past?

'You understood me perfectly well. You—'

He's interrupted by the sound of footsteps echoing down the corridor; the slap of one sandal, then another, on the stone floor. We both hold our breath.

The man with the gigantic turban stops in front of the door to our cell. He brings his face close to the bars, then turns his head away to spit. He fixes me with his eyes.

'We're going to sell you at the market,' he says.

As he walks away, my companion looks at me, puzzled. 'My friend,' he says, 'If you get sold at the market, it's double or quits.'

'What do you mean?'

He looks away and scratches his beard, half of which is white.

'Here, the masters are either very generous or they're barbarians. You could end up living like a king, or like a rabid dog. It all depends.'

He continues staring at me.

I notice there's a patch on his cheek that's free of beard; a smooth, shiny spot in the midst of the forest of silver hair.

'What happened to your cheek?' I ask.

'An accident,' he replies. 'A long, long time ago. In another life.'

I look away. I don't want him to start another conversation about where I'm from.

Sleep still doesn't come.

*

We stop in front of a low platform that's been erected in a square. There are other, similar platforms scattered around the square, all crammed with slaves, each as thin and exhausted as the next, trying as best they can to stand upright in the crush. The slave market is at the centre of a larger cluster of tables and stalls, hemmed in by large two and three storey buildings of white, blue and yellow stone. Two mosques face each other on either side of the street, with minarets that imitate the style of our churches.

Suddenly, something whistles through the air and a burning sensation shoots across my shoulder. I look round and see my seller, his face filled with rage.

'Have you gone deaf, bloody Christian? Get up on that platform with the others!' he barks, winding up his whip.

In my reverie, I'd barely registered we'd stopped moving. I lift my foot in a daze and place it on the platform. It feels cold and tacky. I can't look down to see what I'm standing on, but I can tell it's a sticky liquid. Soon, the metallic smell assaults my nostrils. The floor of the platform is coated in a mixture of sweat and blood.

This adventure is swiftly losing its appeal. I turn to my fellow captives: they seem to be from all corners of the world, and so far none of them speak my language. Some whisper to each other in a tongue that sounds to me like gibberish. The others keep their mouths shut.

As the red clouds give way to a radiant sky, buyers start to pour into the market. Men, and women too, their faces covered with light veils that reveal only their eyes, framed by a strip of vermilion, emerald green or Prussian blue caftan embroidered in gold or silver.

A buyer approaches. Without looking at me, she feels my arms and presses my stomach and torso, testing for solidity. Then she beckons to the seller. When he comes over, she averts her eyes and whispers, 'I want this one.'

The seller gives a grunt, as if he disapproves of selling to a woman, but he gives her my price and she pulls a purse from the folds of her dress. In an instant, I'm hers.

I walk behind her, flanked by two dark-skinned men. At the bend in an alleyway, she stops. One of the guards opens an iron door and pushes me inside. The woman follows me and guides me into a room. She closes the door behind us, leaving the guards outside.

The room is finely decorated: a hand-woven carpet depicting two doves holding a laurel branch in their beaks, coloured silk cushions with mother-of-pearl buttons at their centres, an ornate wrought-iron oil lamp in each corner of the room. Sunlight filters in from a window. I imagine the blue square the moon must project through it at night.

The woman ushers me to sit on a divan piled with cushions and enclosed by gauzy curtains. Finally, she pulls aside her veil. I know her look, her smile, and her voice when she whispers, 'I've found what I was looking for. Now let's get out of here.'

A wave of happiness engulfs me.

She takes off her veil, revealing her jet-black hair, rolled into a bun at her neck.

The *muezzin* begins the call to prayer. She slowly unties a knot in her veil and takes out a wooden die.

Molten gold has been poured into each of the letters engraved on its sides.

She lets me take it and hold it up to the rays of light coming through the blind. The sun makes it gleam.

'When you gave me the die on the beach that day,' I ask her, 'Why did you behave as if it were the only one of its kind when you had one too?'

She makes no answer, but contemplates the object with

me. When she does speak, it's to say something else.

'I need your help, Hardie. We're in great danger. If I don't find all the dice in time, I'll lose my husband forever. My true husband, I mean: the one who was taken from me.'

I raise an eyebrow. 'But Fadili hasn't gone, in the place where we came from.'

She looks away from the die, and turns to me with sadness.

'Whatever life we live, he and I, someone always tries to separate us. Wherever we go, we love each other and get married, but the same person tries to break us up.'

I understand now why she moves between different lives. I wonder who this person is who's so intent on keeping them apart. At the same time, I feel anger brewing inside me. A multitude of questions invades my mind.

'I want you to explain,' I say, raising my voice a little. 'Why did you lie to me? I thought I had something precious, rare, unique. And now you're showing me another die. Maybe you've got lots more of them. Maybe other people have them too…'

'You think you're not important to me? You think I've been making a fool of you?'

Tears well up in my eyes. She's just named the thing that always pained me most as a slave: being mocked.

'Masters sometimes issue special little tasks to ensure your loyalty,' I reply, 'To give you the impression you're important, like no one else could do this thing. It's a way of checking they can trust you before they give you more important or risky tasks, things that require discretion. Then when they no longer need you, they make it clear that what you were doing wasn't special at all, that they can, of course, manage without you.'

There's a short but weighty silence. When Halima speaks, her voice is brusque. 'Is that how you see me? As a master? Do you still think I'm like them, incapable of compassion?'

'No one but Tamu ever showed me compassion. She always said that true love exists only in a mother's heart. Everything else is just a role people play to suit their interests.'

'That's not true,' Halima hisses. 'And I don't believe Tamu said it. I never met her, but the mother you described to me would never speak like that.'

'You promised you'd help me find her.'

'And I will.'

She puts a hand on my shoulder. The warmth of that touch melts my resistance.

Her voice becomes a whisper. She speaks quickly, breathlessly, as if she's sharing someone else's secret. Outside, the sounds of the market mingle with the voices of the children chanting by rote in the *madrassa*.

'The die you're holding in your hand has four brothers. Five dice in all, made from five different woods.'

She takes the die from my hands, holds it up to the sunlight and turns it around between her fingers so I can read each of the letters engraved on it.

Sîn, Aïn, Fâ, Sâd, Sa'fas.

'I have two of them now. I found this one in my husband's safe here.'

'And now you need the other three?'

She turns to me, her eyes filled with anguish.

'If someone gets hold of the fifth one before we can, I'll lose any chance of ever seeing my husband again, and you'll never find Tamu. But there's more, Hardie, there's more than that at stake.'

I'm not sure I understand, but I'm sure of one thing, despite myself: whatever the obstacles, I'll help Halima in her quest.

One question still nags at me, though. I'm reluctant to ask it, because it might make Halima decide she no longer wants to take this journey with me. But I need to know.

'Why me?'

The die seems to have hypnotised her; she drags her eyes away from it with difficulty.

'What do you mean?'

'Why do all of this with me and not with someone else?'

A sad smile stretches her lips.

'Hardie, you think I'm taking you because I want a servant by my side, is that it? I don't need a slave. I'm taking you because I care about you.'

An imaginary snake slithers down my spine and coils itself around my heart.

*

The next morning, Halima rushes into the small room where I've spent the night and shakes me briskly awake.

'We're leaving, Hardie!'

Half-awake, I can't remember my old name. I go on the defensive. 'You're mistaken, my name's Miguel!'

I realise I'm casting her an appreciative glance. The sway of her hips under her grey caftan, the swell of her breasts beneath its silky folds, titillate the senses of the man I am. I slur, 'But I'd be happy to be whoever you want me to be, my pretty one.'

She gets impatient. 'I should've known you'd forget who you were! It's the effect of sleep. Luckily I've worked everything out.'

Suddenly the latch lifts, the door to the room opens and I hear footsteps.

'It's my husband in this life,' explains Halima. 'We have to get out of here!'

The man shouts her name as she pushes me behind a curtain. 'Isabela? Isabela! Where are you?'

Halima grabs my arm with the strength of a dozen sailors. She shouts at her husband, 'I love him, not you! You'll never separate us!'

With the same incredible strength, she pushes some shelves stacked with baked goods to one side, revealing a door I hadn't seen the day before. She takes an intricately-worked key from her bodice and inserts it in the lock. She pushes me into a room and slams the door shut behind us just in time. There's a knocking at the door, followed by furious shouts.

'Wait till I get that door open, you she-wolf! I'll eat you alive!'

We're in a cramped, musty-smelling space.

'This is where they lock up disobedient slaves,' murmurs Halima.

Calmly, she takes the die we were looking at yesterday from her pocket, along with a bottle the size of a hand. From it, she empties a stream of sand on to the floor between us. She places all the fingers of one hand in the sand, leaving five distinct circular marks. Then she grabs my hand and looks into my eyes.

'Repeat after me, Hardie, quickly!'

I do what she says, more out of desperation than conviction.

'*Sa'fas, Qarshat, Hawwaz, Hutti.*'

She grabs a handful of sand and throws it violently to the ground, before whispering, '*Abjad.*'

The last thing I see is the murderous stare of Isabela's husband in the doorway, then I'm plunged into darkness.

*

Coconut milk infused with jasmine. A more distant hint of the scents of lemongrass, bay leaves and wild thyme. The sound of water bubbling to a boil: herbal tea.

Fingers running through my hair, the caress of long nails: I picture the henna-tinted nails that have been tracing wavy furrows on my head since I was a little girl. I hear the laughter of the other workers.

'Since when do slaves braid their hair?'

'Since I had a daughter,' comes her reply, somewhere above my head.

I look up and my heart sings. Tamu, gripping my frizzy curls, slicking them with coconut oil, then parting them neatly with her nails.

'Today, we'll do the pattern of inner knots: the strands are interwoven underneath each other. That's the best trick to protect the hair, and yours needs it. You get so dirty every time you go to Ahmad's Wood.'

Her voice is as warm as milk fresh from the animal. I hear her unique accent; the sounds of the place her grandparents came from, long ago. As she braids my hair, she hums a tune they used to love.

You take the padlock, I'll take the oar
We'll defeat them
And we'll find our way home
Back to the land of the ndovu.

I can't stop looking at Tamu: her eyes, half hidden beneath eyelids lowered in concentration; her mouth, curving slightly downwards when she speaks or laughs. Was it all just a dream? Did she never disappear at all? I ask her what the *ndovu* are.

'The *ndovu* are the most majestic beings in existence. They're huge and phenomenally strong: they could kill you with a single blow from their feet or their trunks, yet they're supremely gentle. They're the guardians of the earth. This is their imprint on the sky.'

As she shows me the constellation of the elephants, something strange happens. The stars seem to spin, then to orbit around each other. Tamu's voice changes, as if it's spinning along with them: her vowels elongate as the stars dance, until they're hard to make out.

Then her voice fades away completely, along with the neighbours' houses, the shrubs next to them, the black stones beneath my feet, Tamu's hands. Everything rushes away from me, and I'm alone, in an immense empty space where I have no foothold, falling.

'Abjad.'

*

The sensation of colliding with stone shook me awake.

Halima was standing in front of me. When I saw her, it all came flooding back: my life as Miguel; my life as Hardie; all the incredible and inconceivable things in between.

I was glad to be home again, but something was worrying me.

'What happened?' I asked. 'What was that world?'

Halima sat down beside me, her expression as peaceful and melancholy as always.

'We were probably at the time of the *nasara*: Arabs who enslaved Christians.'

I nodded. I'd read verses that referenced the *nasara*, as well as the *hud*. Those peoples were said to have been given a divine gift, the aim of which was for them to attain the purest compassion.

I didn't have time to think about that though. I was only interested in Tamu.

'Halima, there was no sign of Tamu on our trip. I think Mlima was right: someone must have taken her and sold her. That means I'm never going to see her again!'

I started to shake uncontrollably. Suddenly, my whole body ached: my throat, which Tamu was so good at soothing with her ginger tea; my heart, which she calmed with her stories. The place where my breasts should have been ached too.

Halima took hold of me by the shoulders and pulled me to my feet. I looked around vaguely: we were in her room, which had gone back to being small and cramped. She kept flicking her eyes towards the low door, as if she was afraid something or someone might jump out, then turning her attention back to me. I felt too weak to ask her what she was watching for.

'Go and rest,' she said at last. 'Those journeys are tiring. We won't be doing another one for a couple of days. And next time, we'll use your fire. Then you'll see how much strength you possess.'

'Agreed?'

'Your wish is my command,' I planned to say once I'd stopped trembling, but I didn't even have time to nod. A voice cut through the silence I'd let settle. It was the hoarse, harsh voice of an angry old man.

We both snapped our heads up in horror. Fundi.

'And where are you planning to travel to?'

Neither of us knew what to say. There was no point even concocting a lie: he'd probably been hiding behind the door for some time, listening to every word we'd said.

He glared at me as I left in silence. If that low doorway had been a hole, I'd have buried myself in it forever. As I walked down the narrow corridor, my shoulders hunched, all my attention was focused on what was happening in the room I was leaving.

Fundi closed the door behind me, then all I could hear was the thunder of his voice, followed by the trembling but sure rain of Halima's. I imagined her, chin raised, trying to stand her ground against her husband.

Then I heard her scream. It was as loud and shrill as an owl's, but infinitely sadder. My blood ran cold. My legs changed direction of their own volition, and in a flash I was back in the room.

Fundi was holding Halima in his arms. She was sobbing and muttering something I couldn't immediately make out.

Fundi turned towards me. This time his look was grave. My heart sank as he said, 'Halima has lost someone. Her father, Fundi Charif Mohamed, has died.'

My throat felt dry. I looked at Halima, slumped against her husband, weeping. I could hear now that she was whispering, 'Forgive me, Father.'

My eyes returned to my master. He was still staring at me, insistent and disapproving. At first I thought it was because of the journey I'd taken with Halima. Then the elements began to fall into place in my mind and I thought I could read his thoughts: *Charif Mohamed died without his only daughter at his bedside, because you, Hardie, encouraged his daughter's whims. Nothing would stop you, not the laws that define servant-master relations, nor fear of me, your teacher.*

I lowered my eyes and turned on my heels. The look on the *fundi's* face followed me all the way back to my room. When I got there, I gathered a few things at random and packed them into a *leso*. Then I left the house.

*

The waves were raging. They'd transformed from crystalline blue to a menacing inky black, rivalling the darkness of the sky. They crashed ferociously against the chiselled rocks. The rocks, like knives, tried to stab them back.

My thoughts circled in a merciless, repetitive dance. When the sea got out of control like this, we said it had lost its mind. I wasn't far off losing mine too.

I'd been there a long time, staring at the sea, when I heard Olympe's voice.

'Not a very clever place to hide,' she said. She sat down beside me.

The smell of coconut milk on her skin turned my stomach. I looked away. Out of the corner of my eye, I saw her bring her knees up to her chin and wrap her arms around them.

'Do you know that Fundi is looking for you?'

I nodded silently.

'So you've heard about your beloved's father,' she went on.

I let out a long sigh.

She waited for me to speak, but no words formed on my tongue. I remained mute, as if trapped in the kind of nightmare where you open your mouth but no sound comes out. What was there for me to say? I'd obeyed my master's wife, and now I was being blamed for her father's death. This was our destiny: to obey and then face reprisals for having obeyed.

'Yes, I've heard,' I finally replied. 'It was my fault.'

'What do you mean, your fault?'

'I didn't know how to say no to her. I went along with her experiments and her father died without her at his bedside.'

Olympe looked at me for a moment, then gave a nervous laugh. 'You afford yourself far too much importance, my friend! Do you think you can prevent death?'

'No, but if I'd said no…'

'If you'd said no, he'd still be dead.'

She let a moment's silence pass, before continuing, in a whisper, 'If you'd come home earlier the other day, you'd still have lost Tamu.'

She'd understood the real source of my turmoil before I had. The death of Halima's father had propelled me back to

Tamu's death. The dagger had met no resistance and penetrated to the very depths of my heart, where it now did secret battle with the sword of my guilt.

But Olympe chose this moment to change my life forever. She chose her words carefully. The sea was still hurling itself violently against the rocks. Was it in pain?

'Did your beloved confide anything else to you?'

I shook my head, thinking a little water would do me good—my throat was so dry.

Olympe let out a long sigh.

'She's expecting a child.'

Weeks went by. I returned to Fundi's house. A strange disease was afflicting the trees, speckling their leaves with black blotches. M'maka, who worked in the fields every fifth day with the other women, tried to remove the stains using water and various oils. The more she rubbed, the darker they became.

She told us this beneath the mango tree in Gerezan, where we now met Fundi one morning a week.

'It's because of our sins,' said Ramla.

'All the *jinns* we summon, the pagan practices,' added M'maka.

'I think it's a punishment from our ancestors because we've forgotten them,' offered Olympe.

'I doubt anyone wants to deprive our land's innocent children of food!' I retorted, irritated.

'Some of them aren't so innocent,' said a male voice behind us.

Fundi approached. He didn't look at us. He was wearing a beige linen *kandu.* His white scarf with red spots was folded lengthways and draped casually over his shoulder. This was the way all the nobles wore it.

He walked past us and sat down at the foot of the mango tree. Under his cloud-white cap, his brow looked tense. He was clearly making an effort to keep his voice calm.

'Where's our sixth member?'

We looked around and realised Mlima wasn't there.

Since she'd been sold to Kaba-il, the wealthy merchant from the capital, Mlima had come more and more infrequently to our nightly gatherings of friends. But she'd never missed a meeting with Fundi before.

'Well, where are your manners?'

We hastened to greet him, '*Kwezi*, our master.'

Fundi let his gaze wander off into the distance.

'You were talking about the diseased trees just then. It's a serious illness. It has nothing to do with divine punishment. We'll start by praying for the recovery of the trees.'

He had us read the *surah* of the opening, then the *surah* of man. As usual, he played with his hands throughout the reading. I read mechanically, hypnotised by the dance of his fingers: he folded two, extended the other three, then reversed and folded the three while extending the two, before changing position again. I knew these movements: Tamu sometimes made them when she was counting the fruit she was going to trade for cloth at the market. I knew why she did it, but why was Fundi counting while we read?

When the lesson was over, I waited until the others had gone. I was wracked with guilt and terrified, but I didn't want to avoid my master.

Fundi just stood there, looking away from me. I spoke up. 'Master, what you saw will never happen again.'

He turned to me, his gaze cold.

'What exactly did I see?'

'I mean, I disobeyed your order. I'm ready to accept whatever punishment you think I deserve.'

He looked at me for a long time. Instead of the contempt I'd expected to see in his eyes, I saw pain and deep disappointment. It was the sort of look Tamu had sometimes given me. I should've been delighted—here was proof that Fundi thought of me as a daughter—but all I felt was shame.

He looked away again.

'Come and find me in my room after your afternoon prayer. And don't say anything about it to my wife.'

'Yes, Fundi. I swear to you, by Allah…'

'No, don't swear by Allah. You should never swear, because you never know if you'll live long enough to keep your promise.'

'Yes, Fundi.'

Olympe was washing one of the mistress' *hamis*, her legs half immersed in the water. The sea breeze carried the scent of bluefin tuna: this was their season. I wanted to dive in, swim briskly until I reached a depth where I could no longer stand, then sink down beneath the surface. There, I'd scan the waters, feeling a burst of pleasure whenever I caught sight of the golden scales, plump bodies and metallic blue skin of my island's tuna. I wasn't interested in catching them; I only fished them for the masters, who were crazy about the flesh, which separated so smoothly into slices when fried. I preferred just to look at them. It seemed to me they were trying to tell me something; a story, perhaps, of sea princesses and courageous turtles.

'Pass me the other end of the cloth,' said Olympe.

I grabbed the other end of the *hami*, which was slapping against the rock with the waves, and helped Olympe to wring it out.

'My mistress is selfish,' she said.

'Selfish? Why?'

'Because she doesn't think about others. She knew what you were exposing yourself to by going to see her.'

'I'm the selfish one. I didn't listen to Fundi. And it's my fault she couldn't go to her father's bedside.'

'But how are you supposed to know who to listen to when everyone's your master? Besides, has she spoken to us about Tamu since that day she sent us to the market to question people? All she gave us was that one mission! Just because she'd "always dreamed of doing that!"'

Olympe was very annoyed.

'Has Halima upset you?' I asked her.

I could see disapproval and disbelief in her eyes. 'Halima'? You call her by her first name now?'

'I meant the mistress. It just slipped out.'

Olympe rolled her eyes. She wrapped the cloth around her arm. Droplets of water trickled down silently as I dried my hands on my scarf.

'I don't know, but I think she's taking your mother's disappearance too lightly. I don't like to blame others, but I think if she really loved you like she says she does, she'd care more about it.'

I wanted to protest, but I didn't dare say any more. The shadows were already lengthening and the *muezzin* was calling us for afternoon prayer.

*

The master's room was opposite Halima's.

It was of identical construction, with the same stone walls, but was more richly furnished. There was a desk in the middle, a wicker chair and a small round table of mango wood for tea. On the desk was a pile of law and prayer books, alongside the brown pearl rosary the *fundi's* students knew so well. Near the door stood a carved wooden lectern, on which a huge Qur'an sat open. Not far from the door and the lectern, against the wall, was an *adas* bench bed with wide legs made from the trunks of palm trees.

Fundi was standing in front of his desk, waiting for me.

'Close the door behind you,' he ordered.

I complied.

He walked to the other end of the room, opened a huge tin trunk and took out a small green velvet bag. He handed it to me and motioned for me to untie it.

Unsure of what I was going to find inside, and feeling intimidated, I looked at Fundi for a moment, as if seeking further confirmation of his order. He remained impassive. I pulled at the cord that held the bag closed. It fell open in my palm. In the centre of the iridescent folds, I saw it.

A die.

My heart almost stopped.

Fundi explained immediately, 'It was given to me by my father. You seem surprised to see it there. Have you seen it somewhere else before?'

I swallowed.

'No, Fundi. Only the ones you showed us under the mango tree. But this one is…'

'Different, yes. It was carved from a very rare wood by an extremely skilled craftsman. Run your hand over it: you won't feel any roughness.'

He was right. This die was as smooth as the one Halima had shown me in Algiers when I was Miguel. But I was careful to appear ignorant.

'Each of these dice has a name,' said Fundi.

He picked it up and held it to the light that shone through the window. I realised Halima might not even know this die existed. To my great surprise, I decided I wouldn't tell her. That would be my only power over her. Without her, perhaps, I could explore even more different lives. Slowly, the idea of an escape began to take shape. I dismissed it: it was too much to hope for. Being let into a secret by one of my masters, a secret the other one was desperate to know, was exhilarating enough. I moved closer to the die.

'It's said that they contain the souls of five princes who possess absolute knowledge,' Fundi went on. 'Five princes from five different parts of the world, all on a quest for transcendence. They don't know each other, but every seven years, fate brings them together in one place and presents them with a choice: to stay apart, and thus leave their knowledge scattered across the earth, or to unite, and offer all the knowledge they possess to the whole of humanity.'

He turned to me.

'Why,' I asked, 'Wouldn't they give all their knowledge to humanity?'

He smiled and opened a *mraha* board. It was a game he'd

confiscated from some young people who were neglecting their prayers. The board had two surfaces, each with five pairs of holes. Some nutmeg seeds were arranged on it in groups of three. He took five of the seeds and placed them in a circle on the desk.

'As long as they remain separate, knowledge is divided between different peoples. Each people suspects that its own knowledge is part of a larger whole, but it also knows that the rest of the knowledge lies elsewhere. To achieve the ultimate knowledge, humans are forced to work together, even if that means they sometimes fight.'

He stretched out his long, gnarled fingers and gathered the seeds from the table.

'Now, let's imagine that all knowledge is accessible, but in only one place on earth. Don't you think all the peoples would want that place for themselves? There would be nothing left to search for. And when there's nothing left to search for, there's no more reason to collaborate. Give everything to humanity, and it will cease to exist.'

A cruel question came to my mind. What about the peoples with no territory at all, like my own?

Fundi placed the die in my hand. On four of its faces, a letter was engraved.

Hâ, tâ, tâ, yâ. Together, the letters formed a word: *Hutti.*

If Fundi knew that I knew, he didn't betray it. I struggled to maintain my attentive expression and conceal my surprise.

'Isolated from the others, each people has a chance to understand the world for itself,' he said, guessing at my question. 'To ensure this, the dice mustn't be allowed to fall into the wrong hands. Hands like those of my wife.'

He was already heading back across the room. He stopped in front of another lectern, wider than the one at the entrance. A book was open on it. As he spoke, he began to leaf through it.

'It's not your disobedience that upsets me. It's what my wife made you do.'

I looked up at him.

'She used your naivety,' he continued, his eyes fixed on the book. 'She used you to travel through time.'

'So you…'

'Yes. I know you've travelled into other lives.'

'But, Fundi, what is it about me that meant she could use me?'

'It takes two to make these journeys. And you…'

His sentence hung suspended, its completion held back by an invisible hand.

When he spoke again, he changed the subject. I was too intimidated to ask him what he'd been about to say. There was another question that was easier to ask.

'Master… how did you know about our trip?'

He turned to me, fire in his eyes. Then I noticed something that made my breath catch: there was a bald patch in his beard, on his left cheek. A small, smooth circle of skin, like the remnant of a scar. It caught the light.

I recognised my cellmate.

He stood motionless in front of me, his gaze riveted to mine.

You're not from here. Not from here at all.

'Yes, it was me,' he answered my silent question. 'Now, listen.'

His words buzzed inside my head. The room began to spin around me.

'You see,' Fundi continued, 'Time is sacred. It is a grave sin to want to cross it for personal reasons. She should never have dragged you into this. But now the damage has been done…'

He stopped on a page of the book, marked it with his finger and brought the book to his desk. He turned it towards me, so I could see the cover.

In the centre of a rectangle of interlocking rhombuses, two words had been written by hand: رفـعج ملع

Ilm Jafr. 'The knowledge of the invisible.'

It was the first time I'd seen another book as richly decorated as the Qur'an. Fundi opened it again and continued to leaf through it as he talked to me. The sun's rays, filtered by the wooden shutters, produced stripes of light and shadow.

'Every message hides another message. Every letter has something else to tell us, beyond what it seems to say. That's what the prophets and the messengers were trying to explain. What's the prayer I ask you to read when you master a new chapter of the Qur'an?

'*Open for me all the secrets of what I have read by your grace…*'

'*Open my mind through your wisdom… and so remind me of what I've forgotten*.'

He'd finished the prayer for me. I thought I understood what he meant.

'Fundi, does this book…?'

'Contain the key to understanding the *true* message of the holy books? The hidden truth that we all know but have forgotten? Yes. I said the holy *books*, not just the Qur'an, because all the holy books have a message to deliver, a message that's hidden behind another, waiting to be discovered.'

'But, Fundi, why hide one message behind another instead of delivering it directly?'

I thought he'd show me the book again and explain. Instead, he began to pace from one side of the room to the other. I looked at the book, which seemed poised to snap shut like an oyster if anyone came near it. I itched to pick it up and leaf through it, to inhale the scent of its pages.

'The Torah, the Gospels, the Psalms, and the books that preceded them that we know nothing about, were all altered by the powers that be. Their message is still there, but it's been obscured by these alterations.'

'What about the Qur'an?'

'Our master Mohammed formally forbade us from touching a single letter of the Qur'an. And since he too had become one of the powerful, naturally people listened to him. They got round it though, by inventing new interpretations of the verses. We memorise these, swallow them whole, without understanding their true meaning. So we seek out people who claim to have understanding. They chew on the letters and the words, adding their saliva and their juices, before spitting them back into our mouths, entirely altered.'

'They make the book say whatever suits them,' was how Halima had put it.

Fundi paused then, for what seemed like an eternity. Outside, the sun was fading. I wondered which chores Olympe would leave for me to do. Dinner? The *fundi's* laundry?

'This book,' Fundi continued, 'Is a guardian. It contains the key to the real meaning of the verses. But to have the right to read it, you have to prove yourself worthy of it.'

'I'd like to be worthy of it, Fundi.'

He gave a little laugh. 'Ah, why so greedy?'

'It's not greed, Fundi. I've never been worthy of anything. Without your kindness, I'd be someone else's slave today, cleaning his toilet, bearing his offspring. It's really you I want to be worthy of.'

Immediately, I regretted my words. What if he asked me again to stop talking to Halima?

'I trained you badly, my girl,' he joked. 'But you're right. I think perhaps you are worthy of it. But there's something I need to make sure of first.'

He leaned towards me and searched my eyes. I had spoken truthfully. Fundi had married my sweet Halima and broken Tamu's heart in the process, but I was incapable of hating him.

Reading once again from the open book that was my mind, Fundi said, 'She promised to find her, didn't she?'

'Who, Fundi?'

'Your mother. Halima promised to help you find Tamu. That's why you joined in with her schemes. Isn't it?'

I lowered my eyes.

'Did you see Tamu? Did Halima keep her promise? In all the lives you've visited, has she mentioned your mother once?'

'N… no, Fundi. She… she hasn't.'

I had to admit it was true. Halima had not helped me to find Tamu. But she also hadn't rejected me when she found out about the strange fire that burned inside me. She'd shown me that inconceivable things were happening in her body too.

I was brooding over the extent of my grievance towards her when Fundi pressed home his point.

'She used you. She used your grief, your fear, your despair.'

My heart clenched. Was he right? Why would my *fundi* lie to me? Without him, who was I? He'd given me what Tamu called the key to freedom: knowledge. No *fundi* had ever done that for a slave, in the whole of Itsandra, on the whole of the island. Why would he tell me anything other than the truth, act other than in my best interests? It was Halima who'd abused me; by asking me to look after the die, then dragging me into her schemes.

'Do you remember,' Fundi continued, 'On our last trip, when I told you the word *waw* reminded me of the number six? In Arabic stories, *waw* is the distance that separates us from God. So does it take six days, or six journeys, to reach God? Six days of creation, six days of searching? Be aware that a journey such as those you've made lasts for one day.'

'You mean it doesn't matter how long we spend there?'

'That's right. Here, it only ever amounts to a single day.'

He leafed feverishly through the book, breathing heavily. 'So it would take six trips. Six journeys…'

'Fundi, what do you mean by "to reach God"?'

That was when he finally decided to show me the contents of the book.

We were sitting on another bed with a rope base, in the alcove that separated Fundi's resting place from his study. Curtains decorated with birds separated the two spaces. The alcove was dark: the only window, on the right-hand wall, was closed, and its wooden shutters let in only a thin sliver of light that died by our feet. The rest of the room was bathed in the dim, flickering light of a lantern. Every evening, after the twilight prayer, I'd take that lantern out to re-fill the oil reservoir, replace the burnt-out wick with a clean one, then replace it on the small carved wooden bedside table. Fundi kept his most precious books in the recesses of the wall, away from the curious eyes of all who passed through his study.

The Book of the Knowledge of the Invisible was as thick as the palm of my hand and heavier than ten wet items of clothing.

Its pages smelled of old wood, with a hint of musk. The first page was covered with dark ink that spelled out the names of its successive owners.

'That's my family lineage,' explained Fundi. 'Here's my name: Ahmad, son of Cheikh, son of Tâhir Hassan, son of Tayib Thabit, son of Zain Abidîn—the Friend of the Birds, son of Mohammed— the Night Camel, descendant of Fatima, daughter of the Messenger of Allah.'

His voice trembled at the mention of the prophet, as did the voices of all our teachers whenever their mouths spoke the name. I'd always wondered whether the ghost of the prophet somehow penetrated their bodies as they said it, whether it was a sort of inherited emotion, or whether they really felt moved.

'I know that the Friend of the Birds and the Night Camel are of particular interest to you. I'll tell you their stories. But that's not what we're here for right now. What I want to show you is this.'

He turned the pages and stopped at an image that occupied a double page. Faded with age, its colours were still beautiful.

On the right-hand page was a nude man whose private parts had been erased for the sake of modesty. His arms were lifted. His skin colour was somewhere between beige and brown, his head was bald. He was surrounded by arabesques, the ends of which were held in the beaks of birds. White circles had been painted on three parts of his body: his forehead, his stomach and his feet.

On the left-hand page, the frame was the same, with arabesques and sparrows. The same man appeared here, only this time he was wearing several layers of clothing, in translucent colours, so that each layer was distinguishable beneath the one above it. He wore different hairstyles too, also layered and translucent.

Fundi guessed the question I was asking myself.

'This is your soul, my soul, the soul of each and every one of us,' he said, pointing at the naked man. 'Here,'—he pointed at the page on the left—'Are the different lives of the soul, all the cultures in which it can live, all the families into which it is born and reborn, by the grace of God who causes us to die and be reborn. Whatever life you choose to live when you return, your soul remains the same. It takes with it the lessons of its past lives.'

I couldn't believe what I was hearing. What Fundi was telling me bore no relationship to any of the lessons he'd given me before.

'But, Fundi,' I protested, 'You told us that we only die once, and that to say otherwise was to sin.'

'Yes, you only die once. Once in each lifetime.'

'But if I die an evil king and am reborn as a defenceless child, when do I pay for my crimes?'

'You carry the sins you committed in your previous life into your current life. You would have to atone for them when you grew up. Allah would create a situation in which you were offended by the people you offended. *Al ayn bil ayn*. An eye for an eye, a tooth for a tooth.'

'And the good marks we get for our good deeds?'

'"Good marks"!' He smiled. 'I shouldn't have put it to you like that. I was treating you like children. You don't earn good marks for good deeds. You earn only peace of mind, and perhaps recognition from those you've done good for.'

I looked back at the pictures. The one on the left, with its superimposed layers, gave the impression of being in motion. As the layers of clothing billowed around the body, it seemed to become clearer and brighter, as if it was ridding itself of everything that encumbered it, right down to the colour of its skin. I found myself wishing the same thing: to see my skin disappear bit by bit, until I was no more than a transparent veil, able to move without being seen. A skin that didn't assign me to any side except my own.

I looked up and saw Fundi watching me. I wasn't sure how long he'd been doing so.

'You understand, don't you?' he asked me.

'Yes. I've travelled in one of these costumes, with Halima.'

'Yes, but do you understand the rest?'

His eyes twinkled. He moved his face close to mine, as if wanting to extract something from my head.

'No, Fundi,' I said. He looked at me again, for a long time, then shook his head. 'Well, it doesn't matter. But you should know that I'm searching for the same person you are.'

'Tamu?'

'Tamu.' He sighed.

'Your wife thinks she's been kidnapped.'

He gave a bitter laugh.

'Kidnapped? Why would anyone kidnap a mature woman? They take the young ones, the ones they can still impregnate. Your mother has already lived.'

'So where is she?'

His eyes fell on the picture in the book, then on me. I shuddered.

'So she is there?'

'Yes, my daughter. She's somewhere, at the gates of time. And I'm going to help you find her. I won't lie to you, not like she does.'

I lowered my eyes. I couldn't find it in myself to blame Halima. Nor was I entirely sure whether I could trust Fundi.

He put a hand on my shoulder. Tears coursed down my cheeks.

'I miss her too, my daughter. If I didn't have something I needed to redress in this life, I'd never have married that temperamental girl. I'd have married your mother. My Tamu.'

I cried harder and blew my nose loudly, like a child. Fundi stood beside me until the smell of musk and peppermint cleared my nose. Only a father, only someone who genuinely cared about me, would do that. Fundi was the only one who could help me.

Suddenly, I felt a pain in my chest, right where my breasts had been ripped out. I resisted the urge to press my hands to the place. A question rose to the top of my mind: a terrible question, but one I had to ask.

'Fundi?'

'Yes, my daughter?'

'Did I commit any serious sins in my previous life?'

He withdrew his hand and looked at me. 'Why do you say that?'

'Because in this life, I'm worth nothing.'

He looked into my eyes. His dark eyes shone. They were damp. His eyes were always damp, as if he were perpetually sad.

'It doesn't matter what you were before or what you are now. All that matters is what you do with your life.'

'But I have no power over my life. I don't even have a life. I won't even have any descendants.'

He scanned my face.

'You know about Halima, don't you? About her pregnancy?'

'Yes,' I sighed. A silence followed. I finally broke it.

'There's nothing I can do in this life. I'm no good to anyone. No-one would miss me if I died.'

Fundi stood up, gestured that I should wait for him, and went over to a corner of the room where his *kandus* were arranged in a neat pile. At the bottom of the pile were the coarse cloth *kandus* that men wore when they were young and single. In the middle were the beige linen and silk *kandus* reserved for newly married men. At the top, the *kandus* of a farmer or a master, made of faded, ochre-coloured cotton.

He took a small tin box from a recess. This was where he kept his sacred charcoal. He cut off a piece and came back to me. He lifted the lid of the bucket that sat by my feet, dampened the charcoal before crumbling it slightly, then detached a small amount of the dark wood and drew a few lines from the chapter of the cow on the palm of his hand:

It is He who causes you to die after giving you life,
Then causes you to be reborn,
Then causes you to die.

With the same hand, he drew some water from the bucket and held his palm out to me.

'If you drink this water, you'll return safely to this life and will, I hope, bring our beloved Tamu back with you. But you must travel with no one but me. Otherwise it may cost you dear.'

I looked at his palm, filled with water glistening with tiny black blobs. I thought about what had happened on the beach. Should I tell him about it? I was desperate to share that secret, to lighten the weight of it. But an obscure instinct told me to stay silent.

Again, I wished I could be totally transparent; accountable to no one; no longer required to please in order to survive; no longer…

Those were things I could only know in other lives. And if I could bring Tamu back, it would be worth it.

I brought my face close to Fundi's and closed my eyes. I opened my mouth. The water, warm and bittersweet, slipped down my throat with disconcerting speed.

The boatman is waiting for me on the bank. I'm ready to cross. His cavernous voice reaches me in the half-light.

'Who are you?' he asks in Persian, the language of my ancestors.

'I am Halima, daughter of Nadjat.'

He looks at me again.

'What are you looking for?'

'Someone I've lost. Fadili.'

'You can only come on board if you answer my riddle. Are you ready?'

'I'm ready.'

'To the north, grains of sand. To the south, grains of sand. In the centre, immaculate whiteness. Who am I?'

'The milk.'

The man smiles.

'You may pass.'

I climb into his boat and we sail into nothingness.

*

I know why my father did what he did. He couldn't stand what the soothsayer had said about me when I was a child: that I was worth ten boys; that I would be called to a great destiny; that I would rescue my people. Worst of all, that I would reap glory for centuries to come. Me, a girl. I think that's what made him angry: the idea that it was my name, not his, that would be immortalised. Because once I was married, I would bear my husband's name.

Yes, I have no difficulty understanding why he did what he did to me.

But my mother? How could she have allowed it to happen?

She could have fought him with the means at her disposal: refused to go to his bed, stopped fermenting the milk, grinding the spices and cooking them with rice and mutton for him. Deprived of *plov*, his favourite dish, my father might have agreed to listen to me, allowed me some time. Just enough time to run away.

But no, she obeyed the worthless man. So here I am, galloping across the steppe trying to escape a forced marriage.

The first thing I do when I reach my own region is remove my wedding bracelet. I let the cool breeze caress my wrist. My mare keeps up a tireless trot across the Alaï plain. I close my eyes from time to time and inhale the scents of thyme and sea buckthorn. I've just descended a scorched green hill, taking care to avoid crushing the sacred medicinal plants, when hunger forces me to stop in front of a Siversky apple tree, the only one of its kind, surrounded by pistachio trees. A small ditch runs between the trees to irrigate their roots. I sit down next to the ditch and open my bag, already looking forward to sinking my teeth into an apple, when I hear a sound that could be the wheels of a cart.

I jump up and conceal myself amongst the trees. It might be my husband pursuing me; though I'd be amazed if he guessed the circuitous route I've taken to get home.

It's not him. The cart is pulled by two Karabair horses moving at walking pace, and is followed by a procession of at least ten men. On the cart lies a body draped in white. It's a funeral cart. I whisper a prayer for the dead, whoever they may be. Then, suddenly, I see the body move. It sits up on the bed of the cart, making me jump. Two men detach themselves from the procession and take the body by the arms, lowering it back down. They don't do it gently; they seem angry. The part of the white cloth that's covering the head slips down over the shoulders, revealing long black hair. I get a glimpse of the face: it's a woman.

Now I understand what's going on. Something inside me crumbles like a clod of dry earth. This woman has been accused of adultery. The men have brought her out here to stone her.

They lead her to a post I hadn't noticed before, directly opposite the pistachio tree I'm hiding behind. They tie her to it so that she's facing me. She looks up; I think she must have seen me, but then her eyes start to wander from right to left, and I get the sense she isn't perceiving much. Her vision must be blurred from the blows she's already received, to which her swollen face attests.

In spite of this, I can tell that she's beautiful.

The men step back and form a semi-circle in front of her. Each one picks up a stone; some spend a little time searching for one big enough to fill the palm of their hand.

I'm trembling, both for the woman and for myself. I'm burning to step out of my hiding place and shout at them to stop, to tell them this is not how the prophet said women should be treated, that there's nothing Muslim about this, regardless of whether or not they strike the ground with their foreheads five times a day or starve themselves during the month of Ramadan.

I'm outnumbered, though. To show myself would be to risk being tied to the post alongside the young woman, to die with her under a hail of stones. Witness or heroine? I've had to make that choice in every one of my lives. When I retrace my incarnations in search of one of the five sacred dice, I'm always faced with the same choice, and I never know which path to take. Hardie would know what to do. When she woke up in the skin of the Bedouin, she knew how to talk to the man who thought he was the master of his wife. What would Hardie do in this situation? What would she say? Would she come out of hiding and risk her life? I have no doubt that she would. But what's the use of a sacrifice like that if it's buried in the depths of a desert for eternity?

Suddenly, the men all raise their arms in unison. My

breath catches in my throat as they prepare to launch their projectiles. The woman stills her features, as if to preserve a semblance of dignity in the face of the vilest human cruelty. Her eyes meet mine. I shudder, terrified my mare will choose this moment to snort or whinny.

Then another group of men appears. These ones are mounted on beautifully-ornamented horses. They wear thick fur cloaks and hats, and their bearing is proud and haughty. One of them, undoubtedly the leader, sits astride a horse even more sumptuously-adorned than the rest: it has a saddle upholstered with velvet, a bridle studded with red and green gemstones, soft leather reins. The man's cloak is wrapped across his chest and tied at the waist with a plaited belt. At the sight of him, the men with the stones freeze, their hands trembling.

'What are you doing?' thunders the newcomer.

The men bow their heads.

'Our respects, *begim*. We are preparing to punish this adulteress, according to sharia law.'

'Do you have proof of her crime?'

'Yes, *begim*. She was seen by four witnesses, two women and two men.'

'Don't our imams say that two women count as one man? So there are three witnesses, not four,' retorts the prince, a touch of mischief in his voice. 'Is there anyone here to argue her innocence?'

'Me, Prince!'

I'm the one who says this. If I'm lucky, this prince will protect me. I can pretend to be the woman's sister, or a neighbour, and try to save her—and myself.

The prince turns towards me. The rest of the men do the same. They stare at me in amazement.

'I saw her, Prince, on the day they say she committed the crime. She was at the river with me, washing her clothes. But someone in her clan wants to harm her. I followed the procession in secret to try and stop these men from stoning her to death.'

I walk up to the prince, ignoring the bewildered look on his face. I hold his gaze. He dismounts and approaches me. He's so close I can smell his scent: incense, cinnamon and jasmine oil. I look into his eyes and my breath catches. They're so piercing, so deep, and yet so melancholy. Could it be him? He returns my gaze, seemingly wondering where he's seen me before.

'Water... water...'

The poor woman's voice drags us back to the present.

'Give her some water!' the prince cries. Together, we watch in disgust as each of the men hides his canteen inside his coat. I go to my mare and untie my wineskin. It's half full of water. I take it to the woman and hold the neck of it to her mouth. She's so weak I have to dab drops on her lips.

'Now get out of here!' thunders the prince.

'*Begim*, you're making a grave mistake before Allah,' mutters the man who picked up the largest stone.

'You're the ones driving people away from Allah with your murderous laws!' the prince shouts. 'Obey your prince and get out of here, or I'll refer you to the Caliph!'

The men scatter, taking their cart with them. I untie

the woman. The prince offers to take her home. She accepts. He turns to me and asks, 'What is the name of she who saves the destitute? What is your name, brave woman?'

'Kurmanjan,' I say.

'Kurmanjan… I'll see you soon, Kurmanjan.'

*

My father is ill. He refuses to drink the warm water I prepare for him to ease his digestion. In his eyes, I'm a traitor. Three moons have now passed since I left my husband. For several days afterwards, rumour had it he was coming after me. My mother supports me, but says she can't defend me: I'll have to manage this situation on my own.

Last night, I gave the tribe's messenger a letter embroidered on cloth. In it, I proposed to the prince that he marry me. I know custom forbids a woman from asking a man to marry her, but I know the prince is the man I'm looking for. He is Fadili, Halima's husband; he will be Ali Datka, Kurmanjan's husband. Together we'll reclaim the destiny that's been stolen from us. I know he has one of the die, but I want to live with him, and if I take the die from him, I'll lose him.

The prince arrives to ask for my hand. That same night, my husband arrives. They dismount their horses and stand face to face. They don't recognise each other, but I recognise each of them: the man I love and the man who covets me.

Today, the latter holds no power. He's forced to let me go with the prince. And he doesn't know where the sacred die is. He and my unworthy father watch me leave, happy and free, at the side of my *begim*.

*

For five moons, my prince and I make perfect love. There's not a single cloud on the horizon. If I let myself get too caught up in this joy, I'll end up forgetting what brought me here in the first place. The sacred dice are starting to seem less important to me. Am I not with the man I love? Haven't I found my Fadili, my *begim*? Nothing else matters.

One night, my prince is woken by the cry of an eagle. I recognise the cry; it's that of the hunter eagle. Every man in our clan has one. This one is not from here, which means it must be carrying a message of the utmost importance tied around one of its talons. In an instant, my husband is awake, dressed and standing at the entrance to our yurt.

One of his men hands him the letter. I approach him and read it over his shoulder. An ominous message is embroidered on the cloth: the soothsayer Rustam, my husband's wise father, has been murdered.

*

The entire province of Alaï has been in mourning for three days. My prince has gone to bury his father.

But my pain is not over yet. On the day my husband is due to return, a messenger comes running with a letter in his hand. It's been hastily embroidered on a thin cotton square; a falcon has carried it from the plains of Osh.

I look at the messenger, then unfold the cloth. Anxiety swells up inside me, like a water lily opening at the bottom of a river.

I sense something is wrong, try to push away the foreboding, but it grips my chest with iron clutches.

Slowly, I read the letter.

My worst fear has been realised. My husband, my prince, my *begim*, has been killed outside the mosque where he always stops on his travels.

I read and reread the lines that inform me of my husband's death. I always suspected he would die like this, killed by fanatics or brigands, because he's always the same, every time I meet him: uncompromising, honest, scrupulous, swift to come to the aid of the oppressed. He'll have stood between two enemy groups to defend some poor, persecuted man, and paid for it with his life.

My grief is immense, so intense that it takes me a moment before I can read the rest of the message. There are three sentences left, stitched clumsily on the cloth by whoever discovered my husband's body: 'We were unable to recover the corpse of the Prince of Alaï for several hours, because a tigress approached it. She did not eat it, as we'd feared, but sniffed it, stuffed her snout between the folds of his coat, then left, carrying a small object in her mouth.'

My heart seems to stop beating for a moment. An object in her mouth… despite the fact that my heart is breaking, I tell myself the time has come.

As night falls, I leave the yurt without my veil or headdress, so as to go unnoticed. I tie up my hair and put my husband's fur hat on my head.

I walk to the horse paddock. My old travelling companion, my mare Ghazal, comes to me immediately: she was already awake when I arrived; it was her turn to stand guard. I wake up her eldest son, sleeping next to her, so he can take over watching the herd. Then I climb into the saddle and we set off across the steppe.

We reach the craggy mountains at the darkest hour of the night.

*

There's no moon: the darkness has swallowed everything. Only a handful of stars deign to cast me a discreet glance.

I tighten my legs around Ghazal and give a sharp tug on her reins. She understands and stops immediately. I dismount and let her forage for food among the plants that have taken up residence between the rocks.

How I envy those plants, so steadfast in the face of adversity, so unperturbed by the natural barriers that stand in their way. Wherever they find a chink of sunlight, they occupy the space, spreading without suffocating, thinning without breaking, until their leaves burst forth into the open air. They're confident in the abundance of this air, this sun, certain they'll reach their destination, even if they have to twist and contort themselves between the stones.

At last, I see the cave, a shining edifice in the deep black of the night. There's a rustling sound close to me. At the entrance to the cave, the odours of grass, skin and blood assault my nostrils.

She's there. The tigress.

Her huge, velvety paws are warming the ground beneath my feet. I can't see them yet, but I can hear their soft, brushing sound as she walks.

I reach my arm out from inside my fur coat, delivering it to the cool wind, and wait. First I feel only the lightest touch, then a whole cheek is rubbing against my palm. I let my fingers run through the thick fur down to her flank.

My throat closes up and tears spring from my eyes. I can barely make a sound. 'Hardie! How did you get here?'

She turns to me and makes a purring sound. I lose myself in her eyes; so green, so bright. I answer my own question: the only person apart from myself who's capable of bringing her into a past life is Fundi. Anxiety seizes me. If she's come without me, and if this is the die that she plucked from Fadili's clothes, how did she know where to find it?

'Hardie, have you told anyone else about our travels?'

She looks up at me for a moment, then shakes her head. I'm about to question her again, but she moves slowly away. That's when I see the two flaming yellow balls of fur behind her.

Her little ones!

'Hardie, you have children!'

My heart explodes with joy for her, and I forget my current preoccupations for a moment. She looks so happy!

She turns to her babies, picks them up in her mouth, and brings them to me so I can stroke them. They close their eyes and nuzzle against me. Hardie has little ones to love; creatures that will not judge her, that will expect her only to be happy and to love them more than she loves herself. I can feel Hardie's love for her offspring inside me, and I rejoice.

'Oh, Hardie, I had to find happiness with my Fadili for you to find it too. We're so intertwined that the joy of one of us leads to the joy of the other!'

*

I long to stay here with her, but I must go back. Hardie doesn't want me to. She doesn't understand. She paces back and forth in the cave, her mouth open, her face bruised.

'I'm sorry, Hardie. I have to go home. We both have

to go home. To stay here would be to disrupt the flow of time. We've already upset it enough as it is.'

She glares at me. She's telling me she knows I used her.

'I didn't use you, Hardie. I… you'll understand one day, I promise. I'll explain it to you. But now we have to get back. Trust me, I beg you.'

She looks at her cubs, curled up asleep against a stone. There's such gentleness in her eyes, so much tenderness I could weep. How can I do this to her? Why should I? If only I had a choice! If only everything wasn't already written.

She stares at me intently. Her face takes on the expression that precedes an attack. Her fangs are slightly bared, throwing white sparks into the darkness of the cave.

'Do you want to kill me?' I ask her. 'Fine, then kill me! But you'll regret it: it will change your destiny in all your other lives!'

She pulls her shoulders up to her ears, then leaps. In two bounds, she's on top of me. We're tangled together on the ground, like in the other life, on our night of love. Her breath is thick, thicker than human breath. Her paws are hot on my shoulders. I inhale deeply, then place my already-damp hands on her. The heat from her fur immediately dissipates with a loud 'shhh' sound. She pulls away, stunned. I stand up, triumphant.

'Water against fire, Hardie. I told you it would be dangerous. Kill me and I'll kill you. Both of us will be reduced to water vapour. Your babies will be motherless.

I can't help defending myself against you; it's in my soul. Water has defended itself against fire since the dawn of time. Lava dies in the sea, water evaporates on contact with it. That is our destiny, and it's a heavy one to bear. That's why I want to unite the dice. To free ourselves from our cursed lives. So you can find Tamu, so I can find my Fadili, so the curse that's made us what we are can be lifted.'

She lowers her muzzle. Her fangs disappear behind her lips. She kisses each of her cubs, then moves towards me. She opens her mouth so I can take the die. My heart nearly breaks at the sight of the family I'm separating. But I have no choice.

The die is in my hand. The letters, sculpted in relief, have been painted with henna. I put my hand on Hardie's back, close my eyes and whisper the name of each cube, until I get to this one.

'*Hawwaz.*'

HUTTI

حُوطي

The fog that blinds me is chased away by the flickering light of a lantern. I scan all around, searching for my babies. Soon I'll have to go and find food. Strange, I can't hear their breathing. But I can hear the whisper of the wind at the entrance to the cave.

I listen more carefully: it's not the wind whispering, but a breath; a human breath, so powerful it seems to envelop me completely. I feel the grip of this human tightening around me. My mouth begins to spit a bitter, black liquid onto a surface of pressed plant fibres.

It takes me a few moments to understand. I am a feather. Someone is using me to write. My life as a tigress is a past life; one I was plunged back into merely to retrieve a die. I had children in that life, and I miss them horribly. I liked the animal existence. And now… I search for memories of my current life. They flash through my mind: I was a proud, majestic bird; a peacock. Then I was gutted, skewered and stripped bare.

My soul and my spirit have survived in the stem of this feather.

I spit out another tear of ink, for my children, now lost.

*

I love to hear the sound of rain on stone. But my master prefers to make me run along paper. He scribbles frantically, pressing my point into the tough, even grain, squeezing me between his fingers as he traces the downward-curving letters. He likes to thicken the line along the curve, leave it thinner at the end. My favourite part is when he places the dots above or below the letters.

There are ten letters with dots in our alphabet. In the old days, before they invented the dots, the letters had to express several sounds at the same time. The tongue had no trouble manipulating the sounds to suit the words, but the feathers and reed pens became confused when translating them into script: should they write *fâ*, *qâf*, *tâ* or *bâ*? They all sounded so much alike.

One day, the wife of a calligrapher suggested the idea of distinguishing these words using dots. All we had to do was let a single drop of ink run along our hollow point; gently, slowly, until it landed delicately on the paper, and we had a different letter.

I fell in love with those dots. I savour the sensation of the ink trickling down my wall, and the soft, velvety sound as it meets the paper. I prefer this feeling to that of my nib scratching across the paper fibres, or of the master's fingers clutching my stem.

I feel his steady breath lifting my filaments. His beard sometimes gets tangled in them, when he uses me to stroke it as he's pondering something. He's concentrating too hard to notice the fly that's circling me. A drop of rain lands on me, blown by the wind.

My master is a well-known scholar in his home town: when he was still a student, he single-handedly challenged several centuries of Muslim science and jurisdiction. In those days, women had no rights at all; they lived their lives oblivious to the prerogatives that had been granted them by the prophet. They suffered their fate as wives in silence, accepted as necessary the departure of their sons for the houses of Qur'anic masters, and prepared their daughters for a fate like their own.

My master found this unjust. He also questioned other precepts he believed had been added to the religion. After several years of teaching and living from favours granted by the *vizier* of his city, he left his country, confused and perplexed, to seek God in the desert and in the vaults of distant mosques. I've accompanied him on his journey, offering him my tip every evening, serving as a receptacle for his intimate thoughts. My companions, the sheets of paper he brought with him, shiver slightly with pain at my touch. I'm sorry to hurt them, but there's nothing I can do: I can hardly break myself to stop their torture. The master wouldn't stop writing in any case. So I make sure I press on them as gently as possible, whispering an apology as I do so.

An apology isn't enough, though. You have to make amends.

I part my filaments so the raindrop will rest there for as long as possible, let them bend beneath its weight. Then I whisper to the fly to approach as quietly as possible, so the beating of its wings won't assault my master's ears. It dances on the wind until it reaches me, and lands close to the raindrop. A sudden movement lifts me; it's the master, who's noticed the fly's presence. His half-closed eyes, weary from sleep deprivation, linger on the insect. His drawl breaks the silence of the night.

'I'm tired of you. You and your friends are always pestering me while I'm trying to think.'

I'm afraid he'll scare the fly away, cause me to fail in my mission. An idea comes to me: if I pull my filaments apart slowly enough, perhaps I can make the drop of water glow in the candlelight. I must try. It's important to try.

The slightest movement from me, imperceptible to human eyes, and the drop begins to glow.

His eyes, too, light up.

'Oh, that's it,' he murmurs, 'You're thirsty. Well, drink up. I could do with a minute to rest my mind.'

The fly swallows the whole drop. When it finally flies away, its thirst quenched, I let the ink flow again.

*

A year has passed since the night the fly visited us. My master lies in a grave whose location is known only to his brother, who buried him. His work, The *Revival of the Sciences of Religion*, is taught in his home town and throughout Persia. They say that one day the whole world will know his name, because during his lifetime he served the cause of God like no one before him.

I rest in his brother's chest, along with his rosary and turban. The brother lives alone, in a modest house he's refused to leave, despite the pleas of the governor, who wanted to give him a larger, more comfortable home as a tribute to the master.

I'm just about to fall asleep when there's a knock at the

gate. The brother gets up from where he was sitting on the low stone wall and goes to open it. Through the gaps in the wood of the trunk, I see the shape of an old man, no doubt one of the brother's dervish friends. After the customary greetings and cup of tea, the old man reveals the reason for his visit. Since I'm no longer active, I listen to conversations to pass the time.

'Brother, I saw the master in a dream. He was bathed in light and bliss.'

'Praise be to God. Did he tell you what it was that gained him entry to heaven?'

'I asked him, and it was his answer that sent me to your house, because I knew you had to hear it.'

'I'm listening.'

'I said to him, "With all the impressive works you've written, everything you've done for the love of God, it doesn't surprise me that He should shower you with His blessings." He laughed, and replied, "Think again, my friend. I owe all my happiness to a fly."'

If I had a body, I'd use it to laugh. As a feather, though, I can still be ecstatic: the master has just offered his greatest lesson of all to his brother and to me: *The means we use to achieve our ends are God's ends. The ends we pursue are His means to His ends. His want is not that we achieve our ends.*

What matters to God is the means we use: as water patiently polishes rock, every step we take towards our goal smooths our soul, until it is exactly the right shape for fulfilment.

*

I was listening to the voice of Fundi Ahmad reading from the Qur'an. I'd just returned to my existence… as a slave. I'd been a peacock feather in the hands of some sort of spiritual master; a man who said he owed his happiness to a fly and a drop of water, and my own meagre intervention.

My heart suddenly raced, and before I could control my movements, I was scanning the room again, searching for my little ones. I knew I was no longer a tiger, but I could think of nothing but finding them and seeking a new home for us. I tugged at the sheets, lifted the pillow and the laundry basket, but there was nothing but the smell of burnt candlewick, coconut oil and musk; only the moonbeams piercing the darkness. My heart felt so empty it was like a hollow crater. Where were my dear little ones? Had their existence just been a dream? The silkiness of their fur; its golden accents; their earthy taste; the warmth of their skin under my rasping tongue; their supple hides between my teeth; their soft snouts pressed against mine; their mouths grasping to suckle. My dearest little ones.

Fundi had finished his oration. He stood up, came over to me and smiled.

'You're awake, my child.'

A strange sensation seized me. I wanted both to throw myself into his arms and to tear out his throat. I recognised him; he was my master.

'So, tell me. What did you see? Who were you?'

But I still couldn't stop looking around for my disappeared cubs.

*

'Then what happened?'

Fundi was becoming impatient with me. He'd barely listened to my lament. All he wanted was the die.

'Did you find anything?'

'No,' I replied casually.

There was a short silence. I stared determinedly at the floor, afraid to meet his inquisitive gaze. He would have seen the duplicity in mine. I closed my eyes and saw my little ones. I sighed, trying to dislodge the plug of sadness in my throat.

'You felt freer in the tiger's skin, didn't you?' Fundi asked gently.

'I felt loved. I had two cubs. They loved me. Like no one has ever loved me before. Without expecting anything, without demanding anything. I was just loved. I'll never feel anything like that again.'

That was what I wanted to say to him. Instead, I burst into tears.

Fundi looked at me for a long time. Finally he took me in his arms.

'Go and rest, my child. We'll go back in two days. Go and rest now.'

I picked up my sandals and headed barefoot for the door. I'd felt weak when he said we would go back.

I'd also felt a familiar, unpleasant feeling. The feeling of being an accessory, a means to an end, a vulgar object. The feeling of being used.

The feeling was so strong that fire shot through my veins. I looked at my hands, my arms; they were streaked with glowing lines. I was frightened. Was I about to explode right there, combust from the inside out? I had to do something about this fire in me; I had to get rid of it.

I needed to get to the beach, to the rocks I could shatter in my hands. I ran out of the house, past the guards at the entrance who looked at me and shook their heads, no doubt thinking, 'That scatterbrain's left something on the hearth again.' I crossed the *baraza* and made my way down the gravel road in the orange light of dusk, until I got to the stone steps that ended in the white sand. I looked around: there was no one bathing, or repairing a *pirogue*, no one washing clothes in the water. I was alone with the stones and my fire.

The sun had disappeared below the horizon, but the sand still held its warmth. Above my head, Mawu projected its white light to guide the fishermen home. But they'd still be a long way off: I had time.

I found a stone hidden behind a large, jagged rock. I picked it up. As soon as my hands touched it, its surface warmed and it began to glow. I thought about Fundi saying, 'We'll go back in two days.' If I'd belonged to the class of women who were free, I'd have screamed at him 'What do you take me for?' But he only took me for what I was—a slave he'd taken under his wing, so no one could abuse me.

No, I thought; it was only thanks to myself, to my own strength, that no one dared abuse me. I didn't let them, because I was Hardie. Also, a quieter voice in my head reminded me, because I'd already been flayed alive, and in the eyes of men I wasn't really a woman.

My hands rested on the piece of rock. My veins were filled with burning blood. Glowing lines appeared on my forearms. My fingers closed over the rock. Immediately, it melted. I shut my eyes and savoured the sensation of molten lava in my hands. I could have died then and I wouldn't have cared: better to die than to live this life in vain. I could give myself over to the fire that emanated from me.

Moments passed that felt like eternities. I told myself that the hell we were promised wasn't so terrifying after all. When I opened my eyes, it was pitch black. I walked to the shoreline.

I heard footsteps coming towards me, but I could make nothing out.

'Hardie!'

Olympe was calling to me from the frangipani trees that lined the beach. I straightened up and took in a deep breath, to swallow down all the fire I'd allowed to escape.

Olympe found me prostrate on the sand.

'What are you doing, Hardie?'

'Nothing,' I said, trying to sound calm. 'I'm resting. What's wrong?'

'You'd better come back. Halima isn't feeling well. She wants to see you.'

*

Halima was lying on her *adas*, breathing as heavily as a turtle about to lay its eggs. Olympe placed a bottle of castor oil on the table next to the bed, then slipped away.

'Your friend loves you very much,' began Halima. 'She keeps our meetings a secret, and perhaps knows more than we think she does. And she's always so kind.'

'Yes. Olympe is like a sister to me. The others too, but… Olympe and I would die for each other. My other friends like me, but they wouldn't do that. And I don't see them so much any more.'

'I'd love to have a friendship like that. I mean, a free friendship.'

She gave me a guilty look. I knew she was thinking about Fadili.

'What you and I share is more than friendship,' she said, perhaps to appease my jealousy. 'We've been friends for so long. But in all our lives, I haven't been there for you as much as you've been there for me.'

I said nothing. What could I say? I was a prisoner of her love. I was unable to abandon her to her fate. She was using me, but that didn't stop me loving her.

'We've got two more places to look and then it will be over. The last two dice will be in one of those two places. I'm going to need you, Hardie. I'm going to need your gift. I know you're exhausted; I am too, but as long as you still haven't found what you're looking for, you mustn't give in to fatigue.'

I remained silent. I itched to tell her about Fundi's die, but I resisted.

She took my hand and placed it on her stomach. I thought I felt a small tremor. Instinctively, I closed my eyes. The image of my cubs appeared again. How lucky she was to be having a child. When I opened my eyes, I saw a mixture of sadness and pity in her gaze.

After a moment's silence, she said simply, 'I'll call him Mustafâ.'

'And if it's a girl?'

'It's a boy. I dreamed it.'

'Mustafâ.'

I'd repeated the name in spite of myself, like an invocation.

*

Halima touched the wall of her room and it liquefied into a waterfall, gushing from ceiling to floor, then rising and crashing down again, in an infinite circle. We made our way to her observatory. On the floor was the rectangle of sand on which she traced her calculations, then immediately erased them. I'd watched her drawing these symbols over and over with her long fingers, which I thought looked thinner than they used to.

I'd begun to enjoy our travels; seeing so many places that were unknown to me, yet welcomed my soul. Halima was with me in a different guise each time, but whoever we were, she always bullied me. Was this love? Watching helplessly as the same careless hand repeatedly took hold of your heart?

I looked at Halima, wondering when she was finally going to explain to me what was going on. Fundi had clarified some of it, but I needed to hear the rest from Halima.

'You want to ask me something, don't you?' she said, without lifting her head from the sand. Her question felt like a drop of rain on a hot day.

'Yes,' I replied immediately. I sat down beside her on the ground. 'What are these places you take me to? And how is it we can have someone else's body and face?'

She smiled sadly.

'Poor Hardie. You're so used to following without questioning. It must cost you a lot to ask. The places we visit belong to lives we've already lived. The faces and bodies are those we inhabited in those lives.'

'I know that,' I replied. But I want to know if…'

'If?'

'Well, if, one day, I'll find you again. I mean for good. If one day, in one lifetime, we'll live together.'

'But we do live together,' she said, smiling.

'Yes, but…'

'We're hiding, you mean? And you'd like it if one day we could love each other in broad daylight?'

I gulped, like a child whose secret fantasy had been uncovered.

Halima placed her hand on mine. 'Perhaps the only way to find out is to go and look. But let's do it quickly, before Fundi gets home. Sometimes he doesn't stay the night with his second wife. We absolutely must get the two dice before he comes back.'

'Why?'

'Because it's all he thinks about. His stupid power of wisdom. Your master wants the dice to impress his fellow men, to improve his image.'

'He wants people like him and me to be seen as equal to people like you.'

It had escaped my lips before I could stop it. In my heart, Halima and Fundi were battling for dominance. She changed the subject.

'Did you know that Fundi is the wind?'

'The wind?'

She grabbed a pebble and began to sketch rapidly on the sand.

'Fundi is the wind, I'm the water, you're the fire. Haven't you noticed that whenever he sits down beside you under the mango tree, you feel a gentle breeze?'

I nodded in disbelief. It was true: Fundi's arrival was always announced by the wind.

'I'll explain the rest of it later, I promise. I'll tell you everything. I'm sorry about your little ones. But you'll find that feeling again, if you come with me.'

I closed my eyes, smelled my babies' fur in my nostrils. I forgot the incongruity of Halima's promise. The smell of damp cotton, dry grass and earth; the smell of love, peace, freedom. My dear little ones.

'Tell me, Hardie,' said Halima, 'If you found yourself back in the life of a mother, would you want to stay there?'

'Yes,' I answered without hesitation. 'It's strange, but it was as if, by loving my little ones, I found a part of Tamu again. I could feel her presence. And the need to be with her was lessened by the happiness of being with my little ones.'

Halima looked at me for a long moment, shook her head, then presented a determined smile.

'I wish so much that I could feel that way about this one in my belly. You're luckier than I am, Hardie. You have a heart made for happiness. You will be happy. I don't know how, but you will.'

She drew some numbers in the sand and considered them carefully, as if she thought they might speak to her. Then she swept her hand over them to erase them.

'I don't want Fundi finding them. I can't tell you everything here,' she whispered, looking around her. 'We're not safe. Quick, give me your hand. He's coming.'

I looked towards the door, my heart hammering. What would I do if Fundi caught us here?

I didn't have time to find out. Halima was already pulling me by the hand. In a voice that was trembling but firm, she spoke the names of the dice: '*Sa'fas, Qarshat, Hawwaz, Hutti...*'

One by one, she dropped the smooth stones on to the sand.

'*Abjad.*'

*

The boatman waits, impassive. In the still of the night, his voice sounds like a millstone turning: our ears are like grains of rice crushed by its movement.

'Who are you?' he asks me in Tamu's language.

'I am Hardie, daughter of Tamu.'

He looks at me again.

'What are you looking for?'

'Someone I've lost,' I answer. 'Tamu.'

'You're lying.'

I turn to Halima, disconcerted. She approaches and answers briskly, 'We've each come to look for someone we've lost. Fadili, my husband, and Tamu, her mother.'

The man's eyes move from Halima to me. He stares at us for a long moment, suspicious. Then he takes a deep breath.

'You can only get on board if you answer my riddle. Are

you ready?'

'Yes,' says Halima.

'*Sha-kutru-uhum.*'

Halima hesitates. Her eyes are telling me she doesn't know the answer. I jump in and say, 'Tripping over a stone!'

The man looks at us again. Distrust lingers in his eyes. Then the line across his brow disappears.

'You may pass.'

I climb into the boat, followed by Halima, and we sail into the unknown. I'm not as unsettled as I used to be. Even in front of the old man, I felt less intimidated. I answered his riddle without hesitation, whereas before, fear would have made me doubt myself. Now I've been a wise Bedouin, a ship's captain, a tigress and the pen of a scholar.

I ask Halima, 'Do you know where the last two dice are?'

'My calculations have shown that they're either in Hellada or Tsumkwe.'

I repeat the words to myself, trying to stifle the shameful voice that's starting to speak up inside me. I've never heard those names before, yet they seem to hold so much promise.

'Hellada is home to beings who master fire, air and water. Tsumkwe is the land of warriors who speak to the stars. Long ago, the two countries were one. But a tragic event separated them. The trace of their shared past is a stone that's found in both places.'

'What was this event?'

I'm no longer content to listen and say nothing. I want to know and understand everything. I want Halima to see me as an equal. She looks at me, sensing the new tension between us.

'All right, listen,' she says. 'There are five dice, and there are five elements that govern the universe: fire, air, water, earth, and the harmony between them all. Separately, these elements cause destruction, but if someone were to bring them all together…'

'They'd have the power to fulfil their greatest desires.'

'Sort of,' she continues. 'If someone brought them together, they'd get to fulfil one desire. Not two.'

She doesn't take her eyes off me. Suddenly I understand.

'Why?' I ask. 'Why can we only have one thing?'

'Because men's appetites are insatiable.'

She's right. Before, all I wanted was to find Tamu. Now I want so many other things.

My little ones.

Fundi's acceptance.

Halima's love.

Freedom.

The kind of freedom Captain Miguel had.

I should never have agreed to sail between lives. I've tasted too many possibilities, all too far removed from my original existence. Now my life as a servant, which I always accepted before, has become intolerable. I've experienced the riches of being a mother, being a man, being a wise man, being loved. Why is my present life devoid of such richness? I feel as if I'm suffocating. If the boatman asked me what I was looking for now, I'd probably still say Tamu, but I wouldn't be sure that was the only thing I sought. My heart has expanded so much since my mother disappeared.

'What about you?' I ask Halima,'What will you choose?'

She opens her mouth, but says nothing. She looks away.

'I know what you want,' I say.

'You're precious to me, Hardie.'

'Fundi says the same thing. But both of you are using me.'

She bows her head.

'Only you have the power to free the dice,' she says. 'All you have to do is be there, and they appear. It's as if they're drawn to you.'

'I still don't understand why.'

She looks at me and shakes her head apologetically.

'I don't understand either,' she says.

There's a long silence. We hold each other's gaze. I try to look past her eyes to the secrets she's hiding, but I find nothing. Our masters never give us a complete answer; it's one of the ways they keep us enslaved.

'We've arrived,' says the boatman.

Halima reaches her hand out to me.

'Everything will become clear, Hardie. I promise.'

She thanks the boatman. We step out of the boat and into nothingness.

The sensation of drowning is so strong that when I emerge from my sleep, it's with a gasp as loud as a wave crashing against rocks. I hear voices around me.

I look down at my body, or rather, the sheets that cover it. They're silky, luxurious, unlike anything found on my island, at least not for a girl of my rank. I sit up, and feel a weight between my legs. I lift the sheet and see a man's member, erect like a soldier prepared for attack. The thing alarms me. I let the silk drop back down over this man's penis, which is apparently mine. I notice that fullness again, that influx, the tingling that's like a thousand bees buzzing in a hive inside me. It's extremely pleasant. I look at my hands: they're white. Am I Miguel again? No, I don't feel like him: I'm a man, but not that one. My arms are hairier, rounder, fleshier. Slowly, I get off the bed, looking for a mirror in which to check my new reflection. But the room contains only tables piled high with rolls of parchment—the word 'parchment' pops suddenly into my mind—and machines I don't yet recognise. I realise I'm aching all over: I could do with a bath. Next to my bed, on a bedside table, is a silver basin. I go over to it and try to catch my reflection in the water. A film of dust has settled on the surface. I push it aside with a mechanical gesture—I must be used to doing this—and see myself.

I'm a white-haired old man. My face is hidden behind a full beard and moustache. Two dark eyes smile mischievously at me. I smile back at my reflection. I rather like being in this body that's lived and seems happy with its life, apart from the cold breeze that sweeps through the room. My *ephebe* from the night before has left, offended by my attitude towards him. I remember the violence with which I greeted his request for a final embrace, so busy was I jotting down numbers on my parchment. His beautiful, kohl-rimmed eyes darkened and he dressed hastily, before braving the night to leave. He ignored my warnings about the over-zealous neighbours. No arrests were made during the night, though, so at least I know he arrived home safely.

Such sadness, all the same.

I wash my face with plenty of water. It's almost icy. I like it that way: it invigorates the muscles in my face; it's what keeps me looking so young, despite my advanced years.

I put on my shirt, drape myself in my scarf and prepare to go and meet… who, exactly? I haven't yet recovered this memory. My name in this life is not Hardie but Theon. And I need to get back to…

'Father,' says a crystalline voice, 'You're late, you're supposed to be teaching me cosmogony!'

I remember. My dear daughter, Hypatia. I remember something else: I must go and light the fire. Otherwise the cold will penetrate this house as quickly as the goddess Athena.

Before I can retrace my steps, the door opens and a hand grabs my arm.

'The fire's already lit, Father.'

I turn round and come face to face with a beautiful apparition. This person calling me Father is exquisite.

She gives me a cheeky smile. A smile I'd recognise anywhere.

My beloved.

I stammer an apology and let her lead me through wide corridors, past huge pillars, to a large room. This one is also filled with parchments.

I marvel at my daughter. Her hair, piled up on her head, is burnished with gold where it catches the light filtering through the stained-glass windows. Her face is perfectly symmetrical, her movements graceful as she picks up two parchments and places them on an empty table.

'Father, why are you looking at me like that? Did you have a bad dream?'

'Have I no right to contemplate my work?' I say. 'I'm

only sorry that it's only for my eyes to see, and that no other man seems worthy of admiring it.'

'Father, don't start.'

'Hypatia, I may die before I see my grandchildren!'

'But you will have seen your daughter begin to spread knowledge through the world.'

I smile. She's right: her light is already shining across the region.

I sit down next to her and unroll a parchment. At the top is an inscription in Arabic: '*The legacy of the five princes*.'

'I found this in the library of one-eyed Tiberias,' explains Hypatia. 'He didn't want to give it to me, but I offered him a very good price. It's about a legend told by a people from Abyssinia.'

I nod, looking at the document. There's something familiar about it, but I'm not sure what. I begin to read it aloud.

Five princes, born of the same father but in five different regions, all left their kingdoms one day in search of absolute transcendence.

The eldest, Sa'fas, found himself in a dense pine forest. He walked for a long time, leading his horse by its bridle, until he reached a calm, blue lake.

Sa'fas was captivated by the flowers lining the banks, the grass still bathed in dew, the tree trunks coated in fragrant moss. He sat down on the bank, admiring the reflection of the sky on the surface of the water. The clouds seemed to float on this limpid expanse, and the sky looked green because the blue of the water was so pure.

He longed to drink the water. He dipped in one hand, then the other. Bending over, he brought his lips to his cupped palms. Coolness and sweetness invaded his whole being. He allowed himself to slip, head first, into the water. The lake bore him up in her undulating arms, stripped him of his prince's clothes, and he was hers, naked as the day he was born. He returned joyfully to the shore, then set off swimming again. The prince and the water both revelled in the fluid, magical dance of their encounter. If anyone had been watching, they'd have noticed the movements of Sa'fas gradually begin to blend with those of the rippling lake. They'd have seen the prince's body drift apart, forming into tempestuous tides, as he melted with love into the liquid blue.

But this lake was poisoned. The poison did not destroy the flesh and cause death on the outside; instead it devoured all the integrity, confidence and peace in a person's soul, destroying them from the inside. As soon as he entered the lake, Sa'fas was so blinded by bliss that he allowed himself to be swept away. His spirit leaked out and melted into the shimmering waters. An insatiable desire rose up in him: to regain his human form and sit on the shore again. In place of his spirit, on the distant shore, a wooden cube appeared. On the sides of the cube were etched, in black charcoal, the letters of his name. *Sîn. Aïn. Fâ. Sâd. Sa'fas.* The symbol of water.

The second brother, Qarshat, came from a family of blacksmiths. He journeyed to a place where an underwater volcano had erupted many years earlier, and islands had formed from its solidified lava. He took up residence there to rest after his travels.

One moonless night, he was watching the stars, wondering what they were made of. He suspected they were distant, erupting volcanoes, but had never dared to voice this hypothesis aloud. Volcanoes had always fascinated him. As a child, he'd learned from his teacher that everything that happened in the observable world was the result of some interaction in the higher worlds.

Qarshat was wondering to himself whether the activity of volcanoes in the higher worlds governed the lives of those who lived on earth. Then it happened.

He heard a thud coming from the direction of the neighbouring island, the profile of which stood out in silhouette against the dark sky. Qarshat jumped up to get a better look. Sparks were escaping from the island's peak: the volcano was erupting! Overjoyed, he rushed back to his boat, leaving behind his astrolabe and the trunk containing all his possessions, and headed for the explosion of lava.

An unparalleled spectacle was unfolding before his astonished eyes. A raging stream of viscous, liquid fire was coursing down the dark mountainside. It flowed into the rocks and cleaved them open, spurting from the cracks. What amazed Qarshat most was what happened when the lava met the sea: it seemed to hurl itself into the waves in a movement like that of a man desperate for relief from a hounding heat. Cured of its own fever, it then re-emerged further out, black, bulbous, and still steaming, but now solidified. A tongue of lava came licking towards the prince. In the grip of fascination, Qarshat approached, stood up on his boat, then plunged without hesitation into the water just as the liquid fire reached him.

In the place where he'd been standing a few moments earlier, a wooden die appeared to mark his soul. On its sides was engraved the letters of his first name: *Qaf, Ra, Shîn, Tâ. Qarshat.*

The third prince was called Hawwaz. His journey had taken him to a land he'd never heard of, a place of rocky mountains and plains. Horses roamed freely, seeking out the greenest grass; shepherds led their flocks to lakes nestling in valleys surrounded by soaring peaks. The landscape had been painted in a bewitching palette of colours: red and ochre to clothe the stones; green to calm the human inhabitants; white to warn them of the dangers of the cold; and a vast, pristine blue promising them eternal rest.

Hawwaz found refuge in a cave in the depths of the mountains. Exhausted from his journey, he fell asleep.

He awoke to the sound of soft, padding footsteps. He opened his eyes, struggling to see through the morning mist. He spotted a flamboyant golden dress with black stripes.

His long-practised reflexes kicked in and he sat bolt upright, gripping his spear.

The tigress contemplated him, unblinking. She didn't seem to want to devour him. Hawwaz, an animal lover, allowed himself to contemplate her back. Hours passed, then days. His horse, waiting for him, began to gnaw at its rope, then approached the cave, searching for its master. Upon entering, the horse recoiled, having been greeted by a nauseating odour, but overcame its disgust and approached.

No horse had ever witnessed such a sight. The tigress lay on the bare earth, asleep or dead. Next to her stood a statue of a tiger. The prince's clothes were laid across its back. At the feet of the statue sat a wooden cube, its sides engraved with the letters of the prince's first name: *Hâ, Wâw, Wâw, Zê. Hawwaz.*

The fourth prince, whose name was Hutti, loved numbers. He'd heard of the great Pythagoras, and vowed that one day he'd find a country in which nature offered up perfect forms, like those he believed the Greek scholar had sought. For Hutti, numbers represented the spirit of the world, and his quest was for a place where nature lent itself to the laws of numbers in the most absolute way possible.

He made his way to Greece where, in order to be accepted as a foreigner, he was obliged to join the forces of law and order, who were responsible for suppressing heretics. Unfortunately, at that time, mathematicians were amongst those considered heretics. Every day, Hutti was required to betray his own cause. He began to drown his sorrows in alcohol. When things got too much to bear, he would lose himself in the woods, where the wind, his constant companion, would refresh him without judgement or questions.

One day, however, he met a woman who was also an expert in numbers. She'd been sharing her knowledge with an ever-growing number of students. Her spirit radiated throughout the region, as did her beauty. But then what had to happen happened, and…

*

'Stop, Hypatia. This text is starting to scare me.'

'Me too, Father. It's about me.'

My daughter looks at me. In her eyes, I see a long-forgotten part of myself. A part that doesn't belong in this place; that's searching for something. But what?

'Hypatia,' I murmur, 'Who are we? I have snatches of memory, but it's all a blur.'

Hypatia opens her mouth to answer, but she's interrupted by three loud knocks at the door. Then it's shoved open and a horde of soldiers enter the room. At their head is Caius. He's the most ruthless legionary in the city. It's said that he arrived in Alexandria as a young man, having deserted from the Greek army.

Caius' heavy footsteps echo on the marble. He drops his huge body on to the sofa, beside the table where we've spread out our parchments. In a monotone, he pronounces, 'Hypatia of Alexandria, you are under arrest. You have betrayed your country and your true faith. You have betrayed God and his representatives on earth. You will be punished in order to be purified.'

He gives a sardonic laugh.

'You know,' he adds, in a voice that's almost gentle, 'The worst part of all this is that I envy you in a way. You two love numbers so much you're prepared to devote your whole lives to them, whereas I could never make that choice. I refuse to accept that to open one door you have to close all the others.'

My memories merge with the tale we've just read. I look at Hypatia, who returns my gaze. She's understood it too, perhaps before me: sometimes stories can merge with reality in a disconcerting way. There's barely time to realise it before history continues to be written; events take their merciless course. Has our reading influenced what's happening to us? Or has our destiny already been set down?

Hypatia's voice is sure. 'Then how else can you expect numbers to reveal their secrets to you? Every wonder of this world deserves our complete and exclusive devotion. That's the price we pay for being its messengers. We study numbers, dedicate our lives to recording their knowledge, and one day someone else will take over from us and decipher their language.'

'What if the heirs to this passion of yours come from elsewhere?' barks Caius. 'What if they use your knowledge to corrupt or to enslave? Did you never think of that? Can you not see what crimes you'd be guilty of setting in motion?'

'Knowledge has no religion, no nation. It's self-sufficient. It is a torch that each people takes from the hands of another, by force or by gentleness. All that matters is that it circulates.'

Caius laughs contemptuously.

'You show such detachment towards what you claim to love. You don't really care about numbers. You're using them as a tool to find something else. Or someone else.'

Caius turns to me and regards me intently, as if probing my soul in search of weakness. I waver between fear for my daughter and pride at her bravery.

My paternal instincts surface, and I rush to kneel before Caius, hoping he'll see in me not just Theon of Alexandria. I implore him with the eyes of a disciple begging his master. He understands what I'm trying to do. 'I am your pupil, your spiritual daughter,' my eyes tell him. 'Have mercy on me. Put an end to this war that serves neither you nor anyone else. Let time take its course, and everything will find its place again, in this life and in others. I beg you to let time, to let life take its course…'

Hidden in my look is also this plea, which I hope Fundi will hear: 'Please, burn me in her place. I'm the one who taught her everything she knows. If anyone should go to the stake, it's me!'

But his eyes are still filled with unspeakable hatred. Fundi has a secret he's never told me, and it controls his every move.

He moves closer to me, until our cheeks touch.

'I'll free you from your life of hard labour. And I'll

take back the power over knowledge that this woman is questioning.'

'I'll never abandon her,' I murmur, lowering my eyes. 'I can't abandon her.'

'You don't know what you're saying. We'll meet again soon, my child. And then you'll come to your senses.'

With that, he stands up and orders his soldiers to take Hypatia away. I try to grab hold of her ankle, but I miss and fall flat on my face on the marble floor.

As soon as I got back, I left the house where Fundi and my beloved lived. I went to the place where no one would come looking for me, the house where Tamu and I had lived together. It took me a little time, but I got there. The dusk was not too dark. Inside, everything was the same.

I sat down on the stone between the house and the outdoor kitchen where we prepared our meals.

My heart was aching. Recent events were replaying themselves in my mind. I'd betrayed my master: I'd looked him in the eye and chosen Halima. Then he'd put her to death.

I looked up at the dazzling sky. I could have lost myself in its setting sun.

As Miguel, I'd been as light as the wind. Not everything I did had serious consequences for me; my actions were not scrutinised or punished; I could come and go as I pleased; could refuse a dish I was served and choose another. I remembered being someone who was served. And those whom I'd served, in my place, had held me in high esteem. I spoke well and moved with grace and agility. My bearing was confident and proud. My body was only ever afflicted through my own free will, when I fought in battles on behalf of my country, so my wounds were both noble and laudable. And they were inflicted by others of rank: every one of my scars was like a mark of gratitude, delivered by the illustrious sailor, prince or admiral I'd fought.

In each of my voyages, a different part of me had been deployed. In the skin of the Bedouin, I'd understood what it was to hold authority; the power that can be wielded over weak minds; the elation that comes from legitimacy. And the responsibility that comes from having choice.

Yet with each new voyage I had the growing sense that I was being reeled in and pulled out of the water. I was suffocating, like a beached fish.

I thought about what Fundi and Halima had told me about the lives we were experiencing. Had I really lived all of those lives? Had all of those things really happened to me? Had I really known Fundi and Halima in several different lifetimes?

The first star appeared in the sky, followed by the second, the red one. I remained sitting on my stone until all the other stars had appeared. I told myself the story of Tamu's people, about the princes in the desert who'd shared the tubers, one of whom had turned into a zebra. Two princes, two dice. Halima had said two dice remained to be found. But I knew Fundi already had one; he was searching for the fifth and final die. Who would get to it first? And which of them would seek to use me next in order to do so?

*

They came knocking at my door in the dead of night. I'd heard their laughter through my half-sleep, but thought it was a dream. It was them, though. My friends. I heaved myself up and went to the door.

They were all there, smiling at me, just like when we were kids.

'What are you doing here at this time of night? We have work tomorrow!'

In reply, they bundled me into the room, followed behind me and closed the door. Each of them was carrying a fairly large object; I couldn't make out what. Ramla placed hers on the ground, followed by M'maka. Mlima unrolled what appeared to be a thick mat next to my own sleeping mat. When they were ready, they all stood up, and Olympe lit a candle, dripped its wax on the ground and secured it. The flickering flame lit up the room. I saw a bowl decorated with blue flowers, a gourd with clear water in it, and a rug with bird motifs.

The scent of spices and clarified butter rose from the bowl. I stepped forward and inhaled pepper, vanilla, cinnamon and dried cloves. The rice had been soaked in the spice mixture for a long time before being cooked in the butter. *Pilao*. It was still warm.

'Olympe told us you haven't been feeling well recently,' explained M'maka.

'So we came to check up on you,' added Mlima teasingly.

They all looked at me. They had no idea what I was going through. But they had understood that I needed them, and they'd come immediately, despite the work that awaited them at dawn the next day, the fatigue from the day's work they'd just done, the risk of being seen in possession of objects that they'd surely 'borrowed' from their masters.

We ate the *pilao*, the new dish imported by Indian traders that was all the rage in the stone houses, and told each other stories about *jinns*. I laughed along with the others, clutching my ribs, at the jokes told by Mlima-of-the-sweet-saliva.

They left well before daybreak. I watched their dark shapes disappear behind the houses and realised my heart felt a little lighter. This, I told myself, was the definition of love: being there for someone, trying to soothe their pain, without asking about its source.

But in the lives we led, soothing things only ever lasted for the briefest of moments; a temporary dressing of banana leaves that dried up or disintegrated after a few days, revealing the open wound beneath.

After they'd gone, I left the house. Dawn was not far off. Without thinking about it too much, I walked to Ahmad's Wood. I took the path I'd been on when I first met her. This was the place where our story had begun. The henna plants were thriving, the dense bushes caressing my knees; lemongrass invaded the path so I had to push its smooth, sharp leaves aside to progress; new nettle shoots nibbled at my feet. I made my way down the hill to Hatov beach. When I got there, I submerged my feet in the foam. I kept going until the water reached my knees, just as Tamu did when she soaked her clothes. A feeling seemed to emerge from the water and take me in its arms. Guilt.

I hadn't found her. Not here, and not in any of the lives I'd been taken to. My friends' visit had reminded me of this: we were all being used, in one way or another. That was our function, and we'd never had reason to question it.

Whatever Fundi and Halima had done, they'd done it for themselves. I'd never done anything for myself. I'd never understood it to be possible. Now I saw the arrogance of the masters. What they were masters of, above all, was their own destiny. I could have fled, could have taken a different route across the waters, could have decided to stay with my cubs. Hadn't I contradicted the man in the desert who wanted to subjugate his wife? Hadn't I spread out my feathery filaments so the fly could drink the droplet of water?

I could have gone in search of my mother.

For the first time, it wasn't the others I was angry with, but myself. It was a strange feeling. To be angry with yourself was to acknowledge you'd had an opportunity, that you could have done something: decided, then acted. But it was also to bear, alone, the consequences of those actions. I'd always imagined being free would lift all the burdens from my heart, but perhaps freedom was the worst kind of prison, because it was challenging: it said, 'Prove that you deserve me by paying the price. Betraying your master for your mistress is not true freedom. True freedom would be betraying them both.'

I fell to my knees. The water danced around my waist. Its steely-grey foam seemed composed of a thousand shining eyes, or a thousand tiny craters. Suddenly I thought: lava solidifies when it touches water.

I closed my eyes and thought of fire. Perhaps this was what the five princes were looking for: freedom from the weight of responsibility; the absence of guilt; freedom from having to earn your freedom.

Nothingness.

Soon I felt vortexes of bubbling blood rolling under my

skin and through my flesh. I tipped my head back. All I could see was red darkness. The fire from my heart spread through my body to my legs, my feet, my back, my arms, my face. I was a human torch. The water around me began to emit a deafening hiss. *Shhhh*... be quiet. Let there be silence. Let there be nothingness.

*

A flinty silence greets me. There's no breeze. All around me is the cottony softness of a strangely familiar presence. The smell of crushed henna leaf reaches my nostrils.

Then I hear the voice.

'Hardie! There you are!'

The voice comes from above. I look up, but see no one.

'I knew you'd try to come here.'

No, the voice comes from below. It's a woman's voice. I look down, but I can't make out a thing.

'Oh, my child. You've always looked for everything outside yourself. You're so convinced everything is outside you.'

I look in all directions. Where is she?

'Close your eyes.'

As I do so, something strange happens: I realise I can't feel my eyes: not my eyelids, and not the places where they rub against the globes I use to see the world. I try to regain awareness of my body, but there's nothing but the cottony whiteness that's all around me. Where by the life of Queen Abé am I? It's as if I've dissolved, as if nothing has any shape or texture. I feel as if I'm inside myself, and at the same time…

'Mother, is that you? Am I dead?' I ask in a panicked voice.

The voice bursts out laughing. 'No, no, my daughter.'

'Have I travelled to another time?'

'No, sweetheart. Time doesn't exist here.'

'But where am I?'

'You're in my kingdom. Where nothing and no one can touch you. Where you're no longer your body. Where you're no longer even Hardie.'

I don't understand. The voice laughs again. The sound is unlike anything I've ever heard. It reminds me of the river swollen with eels as it flows into the ravine, singing of its frantic race down the hillsides of my island, making the stones clatter and the tufts of grass sigh.

'Hardie, you're finally hearing the sounds that reassure you. I'm glad.'

I don't know what she means. 'The sounds that reassure me?'

'You don't understand, or you're afraid to understand, *bo daba*? Let me show you.'

Before I have time to ask how she knows this name for me, the clouds part and the woven palm house where I was born appears before me. Tamu used to point it out to me from a distance when I was little, but when I was ten she decided to destroy it, because I so often stopped to gaze at it and then came home and curled up on the floor. I remember that time, when the sight of that house would plunge me into a pit of sadness I could not escape.

'This is where you left your body and began to absorb other people's feelings,' says the voice.

I watch a woman enter the hut after checking all around her. Her face is hidden by the darkness, but I can see that her hands are shaking. She has an object bundled in her *leso*; it stirs in her arms. Slowly, she undoes the *leso*. On the back of her hand, I see a tattoo of two vertical lines. Inside the folds of the *leso* is a tiny face with closed eyes. The woman is murmuring words in an unfamiliar language.

'Listen carefully,' the voice tells me.

Even though I don't speak the language, I can understand what the woman's saying. 'I can't let you live,' she says, 'You have to die. If I don't kill you, you'll be enslaved by those who enslaved me. You'll be naked, naked, unless you can learn their religion and their sacred book. But who will teach you that? And how can I protect you, when I haven't been able to protect myself? We're alone here, abandoned. No one's going to save us—not the eel god, not Mawu, not Mantis. There's no god for people like us. And I can't offer you the safety you need to thrive. Forgive me.'

She rolls part of her *leso* into a ball. She closes her eyes and then, in one swift movement, starts to shove the cloth down my throat. I shudder in horror to see the infant that was me, shocked and gasping for air, began to wriggle. Then a dazzling ray of light bursts forth from the ground, like a jet of water. It envelopes the mother who, paralysed with astonishment, drops the baby. The child falls, seemingly wrapped in a luminescent cocoon. Then the ray of light fades, the scene darkens, and the image shrinks and transforms. It's the silhouette of a woman, holding the child. Terrified by the spectacle she's just witnessed, the mother cries out, 'The devil, I've given birth to the devil!' and flees inside the house.

I feel my heart following her, unspooling like a ball of string, of which she holds the end. The strange voice had spoken the truth: this was the moment my heart became detached and began chasing after other hearts like the tail chasing the comet. By thinking she was sparing me, and then running away, my mother had condemned me to the very fate she wanted me to avoid.

I look at the woman made of light. She cradles the child lovingly in her arms. Then she lifts her head and fixes her gaze on me. I cry out in recognition: it's Tamu.

'Now you know,' says the voice, with a smile.

I search with my eyes—the presence of which I sense intensely although I can feel nothing of my body—for the voice that's speaking to me. What does this mean?

Remember, Hardie, the tale of Queen Abé. How does she appear to her beloved?'

'She springs up from the ground like a jet of water,' I reply, dumbfounded. 'But…'

'Yes. Yes, you've got it. And then what does she usually take the form of?'

'A human being.'

Everything seems clear now. No, seems is the wrong word: I use it too often, never completely trusting myself, always waiting for others to accord me the right to my own opinion. That's over now. It's as if I've been struck by lightning.

'You're… Tamu,' I say breathlessly. 'And you're Abé. You came in human form to take care of me.'

My voice dies on the final word.

'Why did you leave without telling me?' I moan through sobs. 'Why did you leave me after blessing me?'

'Every master has to know when to disappear so the pupil can find their own way,' she replies. 'You were more than my pupil, though; we were family, and I should have warned you. But if I'd warned you, you wouldn't have been angry at me for leaving. And if you hadn't been angry…'

'I wouldn't have made the fire. Why fire? Why did you give me that power?'

'It wasn't me who gave you that.'

'Yes, it was! It's you who gives me everything, Tamu… Queen Abé.'

'No, I only give you the world inside you and the world outside you, and the ability to choose what you do with them.'

'So who did give me this fire?'

'Close your eyes.'

Again the blur, the cottony softness. Before me appears the house where Ramla's mother works. I immediately recognise the kitchen, the layer of soot covering the walls.

A young girl appears, her fair skin protected by a blue shawl. She's waiting for Ramla's mother, who arrives to meet her.

The girl in the blue shawl is Halima. She has something in a basket; something wrapped in cloth. Ramla's mother unwinds the cloth and extracts… banana skins.

'I've cast the right invocations over them,' whispers Halima. 'Make sure they're well placed on her chest.'

'Thank you, mistress,' says Ramla's mother in a

trembling voice.

'Don't press too hard.'

Halima leaves hurriedly, as if she fears some divine punishment for the act she's just committed.

I see myself arriving with Ramla, innocent and oblivious. *Ma* Ramla buries the banana peels in the ashes, then waves goodbye to her daughter. The rest I know. That's when I remember the scent I noticed when I arrived in the kitchen that day. Jasmine.

As the skins start to burn my flesh, as I try to scream, I ask Queen Abé to stop.

'Do you understand now why you have this fire?'

'She created it?'

'No, you created it. But she needed you to create it. Water, fire, earth, wind.'

'And the harmony between them. I was the missing element.'

The cloud dissipates. The light fades. I reach out with what I think is my hand to grab hold of her, but she eludes me. The time for following is over. I must find my own soul.

'I can see that you're ready,' says Queen Abé.

I am ready. To discover who I am.

ABJAD

أَبْجَدْ

The name of the fifth prince was Abjad. He set off towards the pine forests, hoping to hear the songs of the birds. His obsessions were the sounds of birds and streams, the spring of fresh grass beneath his feet, the tree trunks that welcomed his exhausted back. Abjad loved simple things. He celebrated them in poems that nobody ever read or heard, because simple things have always been difficult to appreciate. They don't bring glory, rally crowds, galvanise armies or inspire revolutions. Simple things are self-sufficient, and only reveal their treasures to those who notice them. They don't lend themselves to quests, but simply present themselves to people who see them while passing by, who don't wish to possess or reproduce them, only to appreciate them.

As Abjad was walking, he was suddenly seized by thirst. He stopped at the edge of a lake with crystal clear waters. Something was sending ripples out out across it. Looking towards the centre, he saw a kind of whirlpool. From a distance, it looked like a body frolicking in the water. Abjad sat down on the bank, took his cup out of his saddlebag and drew some water from the lake.

He took a sip. Droplets from the lake immediately merged into human form before his eyes. The top half of a figure emerged from the depths; half-woman, half-water. Her hair was long, black and wavy. She stretched out a hand towards him. Abjad found her magnificent. He was captivated by her beauty, but he was not a man who was easily tempted. The figure vanished, as if discouraged.

A few moments later, Abjad fell asleep. From his sleep, another human form emerged. A naked man sat on the shore beside him, gazing down at him with infinite gentleness. A song escaped from his lips:

I thought I'd been emptied of my soul
by this poisoned water
But when I see you
I want to claim it back
If one day I find
What the water has taken from me
I swear I will return
To you, my benefactor, my friend.

When I wake up, I'm not in Fundi's room or Halima's. I'm not even in Itsandra. The first thing I notice is the heat: suffocating, overpowering, with no hint of humidity. The heat that's described in the Qur'an as *djahim*.

Next I notice the sand. It's between my fingers, in the creases of my elbows, in the folds of my stomach, between my teeth, on my tongue, under my eyelids. It's everywhere; so fine that an ochre veil falls in front of my eyes when I find the courage to open them. I gather what strength I have and prepare to get up, carefully, so as not to cause any strain. To my amazement, though, my body obeys me immediately and I stand up easily, as if I weren't overwhelmed by the heat, but used to it. I look down. I'm wearing leather sandals. My legs are bare. They're slender and toned. My whole body is naked, in fact, except for my private parts, which are covered with a piece of animal hide. And I have breasts!

They're small and slightly drooping, but they're there. I touch my hair: it's like black peppercorns sprinkled on my head. For once, I look like the person I am in Hardie's life. That feels good. I'd come to wonder whether Hardie was an anomaly, a mistake that had crept in between my many lives, but it's strange; finding myself in a body so similar, here, in this place of sun and sand, makes me want to be Hardie again.

I had my breasts ripped out when I was Hardie to protect me from lust, but then I was coveted for the fire that burns inside me.

A fire that guides me to find the dice that imprison the spirits of the five princes: Sa'fas, Qarshat, Hawwaz, Hutti and Abjad.

All this time, I've been wondering why me, why all of this. Now I understand.

For better or worse, Fundi is the father I never had. He deserves my love, for loving me, and us, when we were nothing. Love sees our flaws and our beauty as one harmonious whole.

Halima was a lost soul, as lost as I was, convinced she needed to be loved in order to love herself. We loved each other; with all our longing, our hurt, our emptiness.

Strange, I think, how we take our wounds to be enemy attacks. How quick we are to complain about them, to try to cauterise them by any means necessary. As if we were frightened of our own insides.

When I was Miguel, I discovered masculinity could be more fragile than I'd ever imagined. The unquenchable thirst to stand out, to be seen, to find the answers to urgent questions even if it meant risking your life, to try to surround yourself with whatever glowed most mysteriously. There were the women—curvaceous and cavernous, ready to engulf you like the depths of the sea—and the men, light and delicate, so tense with the expectations of others and their own, struggling like butterflies to emerge from their chrysalis and take uncertain flight. In Miguel's shoes, I learned that tears are not the prerogative of women, that fragility wears a deceptive cloak.

I lived with the Bedouin. Was it the prophet whose praises were sung at the *shioni*? Or just a kind-hearted man with a tormented soul, as fallible as the rest of us but more aware of it? In that man's skin, I felt the weight of a tribe that had forgotten where it came from, that had become blinded by its status and oblivious to poetry. My heart bled alongside his when that man realised, after delivering his message, that humanity did not need to heal from its ills, it needed to explore them, to contemplate them eternally, through blood, sweat and tears, until… nothing.

Yes, nothing. Nothing but the deed itself, for the love of it.

In the skin of the tigress, I relished my long days spent hunting for muntjac deer, my nights spent in my cave, the feeling of a tree trunk against my flank, the taste of the newly-formed fur of my cubs on my tongue, their play-fighting games. I felt alive; I felt like a queen; I needed nothing. I could have stayed like that, the sun running through my veins, my eyes closed as I inhaled the hot air, dense with red dust. Time could have found me again like that, years later, lying in that same position with my head lifted to the sky, like statues that go on celebrating yesterday's splendours tomorrow. My only concept of paradise was the happy present, an eternal present, beyond death, beyond the end of the world.

I look around me. The sand stretches forever. It seems to extend beyond the horizon and plunge over some unknown precipice. It's orange, clumpy, dry and scorching hot. Still, I love the feeling of its grains scratching my feet.

In front of me are three huge stones, smooth and flat, piled one on top of the other. This is a sanctuary.

My feverish fingers plunge into the small bag that's slung over my shoulder, next to my ostrich egg gourd—now the details of this life are starting to come to me. My figures grasp a cube: the fifth die. My heart stills.

I walk towards the smooth, round stones. The elders say that no one who's tried to climb them has ever come back alive. Some have died trying to get back down from the top, slipping on the smooth surface. Others, too afraid to descend, remain trapped in the sanctuary for ever. To warn off the more reckless among us, the history of our people has been painted on the stones in ink made from a mixture of blood and ochre dust. These drawings shine brightly when the sun is at its zenith, and their warning is clear.

A bare tree stands on the path that leads towards the stones. Its trunk is smooth and cool to the touch, yet no foliage weighs it down. I crouch in front of it. The ground beneath it is cool. I dig there until I meet resistance. I pull out a tuber, then another. I place them on either side of the trunk. Then I taste the liquid that flows from each.

He appears. I'm startled—until now, I hadn't remembered this was our signal—yet at the same time I was expecting it; every gesture feels familiar.

He stands in front of me, naked apart from the strip of hide over his private parts. His skin is ochre-coloured, like mine, his hair planted like grain on his head. But his eyes betray his identity—they're shaped like upside-down cashew nuts.

'You finally found me,' he says. 'I was so tired of chasing through the sky.'

I return his generous smile.

'I'd have looked for you for eternity if need be.'

He smiles even more widely and takes me in his arms. Together we walk towards the stones.

I place one hand on the first stone and we begin our ascent. The slippery surface roughens wherever I touch it with my hot palm. I find purchase for my feet and climb. I'm extraordinarily thirsty, but this mission is too important to pause. The other princes will reach the sanctuary soon, and I must be there too.

'You don't need to hurry,' says my friend, behind me. 'We've found each other now. And you still don't have all the dice.'

I continue to climb, wondering how he knows about the dice. I decide to wait until we get there to ask him. In fact, he's wrong: I have all five of the dice: they were entrusted to me several lifetimes ago.

The climb is exhausting, but we keep going. The sun beats down so fiercely and the air is so dry that my sweat evaporates the second it leaves my pores.

At the end of the interminable climb, a welcome coolness envelops us. We've reached the sanctuary: the Universal Tomb. I step off the stone and find myself on soft, cool, even ground. My friend jumps down too. I breathe in the damp air. He comes closer. He's panting, as am I.

'How do you know about the dice?' I ask him. 'And why do you say I don't have them all?' He turns to me, smiling broadly. His eyes sparkle like those of a child. How beautiful he is. How I've missed him all of my life, all of my lives.

'It took me six eternities,' he says simply.

Leaving me to ponder this, he moves towards a crack between two stones. A shaft of light shines through it. Its beam is interrupted, though: a small object is lodged in the crack. Carefully, he pulls it out. It's a die. He returns to me, caressing it between his thumb and forefinger, a tiny smile playing across his lips. I look at the die. Only one of its faces is engraved. I recognise the secret name that Fundi tried to extract from the depths of my memory, but never succeeded. The name that is the key to everything: water, fire, earth, wind and the harmony between them.

As well as the path to what some people call God, Allah, Abé, and many other names.

For me, there has only ever been one path: the one that led me to my friend. He looks at me, beaming, and I return his grin. He hands me the die and takes a few steps back. The other princes are coming; we can hear their breath on the air.

I place the dice on the floor one by one: Sa'fas, Qarshat, Hawwaz, Hutti and Abjad. I keep hold of the sixth, the one that would allow the princes to become absolute masters of knowledge, to travel between lives without hindrance, to change what they deemed unjust, then return here to observe their work.

No sooner have I arranged the dice than their owners appear. I grip the die of harmony firmly in my palm.

'There you are at last, Qarshat.'

I've known them for so long: we've sailed through life together for millennia.

Abjad approaches me. He puts his hand on my shoulder and looks at me with his soft eyes. I raise my hand and stroke the scar on his forehead.

'You've never been able to get rid of it, have you?' I ask him.

'How else would you recognise me?' he replies in a whisper.

His look becomes serious. He wants us to extinguish ourselves so humanity is spared our vanity.

'Qarshat,' he says gently. 'You've succeeded. Soon the sun will set, the moon will rise and you can burn the dice.'

'I never wanted this,' says a voice from behind me.

'Hutti,' murmurs Abjad. 'You succeeded too. You passed on your knowledge. But your path ends here.'

I turn to Hutti. His face is tender, firm, kind.

Even here, he can guess my thoughts.

'I've loved you sincerely, my child,' he says. 'But I think you'd be making a mistake to burn the dice. We could spread our knowledge throughout the ages. Everyone would celebrate our wisdom. No one would use it to dominate us, or to steal our lands. Knowledge is the most powerful weapon of all. That weapon could belong to us, for once.'

'That's precisely why we need to destroy them,' continues Abjad. 'Together, they do indeed become a weapon, and a weapon can only do harm, even in the purest hands.'

'You're wrong,' says Hutti, addressing Abjad. 'Tell him!' he says to the others. 'You!'—he looks back at me—'Didn't I give you hope by arming you with knowledge? We must wage war against ignorance. I was going to prepare you all for it, but you'—he indicates Abjad— 'are stopping us! You're just scared.'

'Yes, I'm scared. Because knowledge makes men arrogant, and then they destroy each other. They start to believe in absolute power. It makes them sick with envy and greed. They break the hearts of those who love them.'

'All this trouble over a little heart ache?' mocks Hutti. 'Are you joking with us?'

'All of life is a matter of the heart!' storms Abjad. 'Our brother must light the fire within and incinerate these dice.'

'That's enough!' I'm the one who shouts this. The fire roars inside me. The louder the princes raise their voices, the more my fire calls out for something to burn. My brothers look at me, surprised. I've never dared assert myself like this in our assemblies before.

I'm about to ask them what I should do, but I change my mind. I've already decided. I won't listen to any of them. Not even Queen Abé. For once, I will do as I wish. And my wish, selfish as it may be, is to free myself.

I will no longer depend on the love of others in order to love myself. I will no longer feed on other people's feelings in order to fill the emptiness inside me.

I will no longer say that things seem a certain way to me; I will say that they are that way, and will go on being that way until I decide to change my mind about them.

I will no longer be in thrall to the tormented, vacillating hearts of others.

I will wind the ball of thread that is my heart back up inside my chest. I will face its indecisions and torments in the belief that peace can be found. I will accept freedom and gladly pay the price for it, because that freedom will be mine.

For the thread of my heart carries in it all the cities I've passed through, all the dresses I've sewn, all the things I've made for others. I'll unravel that work and they'll learn to clothe themselves. And I will clothe myself, instead of giving away the fabric from my back and stumbling through life naked, like a sightless worm.

Silently, in front of the stunned princes, I ignore the dice laid out at our feet and cross my hands over my chest, holding the cube that bears the other name, the one no one knows, the one that my heart hid from Hutti for all of these lives. I take one last look at my friend and close my eyes. As the fire consumes me, I whisper the name, so that these stones will keep it sealed forever in their cool shelter. I relinquish the mission it assigned me, and accept a new one.

The fire first burns the face that bears the single letter that makes up the name. Then it consumes the rest of the wood, just as the *jinns* consume the souls of humans. Finally, I let it inside me. The warmth rises up from beneath my feet, spreads through my legs, my torso, my chest, my arms, my head. I close my eyes and let the light flood through me. The shadows of the princes before me disappear. I have no idea what they will do.

I kiss beauty on its burning forehead. Already, I can see Queen Abé's bearers approaching in the distance; shadows laden with buckets filled with light. They pour the light over me and my name, inside my mind, inside my heart, melts away.

WAW

The trade winds awaken. The town of Itsandra is fragrant with blossom: mango, lychee, banana. This year, the fruits have agreed to co-ordinate their ripening, no doubt to accompany the festivities that mark the end of the month of Ramadan.

At dawn the scent is at its most heady.

A small hand slips under my back. Without opening my eyes, I make a disgruntled sound. A mischievous laugh answers me, then the little arm moves all the way under my back. I pretend to roll over on top of it. The arm flies out, the laughter continuing unabated.

I grab the little body and start to tickle it vigorously.

We both laugh. I marvel at the stars that light up Mustafâ's dark eyes, even more numerous when he's laughing.

'Mummy, let me go!' he screams

I release him, but not before giving him a kiss.

'Tell the story of the five princes!'

'Just let me look at you a bit longer.'

*

To my astonishment, and the dismay of the princes, when I burned the sixth die, the other dice burned with it. I woke up back in the house I'd shared with Tamu. People behaved as if I'd always been there. I was still a servant, but a few things had changed.

Tamu wasn't there.

Halima was living with Fadili.

I caught a glimpse of him on the verandah of the stone house, stretching in the sunlight. A moment later, his gold-skinned wife joined him, draped in her light veil. They embraced for a long time.

I didn't know it was possible to feel two emotions so strongly at once: to be both ecstatic with happiness and choked with jealousy. Was this what it meant to come back to life? Accepting an existence of both water and fire? Was this my last lesson from Halima, who'd taught me so much?

I took a step towards their house, then changed my mind.

Instead, I went to catch some fish for Fundi. His favourite were needlefish, *mtsumbuu.* Their flesh was exquisite with lemon and chilli.

I tied one end of my *leso* around my neck, then unfurled the other end beneath the surface of the water. I gazed for a moment at the ripples. They greeted me with their small, shining eyes. Soon the sharp, wriggling spikes of the fish were lodged in the fabric. I caught six.

When I came back from fishing, a little voice greeted me in the master's kitchen.

'Mummy!'

Surprised, I went towards the voice. A wave, or I should say a miniature tsunami, hurled itself at me with the savagery of childish affection. Plump little arms grabbed the back of my neck and pulled me forward, supple legs wrapped themselves around my waist in a single bound. Emotion bubbled up inside me: I knew this scrambling ball of love, had returned its love for me for years. I stepped aside to get a better look at him.

Eyes like upside-down cashew nuts; a smile like a string of pearls; big, shiny black curls falling on either side of a fair face; sparkling eyes full of mischief.

'This little rascal is a quick learner,' said a voice behind me.

Another emotion simmered inside me. I turned round to see Fundi Ahmad.

He stared at me, clearly surprised I was looking him in the eye and smiling. I looked more closely. He was the same man, yet something about him was different.

Before I could look away, he smiled back. It was an open smile. There was no anger on his face, no vengeful glint in his eyes. There was one solitary crease in the middle of his forehead; just one wrinkle of worry caused by the vicissitudes of everyday life; no suggestion of timeless struggles. He squinted, then opened his eyes wide, laughing. He was wondering what I was staring at, but was amused by it too. Finally, in a voice as gentle as the whisper of slow-moving water over well-polished stones, he said, 'Let's see the fish you found, my girl.'

Hearing that guttural voice of his calmed me like ginger, lemongrass and laurel tea. It was a voice full of warmth and peace. Perhaps it held a little trembling emotion, too, as it did every Friday just before Fundi delivered his sermon at the mosque.

I showed him the needlefish. He grinned.

'Fry them up with that mixture of spices you make so well. Add some chilli, won't you? And don't hold back on the lemon. Oh, and join me for dinner, you and Mustafâ. My wife can grumble all she likes; you'll eat at my table.'

Off he went, happily humming a song in praise of the prophet.

At the back of the kitchen, battling with the fire, was Fundi's first wife. She was coughing, her cheeks red from blowing in vain on the embers. I went to her and offered to have a go. She looked at me, surprised by my buoyant tone.

'Pleased with yourself because your master invited you and your brat to eat with us? Don't get too used to it!' she snapped, before straightening up, coughing and spluttering.

I couldn't suppress a smile. Some things would never change. It was almost a relief.

I blew out one long breath and a flame immediately shot up with an impressive 'whoosh'. Yellow at the centre and brown at the edges, it saluted me playfully, delicate and shapely as a woman.

At this last thought, my hands flew to my chest, in an instinctive but uncertain gesture. Were they there?

My reality was as flat as the plains of the Bangwa massif: I had no breasts. Of course I didn't: *Ma* Ramla had torn them off. What did it matter? I had a son who was already too grown up to make use of them, no one else to offer them to, and they wouldn't be very practical for running around in the forest with Mustafâ.

Part of me was asking myself if something about this life must be wrong. Everything felt so inexplicably different. I didn't know what to make of the feeling of absolute calm and peace in my heart. Tamu wasn't there to discuss it with. Was I the only one who remembered her? I was itching to ask someone, but at the same time, tempted to say nothing, for fear I might break the spell, if that was what it was.

What would Tamu have said in such circumstances?

You ask too many questions, bo daba. Open your hands and accept whatever Abé puts into them!

So be it, then. I live. I let Mustafâ be the light of my days. I'm Hardie, servant to the most open-minded master on this island. It's a wonderful place and, somewhere in history, I'm queen of it. For now, I devote myself to nurturing this little, bouncing thing. So foreign to this world, and the only trace of my passion for Halima. Not so much consolation as revelation, watching him grow, this anomaly of life who nonetheless has a rightful place in mine.

When Mustafâ is an adult, servants will no longer exist. At least I hope they won't. Sometimes time itself seems to whisper that soon things will change; sometimes I think I can feel the force with which its hands steer the world. I don't know how life will change, but I suspect it will, and that warms my heart.

When I look at Mustafâ, I feel sunlight. That's more than enough for me.

When night falls and the stellar beings start to populate the sky, we go and sit outside the house; me on the stone, him on a *pindo*, and I tell him the stories he likes: the one about the five princes, and others. His favourite is the story of the hunter and the zebra.

He rests his head on my thigh and listens, while his hand plays with a wooden object. I teach him the alphabet. He loves learning so much. 'Mama Hardie, teach me to read!' he says, with the solemn insistence of childhood. I teach him what I know.

'Sa'fas, Qarshat, Hawwaz, Hutti, Abjad.' Like a rosary, the names of the princes roll off our tongues, in a litany that my son will pass on to his own *dhuriya*, his descendants.

As I read, almost in a trance, Mustafâ's head gets heavier on my thigh. Soon he's asleep, lulled by my singing. His eyes are closed, his eyelashes resting against his cheek, his lower lip slightly curled like that of a wise old man, his hands open and outstretched in absolute trust. My heart swells with joy.

I look up, sweeping my gaze over the town where I was born, where my ancestors arrived, snatched from other lands. It seems we're all migratory birds; that even if we refuse to migrate, fate takes care of it for us. Our voyage might be turbulent or calm, but it must be completed; the seas of our lives must be crossed.

Absorbed in my thoughts, I lift Mustafâ, whose body is weighed down by sleep. Just as I give him a little nudge to adjust his head against my shoulder, a shape appears in my field of vision. It towers towards the moonlit sky, and I see its dials for measuring the locations and angles of the stars' beams. Its steps gleam in the night, hundreds of steel struts leading all the way up to the sandy plateau, invisible from where I'm standing. The wall that once separated this place from our world is gone. Here, in this fold of my life, it's surely an observatory like any other, the sole purpose of which is to chart the courses of the stars in the sky and use them to determine our destinies.

Satisfied with this, I move towards the door of my house, when I glimpse a shadow emerging into the blackness of the night. She climbs the steps one by one. She's dressed in something light, white and shimmering. Her hair cascades down her back.

She turns and looks at me.

My heart beats faster. Moonlight shines on her face. Her lips begin to move. Instinctively, mine respond. My heart flies to her; my soul recognises the bond that binds us for eternity, and I know that it's beyond me.

Beyond time,
Beyond rules,
Beyond bodies,
And far, far away
From everything we think we know
And everything we think we are,

I love you.

GLOSSARY

Aahee: interjection used to express exasperation, equivalent to 'pff!'

Abjad: name given to the Arabic alphabet. According to Bedouin legend, five princes helped to write down the Arabic language, which until then had only been expressed orally. Their names were Sa'fas, Qarshat, Hawwaz, Hutti and Abjad.

'Ada: up until the eighteenth century, when sultans ruled the Comoros archipelago, they married with great pomp, involving all the inhabitants of their fiefdoms in the construction of the nuptial home. *'Ada*, meaning 'wedding', is the name of these festivities, which are still widespread. An *'ada* can last between a week and a month, and costs the equivalent of 20,000 euros.

Adas: Indian day bed made from a wooden frame and woven rope.

Asr: the afternoon prayer, which takes place when the sun begins to go down and the shadows lengthen.

Azaïma: 'holy water', made from water and charcoal.

Baraza: in Zanzibar and the Comoros, *baraza* is the name

given to a verandah, as well as to the gatherings that often take place there.

Basmala/Bismillah: the opening formula which announces the beginning of each *surah* in the Qur'an, and with which, in some Muslim countries, people start an action in the hope that it will succeed. Literally 'in the name of God'.

Begim: Kyrgyz for prince.

Bhûta: in Sanskrit, a supernatural creature, usually the ghost of a deceased person, described in popular culture, literature and ancient texts from the Indian subcontinent.

Bo: particle used when addressing someone by their first name, nickname or affectionate name.

Bwibwi: large black veil made of silk or cotton, probably brought from Iran to the Comoros. It covers the head and the back of the body. Thin cords are used to tie it across the front of the body and underneath the chin.

Daba: literally, 'idiot'. Tamu uses it as an affectionate nickname to emphasise Hardie's naivety.

Dhuhr: the midday prayer, held when the sun is at its zenith and the shadows are short.

Dhuriya: descendants, posterity.

Dimku: devil or monster found in stories. Some storytellers describe it as something like a dragon.

Djahim: hellfire. Literally, 'the world below'.

Djayyid: well done.

Glossary

Djuba: long coat of one colour that reaches to the ankles, worn by those who have made their customary marriage (see '*ada*).

Dzindzan: turmeric.

Ephebe: youth between eighteen and twenty years of age in ancient Greece.

Fitako: sedan chair or wooden chair found in southern African countries such as Burundi.

Fundi: master. Probably comes from the Turkish '*effendi*'.

Futra: bread made with coconut milk and clarified butter (ghee), sprinkled with sesame seeds.

Gudu gudu: coconut milk and caramelised sugar dessert.

Hami: white linen or cotton cloth worn by young girls.

Hitima: from the root '*ha-ta-ma'* in Arabic, meaning the end of a cycle. *Hitima* is the end of a cycle of learning the Qur'an, which is declared when the student can read without stumbling.

Hodi: formula for announcing one's presence before entering a house: in the Comoros in Hardie's time (and still to some extent today), doors were not closed.

Hud: one of the names given to the Jewish people in the Qur'an. Could come from the root '*hd*', 'to guide'.

Hudhrung: a cloth of a colour between ochre and orange, used to make *kandus* reserved for men of influence.

Isha: the evening prayer, long after the sun has set and the pink-orange colour of the clouds has disappeared.

Jafr: animal skin parchment dating from the 5th to 2nd century

BCE, on which Mohammed's teachings are said to have been inscribed.

Jinn: also Romanised as *djinn* or anglicised as genies, are invisible creatures in early pre-Islamic Arabia and later in Islamic culture and beliefs.

Kandu: long robe reserved for men, similar to those worn by men in the Gulf States. It is made from linen, fine cotton or cotton crepe (*lasi*), and can be white, beige or orange, according to social class.

Kashkazi: monsoon.

Keffiyeh: traditional headdress worn by men from parts of the Middle East. It is fashioned from a square scarf and is usually made of cotton.

Kofia: cotton bonnet, inherited from the Sultanate of Oman. To make a *kofia*, holes are pierced in a rectangle of white cotton, then embroidered around their edges with gold thread. It features inscriptions, often verses from the Qur'an.

Kusi: trade winds.

Kuskuma: flour cake made with clarified butter, probably originating from India, since on the island of Anjouan one of its variants is called *berede*, probably a distortion of the Indian *paratha*.

Kwezi: customary greeting made to a person identified as an authority figure.

Laesha: another name for the evening prayer, *isha*.

Lasi: cotton crepe.

Glossary

Leso (pronounced 'lesso'): square printed cotton scarf, which travelled from India to Zanzibar before arriving in the Comoros. In Hardie's time, patterns were embroidered on it (paisley, *fleur-de-lys*). Different types of *leso* were worn by different social classes.

Ma (or M'ma): diminutive of 'mama', associated with the first name of the eldest child, as in '*Ma* Hussam.'

Madaba: leaves of the manioc plant, which are crushed in a large mortar before being prepared with coconut milk, chilli, salt and garlic.

Madrassa: school dedicated to teaching Islamic jurisdiction and general knowledge.

Mafe: Sultan, king.

Maghrib: the twilight prayer.

Manamein: a sleep practice that combines Eastern and African spirituality. It is a 'conscious' sleep: the subject knows they are dreaming and can decide to look for someone or for an answer to a question. It has similarities with certain shamanic practices in pre-Columbian America or indigenous Australia.

Maqbadhi: leather sandals with two bands that cross on the top of the foot.

Mbona: the response of a person in authority when greeted with the *kwezi*.

Medina: the old quarter of a North African town.

Mihadji: pilgrims returning from Mecca. Comes from the word *hadj*, 'pilgrimage'.

Mkatra sinia: rice cake with coconut milk.

Mkumi: thick cloth usually reserved for men of influence and religious figures.

Mraha: board game consisting of a wooden board with hollows cut into it in groups of two. It is played with seeds. It symbolises the importance of strategy and agriculture.

Mshendzi: when Islam was first established in Comoros, those who didn't speak Arabic and were not Muslims were called *mshendzi*. This may have been the name of a clan formerly settled in the archipelago; however, over time, the name has taken on a pejorative connotation, and is now used to belittle a person who is dark-skinned or without 'noble' ancestry.

Muezzin: the person who proclaims the call to the daily prayer five times a day at a mosque from the minaret.

Mzee: name reserved for men who are given authority: the father, older brother, head of the family or clan.

Mzungu: often translated as 'white, European'. It actually means 'explorer': literally, one who surveys the earth.

Namaste-ji: Hindi greeting.

Nasara: literally, the Nazarenes, as mentioned in the Qur'an.

Ndawe: greeting ('hey, you').

Ndjeni: nettles.

Ndovu: elephant.

Ndzinyo: riddle.

Pilao: spiced rice served with meat or fish, one of the most popular dishes in Comoros.

Pindo: thick fibre found in the upper part of a coconut shell.

Pirogue: canoe made from a hollowed tree trunk.

Plov: Uzbek rice pilaf.

Pvala: literally, 'over there', or 'there', when referring to the location of an object or person. The word can also be used to introduce a different point of view from others on a subject of discussion.

Pvanu: literally, 'here', to show an object or person. Used to introduce an important but thorny subject.

Qadi: the magistrate or judge of an Islamic Sharia court.

Qarân: secretary.

Rawhân: name of a species of *jinn* in Arabic. Literally, 'carried by the breath'.

Rumbu: *jinn* from Durban or the island of Pemba, near Zanzibar.

Saluva: wide cloth with the edges sewn together which women wear by tying the top edge around their breasts. For festive occasions, it is often accompanied by a shirt sewn from the same fabric: the ensemble is called a *kanzu*. It is worn mainly on the islands of Anjouan and Mayotte.

Sharif: word used to describe the supposed descendants of Mohammed, the meaning of which is close to 'noble'. According to legend, one day when Mohammed was praying, the 'sheet of nobility' descended from the sky to rest on him and those praying with him: Ali, his nephew then aged nine; Khadijah, his first wife; and a cat. In ancient Islamic tradition, felines are respected beings.

Shioni: school dedicated to learning the Qur'an and sometimes Arabic. The term literally means 'in the book'.

Sinia: large round metal dish.

Surah: chapter of the Qur'an.

Suriya: concubine.

Tari: dance, probably inherited from the Bedouins, consisting of mimicking warrior combat: in the centre of a circle of men, two others pretend to fight each other with swords, executing a precise choreography.

Trumba: Malagasy name for *jinns*.

Ulul-albab: 'those who hold the secrets'. One of these words, *bab*, also designates a 'door', suggesting a door to which one holds the key.

Wadaha: dance reserved for the wild rice harvest festival: the women form a circle around a large square. A group of four or five women break away from the circle and move towards the centre, where a mortar and three pestles are placed. Three women each take a pestle and strike the mortar. The complexity (and beauty) of the exercise lies in the moment when the pestle is thrown to the next woman.

Vizier: a high-ranking political advisor or minister in the Near East.

Wallahi, billahi wa rasul: 'I swear by God and the Prophet.'

Wazungu: plural of *Mzungu*.

Yee: all right.

Zari: cotton stole from India, with a variety of designs, once reserved for upper-class women.

Dedalus Africa

Dedalus Africa seeks out high-quality fiction from all of Africa, including parts of Africa hitherto totally ignored by English-language publishers.

Titles currently available are:

The Desert and the Drum—Mbarek Ould Beyrouk
Saara—Mbarek Ould Beyrouk
Catalogue of a Private Life—Najwa Bin Shatwan
Edo's Souls—Stella Gaitano
The Word Tree—Teolinda Gersão
The Fire Within—Touhfat Mouhbare
Tchanaze—Carlos Paradona Rufino Roque
The Madwoman of Serrano—Dina Salústio
The Ultimate Tragedy—Abdulai Silá
Our Musseque—José Luandino Vieira
Co-wives, Co-widows—Adrienne Yabouza

Forthcoming titles include:

Headless in Kita—Moussa Konaté